It was one man's word against another's.

What if McLellan *was* the mole, as Smitty claimed?

Ignoring the bolt of regret that shot through her, Chris slipped back into the engine room. This place she knew. There was a certainty to it, not like people. A machine either worked or didn't in predictable ways.

She could do her part and make sure the device she'd discovered—a device that put suspicion on both men—actually was a transponder. Kneeling next to the tool chest, she made two quick slashes with a craft knife through the block of white sealant securing the box to the floor. Her fingernails just fit inside the slash. She pulled up gently. The box rose slightly as the remaining sealant flexed and gave. Perfect. She'd be able to cut the transponder loose later, maybe park it someplace where it'd confuse whoever was following them.

A satisfied smile welled up in her soul. Oh, if it came right down to it, she could cause a helluva lot of confusion—no matter who was lying to her.

Dear Reader,

Yes, I really can change the fuel filter on a 6V53 Detroit diesel engine! When I was advised to "write what you know," the first thing that came to my mind was to write a story about a woman and her boat. I'm definitely not Chris Hampton—licensed captain, intrepid sailor—though my partner usually asks me to pretend to be "Captain Chris" when a hard-to-reach impeller needs to be pulled off the engine's backside. That, of course, requires me to lie spread-eagle across the engine with my head stuck down in the hold and a pair of pliers in my hand. Evil man.

Perhaps one day we'll head out on our beloved thirty-eight-foot motor yacht for our own ocean-going adventure and I'll write a different kind of book, but in the meantime, I have plenty of other stories to tell.

I hope you enjoy the adventure. Let me know if you do! I love reader feedback. E-mail me at feedback@sandrakmoore.com.

Fair winds,

Sandra K. Moore

Sandra K. Moore

DEAD RECKONING

Published by Silhouette Books

America's Publisher of Contemporary Romance

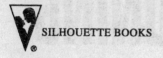

SILHOUETTE BOOKS

ISBN-13: 978-0-373-51414-4
ISBN-10:   0-373-51414-X

DEAD RECKONING

Copyright © 2006 by Sandra K. Moore

www.SilhouetteBombshell.com

Printed in U.S.A.

Books by Sandra K. Moore

Silhouette Bombshell

The Orchid Hunter #35
Dead Reckoning #100

SANDRA K. MOORE

moved from Texas to Wyoming to be closer to the mountains. Summer means hiking, and autumn, camping. "During the long cold winters," she says, "I slide down ski slopes until I have squeezed all the winter out of spring."

For my wonderful editor, Stacy Boyd,
who believed in this story long after I'd stopped.

And for the crews of *Moonstruck,
No Worries, Chances R, Troubadour,
Compromise* and *Salsero*. Fair winds.

Acknowledgments

My sincere gratitude to:

Dave Allen of TNT Yacht Repair, for his
matter-of-fact, down-to-earth lessons on boat anatomy
(and no, I still haven't gotten around to cleaning the raw
water intake filters);

Lem Powell, retired Galveston police officer and
College of the Mainland handgun instructor, for
introducing me to the lovely Ruger 9 mm;

and Ann Peake, Sandy Thomas and
Dawn Temple, for their unfailing patience and
piercing insights, even when reading the
same chapter over and over and over....

For further reading on boating adventures
and other topics mentioned in this book,
a complete bibliography is posted at
http://www.sandrakmoore.com/deadreckoning/.

Any factual errors are entirely mine.

Chapter 1

"Fifty bucks says I finish first!"

Chris Hampton squinted against her racing sailboat's bow spray to eye her nearest competitor.

A few yards away and slightly astern, Dave Mitchell's identical Laser sailboat clipped through the bay waves, gaining. Sitting sideways, he leaned backward to keep the sail upright and full of wind. He grinned over his broad shoulder at her, his brown ponytail flying like a banner. "You don't stand a chance!"

A gust of wind snatched her laugh. She adjusted the tiller. "Put your money where your mouth is!"

"Make it a hundred and you're on!"

"Deal!"

Chris loosened the main sheet to put more curve in the sail. Her Laser had the wind behind her and wallowed a little in the light chop of the inlet feeding into Galveston

Bay. Another spray of water leaped up onto her back, soaking her black-and-royal-blue wet suit, chilling her. She blew water droplets from her nose and settled down to her sailing. Dave had beaten her twice this season. Let him win this last race of the series *and* lose a Ben Franklin? No way.

Just a hundred yards to the final buoy and then the sprint for the finish. Dave was the closest sailor, but a few yards behind him lurked the kid called Ferret. Ferret not only had his namesake's sharp features and close-set eyes, he had a habit of weaseling between boats. The kid was a born tactician and Chris didn't underestimate him. Behind them, the rest of the racers jockeyed for better wind. At the buoy she'd just cornered, the committee boat, a twenty-five-foot cabin cruiser, signaled the race course's ending point.

Chris ducked her head to look under the Laser's boom at the big orange buoy marking the final leg. Fair running, but she'd have her hands full once she rounded the marker. She'd take the wind almost directly on the nose in a close beat to the finish.

She glanced over at Dave. His Laser skimmed easily beside hers and she was beginning to see more of his back than his side as he drew even. *Come on,* she goaded him. *I'm going to bury you right here in this race.*

One boat length. That's all she needed. Heart pounding, she nudged her boat a little further to starboard, closer to Dave. A fresh wind gust cooled the side of her neck. She tightened the main just a touch as the wind strengthened. Her little sailboat leaped ahead as Dave fell back. He was slowing to tack, but she'd chance a spill to gain some distance in the turn.

The buoy sped toward her. As her boat came even with it, she pulled on the tiller and ducked while switching sides of the boat. The sail's boom swung over her head into position on the port side. She yanked the mainsheet taut as the Laser pivoted, stalled and lifted its starboard side—where Chris now perched—out of the water. Chris leaned backward, fighting not to fall forward as the boat tipped her into a standing position.

"Come on, baby!" she coaxed.

The light sailboat hovered on edge, perfectly balanced. Chris braced her feet on the gunwale and leaned farther back. The boat couldn't take another inch. For a split second, Chris felt the boat tip past the sweet spot.

The wind eased. The Laser paused, then dropped back onto her bottom. Chris scrambled to adjust her weight. The sail snapped twice, then caught the breeze. The Laser shot away from the buoy.

"Woohoo!" she heard Ferret yell. "Bitchin' corner!"

Chris grinned, adrenaline surging. The fastest turn she'd ever tried. And the luckiest. She glanced back. Dave's hull rocked bottom-up. He was out of their little match race. Easy hundred bucks for her. Ferret's Laser shot past Dave's bobbing head and executed a picture-perfect tack.

Now it was just her against Ferret for the finish. She tightened the main, trying to get a little more speed out of the Laser. The boat had her shoulder in, really cranking, nipping through the little wave tops. The finish mark was only a couple hundred yards away.

The high whine of a small powerboat's outboard engine, like a giant mosquito, cut through the rushing wind. Chris glanced around but saw nothing. It wasn't the committee boat, which had a gutsier inboard. Just somebody out on the inlet for a joy ride. The next moment, Ferret shouted something incomprehensible. She'd gotten too far ahead to hear him. She licked the salt from her lips and glanced again. Nothing but the committee boat, horn blowing. She ducked to look under the sail and froze.

A power runabout, maybe twice her boat's length and much, much heavier, sped toward her. A hundred yards away but closing fast on an intercept course.

Her heart lurched. If she dropped the sail, she'd stop but couldn't maneuver. The runabout, a flash of red-and-white fiberglass against blue sky and water, bore down, engine screaming. The driver frantically waved his arms, yelling. Chris caught the word "steering," but nothing else.

"Kill the motor!" Ferret shouted. "Hit the kill switch!"

Chris had to change direction. A tack wouldn't do it. It'd have to be a dangerous jibe, letting the wind completely control the boom's movement and position. She turned the Laser away from the wind. The little boat pivoted its nose toward the runabout, then back toward Ferret.

"Come on!" she shouted at the wind. A gust caught the mainsail. Chris ducked. The boom snapped from port to starboard with killing speed. The Laser lurched, then heeled over. Pointed back toward the other racers, it slowly started moving.

A flash of red. The driver's voice, high-pitched, shouted. She glanced over. The runabout had been headed toward her forward position. Now it veered toward her again. Its bow grew quickly as it bore down on her. The driver's thin face stretched wide in a grimace of fear. Her fingers fumbled for her life jacket's straps. She yanked the vest off. A sickening gust of gasoline-scented air rushed over her. Her gut clenched. He was going to hit her. She didn't stand a chance.

She dove.

Cool water shocked her skin, tore her breath away. She stroked hard for the bottom. Water filled her ears, blunted her hearing, but overhead, fiberglass thudded and cracked on fiberglass. Instinctively, she ducked. The runabout's sharp-bladed propeller churned and roared over the little sailboat, chewing it up.

She turned and opened her eyes to stinging salt and murky, silty water. Torn pieces of her Laser drifted down. The sail eased and billowed like a giant jellyfish, tugged toward the bottom by the wrenched mast. The runabout's roar faded, lowered an octave, then quit. Her life jacket floated idly on the surface, its stuffing protruding from the blade-sliced neoprene.

Chris stroked upward. Surfacing, she sucked in air and shook the water from her stinging eyes. Her body trembled, hungry for air and warmth.

"Chris!" someone shouted. "Chris!"

She raised her arm, kept it up like a beacon. "I'm okay!"

The committee boat moved cautiously toward her. Its pilot killed his engine as he drew near and pivoted the boat. When the swim ladder came into view, she side-stroked over and climbed onto the platform.

"Not hurt?" Gus Perkins asked, giving her a hand into the open cockpit. He held her shoulders for a moment in his gnarled hands as his gaze swept her head to toe.

"Nah. Scared. But that's it." She shrugged him off, then shoved aside a boat hook and a stack of flags so she could collapse on the vinyl bench and concentrate on breathing. Her eyes watered when she sniffed and salt water shot up her nose. She cleared her throat. "Where'd that guy come from?"

Gus's weather-beaten face screwed itself into even more wrinkles as he hoisted the blue-and-white checked Abandon Race flag. "Hell if I know. Guys like him shouldn't have a boat. Didn't know how to kill the engine. Dangerous bastard."

Chris tried to comb her fingers through her tangled hair. "I agree completely. Let's go have a chat with him."

"Wait just a minute. Let's make sure you're all right."

"I am."

"Well, you might think so, but you nearly got killed, so let's just take a minute here." Gus disappeared into the cruiser's tiny cabin and came back with a massive towel. "Dry off some. Take it easy."

Chris took the towel. "I'm really—"

"Let's make *sure* you're all right." He grabbed his navy Houston Astros cap off his head, ran his hand over his bald head and replaced the cap. "Let's wait for the police."

The cruiser bobbed soothingly. The runabout, now dead in the water, its bow gouged and scraped, drifted aimlessly. Its driver clutched his face with his hands. The Lasers, race abandoned, rushed back to the clubhouse like a flock of scared seabirds. Dave and Ferret were tacking their way over to the cruiser.

Chris scrubbed her face with the surprisingly soft towel. Gus was right. Relax. She breathed deep, the towel covering her face. Her heart, she realized now, still raced. Her arms and legs still tingled. Adrenaline. Reaction. Reflex. The sailboat would be settling into the inlet's mud bottom, shattered.

As she would be, had she not jumped.

Her chest abruptly warmed. Not now, she told herself. No crying. It was all over and she was safe. What would be the point in crying? It was bad enough her hands were shaking. Why did she suddenly feel so weak? She took another deep breath from the towel.

Only then did she recognize the scent. Peaches. Like the sachets her mother had used. Her parents' house had smelled like peaches until Chris had turned eleven, when she and her sister had gone to live with Granddad.

Chris dragged the towel from her face and mopped the

back of her neck. No wonder she felt weak. She didn't need another reminder of that loss. She'd had a reminder every day growing up, every day she'd gone downstairs to have breakfast with Granddad and Natalie—his beloved "real" granddaughter—and confronted his resentment. His message was clear: *You're not flesh and blood. You're not welcome here.*

At least Natalie had always treated Chris like a real sister. Chris was ten when Natalie surprised their parents by being carried to term. Natalie, though impressionable, had never picked up their grandfather's disdain for Chris.

Chris tossed the towel on the seat. *Screw self-pity,* she thought. Her adoptive parents' love, when they were alive, had more than made up for the old man's attitude when they were gone. And she'd become stronger, more focused, from constantly battling to live the life she wanted. Her life with her grandfather was just the luck of the draw. She wiped a rivulet of salt water from her temple. Chris believed in making her own luck. Like she had ten minutes ago.

"Galveston's here," Gus said from his captain's chair.

Chris watched the green-and-white Galveston Bay police boat glide up to the dead runabout. One cop eased the boat near the red-striped runabout and the other rigged lines to lash the two boats together.

The driver looked up then. Even at fifty yards' distance, she saw how thin he was. How shaken up. His white face a mask frozen with that same grimace of fear. Dread oozed through her stomach and lifted bile into her throat.

"You still want to go over and give that guy a piece of your mind?" Gus asked.

The thought of listening to the man's stammering apology sent a shiver down her spine. What good would it do to hear him say he was sorry? It wouldn't erase what had happened. Chris shook her head. "I just want to go home."

She couldn't, though. She had to give her statement to the police first, then watch a salvage crew pluck her destroyed boat from the inlet's waters while she stood hugging herself against a delayed onset of the shakes. The runabout driver, the police told her, would be severely fined for operator neglect. Because neither competency tests nor licenses were required for powerboat use, as Chris well knew, the driver would be free to take his runabout onto the bay again whenever he wanted, after he took the U.S. Coast Guard's Power Squadron course. Like defensive driving, but with a better chance of actually teaching the violator something he didn't know.

After finishing up with the authorities, she walked outside the racing club, where Dave sat on the porch step, waiting for his ride home. "Stick a fork in me," she told him.

He stood as she joined him. "Think he'll pay for the Laser?"

She shrugged. "If he doesn't, his insurance better. I'm putting the cash directly into *Obsession*." Chris jerked open her ancient Chevy pickup's driver side door. "That dead sailboat will pay for a lot of yacht repairs." She scooted onto the still-warm vinyl bench seat and shoved her gear bag onto the middle floorboard, away from the rusty patch under the accelerator where she could see the asphalt.

"Helluva way for the last race to end," Dave commented as he slid in.

Chris turned the key with hands that still shook a little. She concentrated on how the big 454 rumbled, smooth as butter, and felt some of the residual fear drain away. She smiled at Dave. "I guess I don't get my hundred bucks."

He winked. "You might get a break on your tub's yard bill."

"I'll take what I can get," Chris said, thinking about the decrepit motor yacht she now lived aboard—the only material possession her wealthy grandfather had left her at his death nine months before. The big girl sat on boatyard jack stands for her very first maintenance while in Chris's custody. Living aboard while the yacht was propped up on dry land wasn't a particularly pleasant experience. The yacht's AC system was water-cooled and with no water under the hull, no air-conditioning. Besides, the yacht's soothing rock on the sometimes restive tidal bay was better than any lullaby.

"How far'd you get today while I was in town?" Chris asked as she pulled into traffic.

"Her bottom's painted. Topside polish tomorrow, hull polish on Friday."

"She needs a hull *painting,* not a polish."

"Ain't that the truth. But she's pretty sharp for a hunk o' junk."

"She'd clean up a lot nicer if I had some real money for repairs."

"You could say that about every gorgeous lady."

Chris cranked down the pickup's window. *Gorgeous* might one day in the far, far future describe *Obsession,* but it certainly didn't describe Chris, a scruffy dishwater blonde with too boyish a figure and a brain made for breaking down and rebuilding engines. Natalie was a different story, the spitting image of their long-dead grandmother—wide almond-shaped eyes, an exotic and sumptuous beauty and a flirtatious way with men and money.

When Chris had pulled into the boatyard parking lot and stopped the pickup, Dave grasped her hand. "Are you gonna be okay tonight?" he asked.

She let her fingers lie in his for a moment—he was a

good friend and always there to help—before she pulled free. "Yeah. It scared me, but I'm okay." When his brows registered doubt, she smiled. "Really. Stop worrying."

"Call me if you need me. I mean it. Any time."

"I will." She kicked open the Chevy's rusty door, then scowled as teenaged boys—two Hispanic, one white— sprinted across the yard in front of her. They ducked under a sailboat's hull and disappeared. "What are those hooligans doing now?" she muttered. "Don't you have a policy against letting kids run around a working boatyard?"

"They're harmless." Dave cranked his door open. "They haven't stolen anything."

"Yet." Chris grabbed her gear bag from the floorboard. "When do you think *Obsession* will splash?"

"Saturday at the soonest."

"Good. I'm ready to have her back in the water where she belongs."

He swung out of the truck. "You got any charters lined up yet?"

"I've got to get her dressed up a little before I can start the day cruises, probably another month," she called over the cab. "It'll be next year before she's ready for the pricey weekenders and vacation cruises."

"Sounds like a lot of cash."

"I'll get there eventually."

"You could take out a loan to get her in shape right away," he said as he rounded the Chevy's blunt nose to stand next to her.

"Using what as collateral? I don't own anything. Besides, I don't like being in debt." Sure, she'd saved a lot of money living at her grandfather's, which she'd done mostly to please Natalie, but she'd used much of those savings to overhaul the engines and get *Obsession* truly seaworthy. She was living off the rest until she was ready to launch her charter business.

Dave nodded, then squinted at the sky glowing yellow, tingeing into orange. "Will you be okay living aboard in the yard another few days?"

"Yeah. I've got box fans."

"If you get hot," and he winked, "you know where I live."

She smiled as she shrugged her bag onto her shoulder. Dave waved and strode off to the shabby apartments adjacent to the marina. A moment later, only seagull cries and the occasional metallic clang of a loose sailboat halyard slapping its mast pierced the air. Early evening, the sun was just thinking about dropping behind the western shed housing the covered boat slips. Seagulls arced overhead, headed home.

Chris walked past the line of small boats propped on jack stands in dry dock. At the yard's end, *Obsession* loomed over them. The yacht's deep-V hull gave her a beefy, broad-shouldered attitude. In the water, she was a large boat. Out of it, she was a behemoth.

Dave had been right. The fresh coat of black bottom paint made her look good, at least from the bottom down, kind of like a nice pair of heels on a bag lady. But it was a start. Beneath the bent railings and chalky fiberglass, the cracked windows and dubious plumbing, a grande dame waited to emerge. Chris ran her hand along the yacht's side as she walked toward the tall ladder that led up to the aft deck.

Home.

Chris knew in her bones the old man had intended the yacht to be an insult but he didn't know *Chris*. And he certainly hadn't known she'd love the boat at first sight. The yacht was fundamentally sound—solid hull, reliable engines, no severe water damage—despite being neglected for the better part of two decades. For Chris, abandoning her offshore rig mechanical engineering job to get her captain's license had merely traded one hands-on skill for another.

The old man had hoped to leave her a money pit but she'd turn his insult into a gift if it killed her.

After living aboard since her grandfather passed away, she could tell which bilge pump was running by sound, when the water tanks needed freshening by smell, and when the engine oil needed changing by feel. She'd crawled all over the yacht—into every bilge area, into every nasty, stinking little hole—to see for herself what needed to be done. Now if only she had a lot more cash, she'd be able to do almost all of the restoration work herself.

Just over seventy feet from bowsprit to swim platform, *Obsession* had been built along the lines of the old classic motor yachts. From the bow, the pilothouse, which contained the lower helm station, swept back to the main living area. The living area had a facing dinette and galley, and behind them a salon—a living room, as Chris explained to landlubber friends—that stretched the width of the boat's interior. Further aft, the salon's rear sliding door opened onto a spacious covered deck. Atop the pilothouse and salon was the bridge deck, where Chris planned to steer at the upper helm during nice weather. Down in Galveston, that was ten months out of the year. Most of the sleeping quarters were below, deep in the hull: two large cabins and two crew cabins.

She swung up the ladder to the aft deck and dropped her bag on the teak table she'd recently coaxed from weathered and stained back into golden glory. Her first varnish attempt, and it looked pretty darn good. Now if only the rest of her "little projects" would go as well.

Her heirloom quilt drooped across a pair of deck chairs

in the shade, drying after a careful hand wash early that morning. She tested the material between her thumb and forefinger. Yes, nearly dry, the fabric just as fine and solid as the day she and her mother had pulled it from the quilting frame after months of hand stitching. Chris traced the intricate mariner's compass that emblazoned the exact center like a bull's-eye. Funny how all things come together, she thought. Never in a million years would she have imagined at the age of eight that she'd live on a boat or drape the mariner's compass across her stateroom bed or have earned her captain's license.

Snagging a bottled water from the minifridge, she settled into a third deck chair and tried not to see visions of her destroyed life jacket, its yellow-white stuffing sticking out like a half-popped kernel of corn. At least her hands had stopped shaking.

Her cell trilled and she fished it out of her bag with a sigh. The screen flashed UNKNOWN. Probably Natalie, calling from overseas on the never-ending, globe-hopping honeymoon.

Natalie, perfect granddaughter that she was, had followed their grandfather's wishes and married a rich businessman. It was like Natalie to do it a mere two months after meeting the guy at the old man's funeral. There'd been plenty of business acquaintances, but Natalie had latched onto the blond bodybuilder type's arm and held on with a bulldog persistence that somehow managed to be both feminine and suitably mournful. Predictably, she had failed to introduce him to her sister.

It was like Natalie to get everything she wanted at the drop of a hat, Chris thought. And she had impeccable timing, too, always knowing when Chris would be home and available to talk.

"Chris?" echoed hollowly over the connection when she picked up.

"Hey, Natalie. Where are you this time?"

Natalie gave a slightly breathless laugh. "Rome! I never thought I'd be here. It's gorgeous. You'd love it!"

"Last week France, this week Italy," Chris said, feeling the accident's presence fade from the edges of her mind at Natalie's energetic voice. "Where to next?"

"Who knows? Jerome always surprises me. Greece, I'm hoping. They've got some great bazaars there."

"Shoes and designer dresses, right? Scarves and figurines and upholstery fabric? Not that you need to upholster anything," Chris teased. "You don't stay in one place long enough. At least you're out of the Far East."

"Hey, we'll make it back to the States. Eventually. But wait till you see the clothes I'm shipping to you. Don't you dare wear them to work on that awful boat."

Chris grimaced. "Frilly girlie-girl wear."

"A more feminine style, yeah." Natalie laughed again. "Something that shows off your legs, proves you have a waist, attracts men. You know."

Chris let her groan signal the end of that bit of conversation. "Tell me about Rome."

"You'd love it. Crammed full of smelly little cars and everyone driving too fast. Jerome says he's never seen chaos on the road like this."

"Sounds like Houston," Chris remarked dryly. "Except the cars are SUVs here. How is Jerome? Still treating you like a queen?"

"You know how it goes." Natalie's voice dropped. "Sometimes the honeymoon's over even when it's not."

Chris frowned. The strained note in Natalie's lowered voice was always the first clue that something huge was going on. Had it truly been nothing, she would have laughed it off. "What's wrong?"

"It's okay, really." A pause, then she said brightly, "Rome is so gorgeous. I'd love for you to see it."

Chris hesitated a beat. Natalie typically spoke her mind, no dancing around the subject. Did her avoidance of the question mean she couldn't talk about it? Was she afraid of something?

An old protective instinct flared in Chris. "Tell me more."

"It's a place you'd have to see for yourself. In person."

Meaning Natalie wanted her to come to Rome?

The silence was filled only by a rush, like holding a seashell to the ear. Natalie finally said, "This connection is crap. Let me call you another time."

The phone died. What the hell? Chris stared at the flashing numbers onscreen for a moment. The connection had been fine, so why had Natalie hung up on her? She put the phone down. With no caller ID, with no number to call, Chris couldn't call her back.

Her cell trilled again and Chris snatched it up. "Natalie?"

"Yeah, it's me. I had to switch phones, get outside." Behind her voice, faint road noise: a car engine growling up a hill, tires hissing on wet pavement.

"What's going on?"

"I guess I didn't really know Jerome when I married him," Natalie confessed, her voice now at normal volume. "You hear about men changing after they get married, and he's one of them."

"Changing how?" Chris rose from her deck chair, too keyed up to sit.

"He used to be proud of other men looking at me and making comments, but now…" Natalie sniffed. "At first it was just little things. We'd be at a friend's party and he'd smart off to another man when the guy said something about how I looked. Just a compliment, nothing out of line. I told Jerome he was being silly. I married him because I wanted to be with him. Period. That would usually settle him down, but then after a while it didn't."

"Why didn't you tell me about this when it was happening?" Chris asked, trying not to sound accusing.

"Because it's a drag. I know you, Chris. You'd just worry about me and it wasn't that bad."

"And now?"

"It's worse," Natalie admitted, her voice quavering a little. "He got into a fight last month, nearly got arrested for punching out the party host. He'd been drinking, which never helps. Now we don't go to any parties at all. A bunch of his friends who were traveling with us left last week and went off on their own trip."

"Is he treating you badly?" Chris paced to the railing, stared unseeing over the boatyard.

"He won't let me go anywhere without either him or one of his bodyguards. I have to take a bodyguard with me when I go shopping and the whole time the guy's watching to make sure no one even looks at me the wrong way. I can't even go pee without asking his permission." Natalie sniffed again. "I used to think having a bodyguard would be fun. You know, a status thing. But it's more like being in prison."

Chris scrubbed her face with her hand. Yes, Natalie would think having a bodyguard would be "a status thing." She'd directly inherited their grandfather's penchant for power, except now she was seeing firsthand what that kind of power, misused, could do.

"Have you talked to him about it?" Chris asked. "Told him you don't like having a guard?"

"He won't listen. I can't get through to him."

Just like their grandfather. "What are your plans?" Chris asked.

"We're spending another three weeks or so in Europe, then flying to some private island one of his business associates owns."

"Private island? Where?"

"I don't know. Somewhere south of Florida. I don't really care about it. Just a bunch of guys drinking and fishing."

"Visit me instead, then. It feels like forever since I've seen you. Let Jerome go to his buddy's private island and you come here."

"I can't. I mean, I want to, but Jerome…he has plans and we have to keep to his schedule. He's doing a lot of business and I need to be with him. You know."

No, I don't, Chris thought, annoyed with this man she'd only ever seen at a distance. Why did they have to get married in London? Without family present? Why would he care if Natalie saw her sister? "Can't he give you a couple of days to see me? It's not much time. And it's not like it's a horde of people. Just me."

"You don't know Jerome very well." Then the connection echo was so bad Chris heard her say, "Neither did I" twice.

Chris suppressed a sharp retort. Yes, Natalie had acted, as usual, on impulse. Last year, it was the Jaguar. The year before that, the high-priced condo. In both cases, Chris had managed to get Natalie out of the deal during the three-day grace period. But buyer's remorse wasn't so easy to remedy when you suddenly realized you were married to the wrong man. And bitching Natalie out about it now wouldn't help.

"Listen," she said instead, "why don't you and Jerome stop here before going to the island?"

"That's not a good idea." The strained note was back.

"Why not?" When Natalie didn't answer, Chris's stomach felt heavy. "Why not?" she asked again.

"I told him I wanted to see you and he…didn't like it."

Chris took a deep breath. "What do you mean?"

Silence.

"Talk to me, Natalie."

After a moment, she said, "He…*really*…didn't like it. Look, it's nothing."

"Nat," and Chris's breath curled with dread as she forced herself to say the words, "is he hitting you?"

"I—I should get off the phone."

Fighting down the rage threatening to boil up in her chest, Chris made an effort to speak calmly. "Listen to me. Are you listening?"

"Y-yes."

"Is he hitting you?"

Natalie's indrawn breath shuddered over the line. "Just that once."

"Goddammit!"

"It was just one time, Chris," she cried, her voice high, rattled. "He didn't mean it. And it's not like he broke anything—"

"There's no excuse. None." Chris gripped the mahogany railing so tightly her finger bones ached. "Do you want to come home?"

"He'd never—"

"I don't care about him. I'm asking about you. Do you want to come home?"

"That's what I'm trying to tell you," Natalie said in a low voice, tears clogging her voice. "He won't let me. I tried once. That's when he got so angry and he…" She hiccupped a sob. "He's jealous of everybody. Even you. He knows how close we are."

"Oh, God, Nat."

"I have to get off the phone before he comes outside. We have to move again."

"Move again? What do you mean?"

Natalie's breath hitched as she inhaled. "He won't stay in one place for more than one night. I never know until he comes home and then we pack up and go. Or sometimes he just calls and I have to go meet him."

"What the hell does he think's going to happen?"

"I don't know. But I hate this! I hate living out of a suitcase." A loud sniff sounded. "Look, it's been long enough for me to have a cigarette. I have to go back inside."

"Answer my question, Natalie. Do you want to come home?"

"You don't understand. Jerome will never let me leave."

No, Chris thought. There was always a plan. There was always a way of getting out of places you didn't want to be. It just sometimes took brainpower and usually needed guts.

Where there's a will, there's a way.

Chris's voice was calm as she said, "Fuck Jerome. I'll come get you."

Chapter 2

"What you're proposing, Ms. Hampton, is suicide."

Chris lifted her chin, annoyed by Antonio Garza's pronouncement. As a private investigator, he was there to inform, not to advise. "What I'm proposing is saving my sister from an abusive husband."

She surveyed Garza's small conference room where she sat with her friend, Gus Perkins, Antonio Garza and an innocuous-looking man who'd been introduced to her as Special Agent Smith of the DEA. "The fact her husband is an extremely dangerous drug smuggler is news, but it doesn't mean I'm giving up."

She clasped her hands together on the conference table's edge and willed them to stop trembling. The shoulder squeeze Gus gave her felt affectionate, supportive. As well it should, all the years she'd taken sailing lessons from him after he retired from the Houston Police Department. She trusted him, at first with her safety on the water—he had never let her down—and now with this.

When Gus had told her his old partner had become a P.I. based in Galveston, she'd hoped to get some information about Jerome Scintella before she headed out after Natalie. Did he, for example, have a history of violence? Have an arrest record? Own a gun?

"Extremely dangerous drug smuggler" pretty much had all of that covered.

Suddenly she wasn't just talking to a P.I. about snatching her sister. The minute Gus and Antonio Garza heard Jerome's name, they'd been on the phone to old contacts at the DEA. Hence Special Agent Smith, who reminded her of the boy who used to live next door.

"It's clear we can't take him in Rome." Smith rose, tall and lean, to pace to the window. He braced his arm in the window casing as he said, almost to himself, "With Scintella so jumpy, moving around every night, it'll be next to impossible to get a fix on him."

"That's why I'm proposing my 'suicide' mission," Chris retorted. "Natalie's too hemmed in by her bodyguard to ditch him, so I couldn't go to Rome myself and have any chance of getting her."

"And you think taking your motor yacht to this private island improves your odds?" Smith asked the window. "It'll be covered up with armed guards."

"It's a very long shot. And dangerous." The private investigator's deep brown eyes were soft with concern, as though he was practiced at cautioning others. Given that Garza specialized in finding missing children, Chris suspected he might be.

"I knew it was going to be difficult before you told me about Jerome," she said. "But I can't just let this chance go by without acting on it." Smith's longish blond hair raked his collar as he turned to look at her. She continued, "Natalie phoned again this morning and said she'd sweet-talked Jerome into telling her the island's name. She's not sure if Isladonata is in U.S. waters. I checked the charts but didn't find it. Maybe Isladonata is a nickname. I'll ask around the transient cruising people in my marina and on the newsgroups to see if they know anything."

"So she's able to get *some* information from him." Smith's words sounded almost like an accusation.

"Every question she asks is a risk," Chris retorted. "Jerome gets more suspicious of everyone around him every day. I don't like asking her to stretch that envelope."

Smith sighed and returned to the table. His white shirt, tucked carelessly into snug jeans, both set off his tan and made him look more like a horse trainer than a DEA agent. "I hope I don't sound like I'm asking you to do that," he said as he dropped back into his chair. "It's good she's able to find out a few things for us. It'll help us find Scintella."

And get her out, Chris thought.

"But," his tenor deepened slightly, "there's no guarantee she'll take the chance of leaving even if you show up with your boat. No telling what orders the bodyguard will have been given by Scintella."

Chris's stomach clenched with fear. Would Jerome order Natalie's bodyguard to kill her if she strayed? God, why would he not? He seemed to see Natalie as a possession, not a wife.

"How were you planning on finding Isladonata?" Smith asked.

"All I need is a fifty-square-mile window. In theory, I could track other boats or choppers from the mainland and project which island they land at, then dead reckon my way in." Though her chances of actually succeeding, she knew from having been in the Gulf of Mexico, were incredibly slim. Too much water, too many islands, too little time.

"Navigation by the seat of the pants is risky," Gus said.

Smith nodded. "It'd be better if your sister could get us the exact location."

Chris studied her hands, resting so still and lost on the wood tabletop's vast, empty expanse. "I'm sure it would. But I don't like asking her to take that chance."

"Understood," Smith replied softly.

She looked up to find him staring at her. He was handsome in a vague way, as though the artist painting him had left him unfinished. It showed in the way his hair roughly brushed his neck, in the slight unevenness of his lips. His eyes, she realized absently, were the color of her own.

"And your yacht can make that trip?" he asked.

"*Obsession*'s not a true blue-water boat, so she can't take on an ocean," Chris admitted. "But she'll handle the Gulf of Mexico and the Caribbean just fine. An old ship's log I found aboard said she made two trips down and back in the seventies."

Gus snorted. "The seventies? A little time has passed, hasn't it?"

"I tore down and rebuilt both engines myself," Chris replied. "She'll make it. It's the cosmetic work I'm worried about."

Smith leaned his brown forearms on the table. "What do you mean?"

"If these Isladonata guys are high-dollar bad guys, they'll have high-dollar hobbies. When I inherited *Obsession* nine months ago, she needed a lot of work. I've got her mechanical systems in order, but it's the spit-and-polish that'll convince them she's legit and get me onto the island."

"What were you planning on doing once you were there?" Garza asked.

"I'm going to have to look like a private captain on my way to drop off or pick up someone important."

Gus grunted. "If Scintella's going to be on the island in three weeks, that's not much time."

"Two weeks to dress up the yacht, one week to get down there," she confirmed.

Garza scribbled some notes. "Is that enough time?"

"Not really," Chris admitted, thinking about chalky fiberglass and cracked windows. "And I need a lot more money than I have to make it happen."

"How much?" Smith pulled his hands from his jeans pockets and crossed his arms.

"This is where my plan needs some work." She ballparked the repair price tag. Gus whistled softly. Once Garza's brows dropped back from the ceiling, she said, "Look, a brand-new yacht of her build quality would cost upwards of five million. *Obsession*'s old and needs a serious facelift, but she's fundamentally sound. I've worked on the basic systems myself and sunk most of my savings into her. All I need now is the window dressing."

"That's a helluva dressing," Smith muttered.

"She's a helluva window," Chris retorted. "I'm not talking about installing Waterford chandeliers. Just reasonably good quality furnishings and carpet to make her look like she's been pampered. The external work includes a full-on paint job, replacing windows and railings, that kind of thing. I could do it all myself if I had the time."

She glanced out the window. Her rusted Chevy pickup, the truck she'd bought as a hobby project but that was now all she had for transportation, stared back at her blankly. "And the cash," she added, thinking about how soon her remaining savings would run dry even paying only her living expenses.

"You have your captain's license. Can't you just rent a vessel?" Garza asked.

She shook her head. "Large vessels carry their own captains and crew. Even with a license, I'm an unknown, an insurance risk. Nobody's going to let me hire a yacht that size even for twice the going rate without taking their crew. And maybe I'm assuming here, but I bet if I show up in anything shorter than seventy feet, I won't get within a mile of the island."

Smith settled back into his chair and studied her for a long moment. "Let's say money's no object," he said finally. "What would your schedule look like?"

Money no object? Fighting down the hope swelling in her throat, Chris forced herself to concentrate on facts, not pipe dreams. "Two weeks in the boatyard for as much as we can get done here in Galveston, then a shakedown cruise to New Orleans to make sure everything's working. If there's any cosmetic work left, we may be able to get it done in New Orleans if they're not still covered up with hurricane repairs. Then I'll head south for Isladonata."

"We could take a page from your book and bluff our way onto the island," Smith mused. "Maybe say we're coming to drop off a player."

Garza nodded. "One of the Delacruz family. Enrique Delacruz."

"They wouldn't see us coming."

Gus's chin jutted like a battering ram. "A private island's going to be heavily guarded. They'll be running radar and spot a fleet of choppers and cutters coming from two hundred miles out. Scintella will be gone before you get there."

"It doesn't have to be a major operation," Smith replied.

"You're not going to sneak up on him." Gus shoved his creaking chair back and stood to glare down at Smith. "Not on an island."

Smith raised his face to meet Gus head-on. "We can set it up. With the right hardware, the right men, we can take this guy."

"And his army?" Gus asked. "Sounds like you'll be taking in your own army to handle it."

"Scintella won't be the only target on that island," Garza pointed out.

Finally. Let's talk about Natalie. Chris crossed her arms and willed herself to relax.

Then Garza said, "If he's doing business you'll have the Mendoza family on your hands, too. That's a lot of firepower in one place."

"If you can even get there." Gus thrust his hands in his pockets and started filtering change through his fingers. "I'm tellin' you, he'll catch you on radar. By the time you get there, the only people left on that island will be the cook and the gardener."

But not my sister. Chris tried to still her nerves but the jingling coins might as well have been dancing in her dental fillings. If the DEA spooked Jerome with their he-man tactics, Chris thought as the men continued to argue, Natalie would be swept away, as though she'd never existed. She listened to their voices, heated now, Special Agent Smith standing to square off against Gus. Guns, choppers, ammo. Always Scintella. Always his arrest. Never a word about what really mattered.

"All I want is my sister," Chris said loudly into a break in the argument. "I can get onto that island myself, one way or another, before you bring in the cavalry. Give me that chance to get Natalie out, and you can do whatever the hell you want after we're gone."

"That's a good way to get yourself killed," Garza remarked.

"If I do nothing, Natalie gets killed. None of you sound very interested in her except as a source of information."

For a long moment, no one spoke. Gus's face screwed into his characteristic scowl. Antonio Garza stared at his shoes beneath the table.

"I'm not leaving my sister at Jerome Scintella's mercy," she said quietly. "I'll take *Obsession* to Isladonata if I have to do it on my own."

Long seconds passed while she held Smith's gaze. She wasn't bluffing and she knew that showed in her face—she was scared, but she wouldn't back down. She didn't trust this agent to look after Natalie once he and his team had Scintella in view. Sure, they might be honorable men. But her experience had taught her to be wary. The nice mutt sitting placidly with you on the front porch one minute could become a mindless part of a howling, uncontrollable pack when the quarry was sighted.

She was the only one in the room putting Natalie first.

Smith must have read her correctly because he said to Garza, "I need to make a phone call. Can we talk outside?"

Garza sighed and faced her, his dark eyes soft with what looked like fatherly concern. "Do you mind waiting?"

"Go ahead."

Garza grasped the cane that leaned against the table and levered himself from his chair like a much older man. After he'd limped from the room behind Smith, Chris asked, "Was he injured in the line of duty?"

"Domestic violence case. Guy beatin' up his wife, the neighbor calls, we go over there. We've got the guy cuffed and headed out the door when the wife goes ape-shit with a handgun 'cause she wants to 'save her man.'"

Chris heard again Natalie's voice: *He didn't mean it. It's not like he broke anything.*

"God," she murmured.

Gus shook his head. "I don't know. I'm no shrink. I just know it happens sometimes. They usually don't come out firing, though. Tony got a bad break."

She was silent for a moment before she asked, "What do you think they're talking about?"

His heavy sigh could have been anything: fatigue, resignation, exasperation. "I don't know," he said finally, kicking his chair back onto two legs. "I got an idea but I never cared much for guessin'."

He had a point. Guessing invited a lot of wondering, and that would turn into worrying. She had enough of that on her plate already.

While Gus jangled quarters and dimes, Chris tried to concentrate on not wondering if Jerome was hurting Natalie. Live today, right now, she reminded herself. Maybe it was time to go back to meditating. That practice had helped when she was having a tough time with the rig roughnecks. Funny how the simplest things got so easily swamped by worry and fear. You get busy, then you forget how to stay centered, sane.

"What I don't understand," Gus said abruptly, "is why these boys sound like they need your boat. The DEA could use any old tub they've seized recently."

"I thought smugglers used Cigarette boats and fishing trawlers," she said, thinking back over cruising posts and magazine articles she'd read.

"Then why don't they take a damn go-fast boat then?"

"You know I won't let them go without me," she warned.

Before Gus could work up a head of steam, the office door opened. Chris watched Smith and Garza file back in and settle across from her again. Gus tipped his chair onto all four legs, clearly ready to do battle.

"Ms. Hampton," Smith said, "you've given us the best chance in years to put our hands on Scintella. It's a major break for us."

"I'm sure of that," she said flatly. "What about my sister?"

"We want to see her home with you safe and sound."

That she wasn't sure of. Smith didn't seem to notice.

"We'll put a team together and go to Isladonata, intercept Scintella and bring your sister back."

"On what boat?"

"I phoned my partner, Special Agent McLellan, while Mr. Garza and I were outside. McLellan wants to pay for the upgrades in exchange for using your yacht."

"Why can't you take a seized boat?" Gus demanded.

"Logistical problem," Smith snapped. "Last year's hurricane season took out our suitable yachts. Ms. Hampton's right. We need something that won't make them suspicious."

"And you'll find a captain who can handle a hundred-ton vessel?" She ignored the yank on her gut at the thought of handing the yacht—her home—over to a bunch of weekend sea cowboys she didn't know.

"It might be tricky," he admitted.

"How will you find the island?"

"Hook us up with your sister and we'll take it from there."

She shook her head. "It's not going to work that way."

"Why not?" Smith asked sharply.

"She won't talk to anyone but me."

"That's not wise—"

"Of course it's wise. She doesn't know you. She doesn't know your voice. What if Jerome tricks her into talking to one of his thugs? It's bad enough that he could tap her phone." Chris paused, lifted her chin. "But she knows me. She trusts me. If she does happen to come up with fresh information, she'll call."

Smith hesitated, clearly tempted. "We can set up a phone relay."

Chris shook her head. "Not good enough. I'm going with you or there's no deal." When she saw that mule look come over Smith's open face, she added, "This isn't negotiable."

"You don't understand." Smith leaned forward. "Two operations failed to bring Scintella in. Believe it or not, the long shot you've dropped in our laps may be our best opportunity to nail him. He might anticipate his men turning on him, but he might not guess that his wife would."

"I just want to know Natalie's going to be safe. If it comes down to a choice between catching Scintella and saving my sister—"

"There aren't any guarantees where Scintella's concerned," Smith said bluntly. "Except that he's dangerous and he'll fight being brought in. He'll do everything he can to stay free."

And the DEA agents, no matter how well-meaning, would have their sights set first on Scintella, then on Natalie. *I'm the only one who's going to be looking out for her.*

"I'm captaining my vessel on this trip," Chris told Smith as she stood. Before he could start lobbing objections her way, she said, "When you and your partner come out to the boatyard, I'll be prepping my yacht." Then she turned on her heel and walked out.

The small, silver key dangled on a chain held lightly in Special Agent Smith's fingers. Behind him, late afternoon sunlight swept into *Obsession*'s salon, haloing him, making his blond hair almost golden, his roughly sculpted features classically Grecian in their shadows and highlights.

"I wouldn't deposit or spend this all at once," he said around a smile.

Safety-deposit box key.

Chris scrubbed her hands with a shop rag, feeling suddenly as if plucking that key from his fingers would change everything, that she'd be cast out into the perilous unknown. The end of innocence. The end of everything she knew and the start of a journey she might not complete.

The rising tide of fear was swallowed by the image of Natalie holding out an ice-cream cone to Chris. Chris had been fourteen and Natalie four. "Share!" Natalie had shouted and laughed, tossing her dark, curly hair.

Leave everything she knew behind? Risk her boat and her life to save her sister?

So be it.

She took the key from Smith's hand and shoved it deep in her shorts pocket. "Thanks."

"My partner doesn't like the idea of your captaining us." Smith stepped farther into the salon, abruptly losing his godlike demeanor as he glanced around, seemingly taking everything in at once.

"You told him I won't take no for an answer."

"Yes." He paused. "For what it's worth, I'm in your corner on this."

Surprised, she glanced at him. His face showed nothing but the certainty of a man who knew what he wanted to do. "I appreciate that," she said. "Where is your partner?"

"Busy. He'll show on Monday." He flashed a quick and charming smile. "Call me Smitty."

She relaxed a little. Funny how nicknames knocked people down to size or elevated them into legend. Thank

God his nickname hadn't been something like Nine-Fingered Sam or Chainsaw Larry. "Smitty" was a guy you could trust. Like "Gus."

Then she asked the sixty-four-dollar question. "How much boating experience do you have?"

"I've done a little Coastie work up the eastern seaboard."

"Coast Guard, huh?" she shot back, surprised. "What'd you do?"

He shrugged, wandering past her to the aft deck's sliding door. "A little search and rescue, a little cruise ship escort, stuff like that. Nothing too exciting."

"Not exciting?"

Smitty chuckled. "If I never see another drunken offshore fisherman with a bad bilge pump, it'll be too soon. Can I have a tour or are you in the middle of something?"

"No, I've got time. You've seen the aft deck there."

"Yeah, it's a great space." Smitty's gaze automatically moved from the port cleat to the storage compartment marked LIFE JACKETS to the round life ring and its attached line. His priorities fit hers, she noted with approval.

"She was under a shed and neglected for almost twenty years," Chris said. "I'm surprised she even floats."

"Old girl like this? She'll never sink. That your distribution panel?" he asked, hooking a thumb at the sliding wooden door in the salon wall.

"Yes."

She slid open the panel's door to let him study the shore power switches, generator start-and-stop mechanism, the breaker switches for all the boat's electrics.

"Nice setup. You wire all this up?"

She nodded. "The electrical wiring on the old panel was so frayed I'm surprised she didn't burn to the waterline when the surveyor switched on the shore power." She watched him close up the panel as she said, "I still have some wiring to check. There's a light switch here in the salon that doesn't work."

He stood again and his gaze traced the probable route from the distribution panel to the light switch on the other side of the salon. "Take half a day to track down, probably."

"Low priority," she replied. "Come on down below. I'll show you the engine rooms."

Smitty might turn out okay, she thought as she led the way down the spiral staircase to the lower passageway. He seemed to know his stuff and appeared comfortable with the fact this was her vessel. Even Dave had wanted to jump in and fix things for her rather than wait for her to ask for help. But Smitty just put his idea out there—half a day to fix the light switch wiring—and left the decision up to her.

She opened the starboard engine room door and squinted against the door's piercing screech. *Note to self: Oil the hinges.* She flicked on the overhead light and the starboard engine's massive bulk sprang to life.

"A Detroit!" Smitty said, clearly pleased. "Twelve-vee-ninety-six?"

"Yep. Naturally aspirated, no turbocharging. One thing I wanted to do was paint the engine room floor here before the shakedown cruise so the leaks would show. I overhauled both Hortense and Claire, but—"

"Excuse me?" Smitty asked, turning from his examination of the engine's coolant, collection tank cap in hand.

"Claire's the starboard engine. Hortense is the port, just across the hall in her own engine room."

His grin split his mobile face. "Claire and Hortense. Named after…?"

"Great-aunts on my father's side." Chris smiled, faintly remembering lemon squares and tatted doilies and sunshine on a back porch surrounded by maple trees. No faces anymore, but feelings of warmth and contentment. Happiness.

"Nice to meet you, Claire." Smitty patted the engine's solid block, then turned back to Chris. "I'll paint in here for you."

Chris looked around the engine room's still stout flooring, at the little worktable sitting below the pegboard she'd organized just last month, at the tool cabinet and hatch leading to the bilge compartment, all smeared with grease and ages-old dirt. "Nasty piece of work."

"That I am," he said with a grin, "but I'll do my best."

Friday evening, Chris eased her pickup onto the Galveston-Port Bolivar ferry and parked where she was directed by a bored ferryman. After an afternoon spent poking through Old Man Templeton's salvaged spares, she was ready to get home and snag a late dinner. She'd found several items she could use, including a fuel pump to replace Hortense's aging one. But she hadn't found a propeller. The starboard prop was so gouged and chipped that the shaft had started vibrating. A few hours of that and Claire, the starboard engine, would shake to pieces.

Leaving the pickup's windows rolled down and her wallet and cell phone under the seat, she slammed the door, then headed toward the bow where a small contingent of hardy souls braved the still-warm breeze. In a few minutes the last car came aboard and the ferry cast off.

The ferry's bow wave arced below her as she leaned over the rail. Texas City refineries plumed white smoke into darkening sky. Laughing gulls shrieked as they careened toward her, then banked and slipped back to the wake to fish for minnows stunned by the ferry's engines.

She turned to watch the birds. That's when she saw

him, leaning casually against the shoulder of a dark blue Buick, watching her. He wore a white T-shirt, jeans and black biker boots, his clothes a size too big for his rail-thin frame. His thin blond hair lifted in the wind. One hand rested on the Buick's hood; the other fingered a cigarette. He could have been anyone.

Only she'd seen him before.

She pivoted slightly as though looking back toward Port Bolivar, not moving from the rail. He raised his head and looked at her, squinting against the ferry's bright house lights. His thin lips stretched over his gaunt face in that same grimace of fear she'd seen as his out-of-control powerboat veered toward her. Except she'd changed her sailboat's direction, and his powerboat should have kept going the way it was headed.

But it hadn't. It had changed direction, too.

She looked again. The grimace wasn't a grimace.

He was smiling.

Eugene Falks, she thought. *The name on the police report was Eugene Falks.*

"Nice evening," he called. His voice was thin and razor-sharp, like him.

She said nothing. Her pickup sat directly behind the Buick. She'd walked right past him and not known it was him. He could have touched her. She shuddered.

She folded her arms across her chest, but that made her feel vulnerable—not easily able to move or defend herself—so she relaxed enough to let them drop to her sides again. Better. Deep breaths. *Keep him in view but don't let him rattle you. Settle down and wait.*

Consciously, muscle by muscle, she released the tension from her body. The ferry plowed through the darkening water. Over the opposite railing, Chris watched whitecaps kick up. The man tucked one hand in his front pocket and hunched farther against the car, still watching her.

Was he a stalker? Had he picked her out in the grocery store parking lot and decided for whatever twisted reason to target her? Maybe being a natural blonde, dishwater or not, wasn't such an advantage after all.

As the ferry pulled up to its dock, she faced Falks. He pursed his lips and sniffed, tossed his cigarette onto the ferry's deck and toed it out with his boot. Then he reached into the front seat and pulled out a cell phone. In a moment, she heard her cell trilling in her truck.

He knows my phone number.

People streamed back to their cars. Chris gripped the railing with one hand as the ferry jolted into place. Falks snapped his phone closed, then yanked his Buick's door open and folded himself inside.

The good news was, Falks would have to drive off first.

The bad news was, there was no guarantee he wouldn't follow her.

Don't walk like a victim. Chris strode toward her pickup, head up. She'd have to walk past his car again, but she'd do that on the passenger side, where he couldn't reach out the window or door. At least it'd be harder.

She braced herself as she walked around the car's nose. When she drew even with the Buick's passenger side headlight, the car's engine spat and clattered to life. Falks didn't move, didn't look at her, didn't put the Buick in gear. She dug the keys from her jeans pocket. On impulse, she took a couple of steps back from her pickup until she could read the Buick's license plate. Falks made eye contact in his side mirror.

He didn't grin this time.

The first cars started bumping up and over the landing ramp. Behind her, an SUV revved its engine. She waited until the Buick eased forward, then quickly opened the pickup's door and hopped inside. One tap on the accelerator and the Chevy roared, settled into its purring rhythm.

"Go ahead," she muttered at Falks as she put the pickup in Drive. "Follow me."

Because her first stop would be the Galveston Police Department.

Chapter 3

Chris woke instantly. Someone was aboard.

She lay perfectly still in her cabin, holding her breath and trying to listen beyond the hum of the corner box fan. The boatyard's shed lights glowed outside the open portholes.

Damn kids. She knew Dave should have run the little heathens out of the boatyard. Probably stealing electronics.

Footsteps above, in the salon. Heavy. Not a kid's. A man's.

Her skin tingled with fear. The face of the cadaverous man, pale, thin, eerie in the new moon's light, floated in her mind's darkness. Eugene Falks. She'd have to do something, not just lie here waiting for him to find her. Her arms and legs lay like stones. Was it really Falks? How strong was he? Could she fight him? God, she hadn't hit anyone since seventh grade when awful Jimmy McAllister tried to French-kiss her in study hall.

No way was she going to let some weirdo come onto

her boat and steal something or attack her. This was her home. *Her* home. No freakin' way.

The molten lead that had filled her veins a moment ago surged into adrenaline. What were her options? Her cell phone was in the galley. Her tools were all put away. There was nothing in the stateroom she could use as a weapon. She hadn't oiled the engine room doors, so opening either of those to grab a tool would alert the intruder to her presence. Still, he might not expect her to be aboard while the boat was in dry dock. She could take a chance on the noise.

The wrench. She saw it clearly propped up behind the door to her ensuite head. She'd used it yesterday and forgotten to put it up. Fortunately, it was a nice, hefty seven-eighths.

She slid out of bed and pulled on her robe, belting it tightly around her waist. She retrieved the wrench from the head, paused. Silence upstairs. Whoever was up there had stopped moving. She eased open her stateroom door, crept into the hall.

She paused again by the spiral staircase, heart pounding, to listen. A familiar click and shush told her the door to the port side office had opened. She switched hands on the wrench, then flipped it around so the open end—the end that made two prongs—was the business end. Swing or jab, it would work fine.

She crept up the staircase, skipping the step that creaked. The upper passageway loomed, dark and empty. On the port side, the office. On the starboard side, the galley. Aft, the salon, whose sliding glass door opened onto the aft deck. Dim light from that door cast long shadows of sofa and chair onto the floor. Beside her, the office cabin door was ajar. She sidestepped into the galley. The smooth tile cooled her bare feet.

Shoes. She should have put on shoes.

Without taking her eyes from the office door, she

reached for the counter beneath the starboard window where her cell phone lay. Her hand found a notebook, a pen, the bowl of fruit. Chris tore her eyes from the office door's sliver of darkness. The cell wasn't on the counter.

Yelling wouldn't do any good. Nobody hung around a boatyard after midnight. She hefted the wrench.

Knife?

She shuddered. No. No knife.

Leave.

Now there was a plan. But if Falks was after her, and if he happened to hear her, she'd never outrun him on foot. Not barefoot through a debris-strewn boatyard. She needed her car, to get to the police substation.

Car keys? She slid down the starboard cabinet to the floor, facing the office and willing herself to be small and unnoticeable while she tried to remember where she'd left them. After a frustrating and fruitless visit to the Galveston cop shop about Eugene Falks (*Sorry, ma'am, we can't post anyone at the yard, but we'll send a patrol car by once in a while*), and an equally frustrating call to Garza (*Please leave a message*), she'd driven home, climbed up the ladder to the aft deck, come inside, made sure all the doors and windows were locked, then tossed her keys in...

...the office.

Dammit.

She'd have to chance it on foot.

Chris turned the wrench in her grip. Right. Just slip around the L-shaped counter that separated the galley from the salon, walk across fifteen feet of carpet, ease on out the open door to the aft deck, then down the ten-foot ladder to the ground. No problem.

Except she was sitting on the galley floor, butt frozen to the tiles, legs locked in place, eyes riveted to what little she could see of the office's dark doorway. The only part moving at any speed was her brain, imagining Falks coming through that office door like a storm, his sickly grin plastered on his face.

"Move," she whispered.

She stood. Her heart banged away at her chest wall, fouled her hearing. Crouching, she slunk through the galley, paused briefly at the salon's edge to silently suck some air into her lungs. Her trembling hands clenched. The wrench felt like a puny baseball bat. *Note to self: Buy a Louisville Slugger.*

She straightened and took a step toward the salon door. Dark movement flashed on her right.

She swung, head-high.

A soft thunk—metal on flesh—then a muffled grunt. Chris recoiled, ducked instinctively into the shadowy galley rather than the backlit salon. On the other side of the L-shaped counter, just in front of the office door, the intruder wheezed.

Had she hit him in the *throat?*

She gripped the wrench tighter. Outside. She needed to get outside. The wheeze moved from the hallway toward the elbow of the counter's *L.* He'd be an arm's length from either the salon or the hallway. She remembered Falks's long, spindly, angular arms. *Come into my parlor.*

The wheeze permeated the air like a metronome: *Hiiiss, ruuush. Hiiiss, ruuush.*

Options. Right. A galley door led forward into the pilothouse. But the door, like so many on the yacht, would creak when opened and Falks would know instantly what she was doing. She'd never have a chance. Nor was she fast enough to reach the office and grab her cell.

She had another option.

She could attack.

Chris breathed silently through her mouth while she laid the wrench on the linoleum next to her right foot. She felt behind her for the cabinet door she wanted, the one with the little plaque on it.

Hiiiss, ruuush.

Falks started moving again, inching along the *L* toward the little passage between the galley and the salon. A shaft of boatyard light speared the passage.

The plaque's sharp edge pricked her fingertips. She opened the cabinet door and reached inside.

Hiiiss, ruuush.

Falks's fingers curled around the cabinet's sides. Chris's own trembling fingers found the smooth, cold cylinder she was searching for. Falks eased into the light—an ear, a stretch of pale skin, one wide, pale eye.

"I see you," he whispered.

Calm wrapped itself around Chris like a cloak, as it always did the moment before an irrevocable action: a softball arcing toward the plate and her waiting bat, the red-circled target coming into focus just before she squeezed the trigger, pen poised above paper as she prepared to sign her resignation. It was the moment anything was possible.

Falks was a man. Only a man.

Chris smiled. "Come and get me." She drew in a deep breath and held it.

He leaped. She wrenched the cylinder from its holding clips and yanked out the safety pin. By his second step, she gripped the mini fire extinguisher's handle, and by his third—he fell toward her like an avalanche—she shot a hard stream of chemical agent into his wide and glaring eyes, then skittered away, out of reach.

Falks shrieked, jerked away. "Shit!" he shouted, scrubbing his face, tearing at the smoky dust. "You bitch!" He collapsed back against the counter, reeling. Chris let out her breath, extinguisher raised and ready to strike. He fell backward into the salon. His curses stuck in his throat, then the coughing started as white smoke drifted around his head like a veil.

Chris bolted into the office, snagged her cell. Fire extinguisher in one hand, she punched 911 with the other. Falks's coughs rasped, fading.

"Come on!" she shouted at the phone. Why weren't they picking up? She looked at the phone's LED screen. Because she'd dialed 991.

A thud and the crash of shattering glass, then a scrabbling on the aft deck.

The bastard was getting away.

Chris skirted the dying edge of chemical smoke as she ran from the office into the salon. She stopped short at the aft deck doorway that glittered with broken shards.

Falks's long, white hand shone like that of a picked-clean corpse before it slipped from the deck railing and disappeared.

Chris studied Smitty's lean back from her sofa vantage point. He stood in front of the salon door's remains, hands stuffed in his shorts pockets, his shoulders hunched as if against a cold wind. Or blame.

"I should have been here," he said to the spray of glass at his feet.

The breeze kicked up by the box fans blowing from the galley ruffled his shirt sleeves. Outside, the predawn darkness carried a hint of dew. The cops had long since taken down their notes, given their assurances they'd find

Falks and gone. They'd stayed almost as long as the residual chemical smoke, which had left a film of mica dust over the floor where Falks had jumped Chris.

"Are you sure it was Falks?" Antonio Garza asked. He leaned from his chair to scribble on his ever-present yellow legal pad.

Chris wrapped her fingers more tightly around her coffee cup and drew her legs onto the sofa. "I'm positive. No doubt."

"I'm sorry, Chris," Smitty said for the fourth time since he'd arrived.

Garza sighed. "It's not your fault. It's mine. Had I picked up my messages in time—"

"There's plenty of blame to go around," Chris remarked. "Galveston didn't send a patrol car, you didn't pick up your messages, Smitty isn't clairvoyant, and I should have gotten a motel room once I got the impression Falks was stalking me. That's not the point." She set her cup on the table, finally able to trust her hands not to shake. "The point is I don't know what Falks is doing."

"I've got a call in to McLellan," Garza told Smitty's back. "He's running Falks's name to see if it comes up connected to Scintella."

"You think Falks is stalking me because of Natalie?"

"The timing's right," Smitty said without turning.

"But he tried to run me down before I even found out what was going on with her," Chris pointed out.

Garza's head shake looked tired, resigned. "It's still possible. Scare tactic. Scintella knows Natalie would call you for help if she needed it. Maybe he was trying to make sure you wouldn't pick up the phone."

"Yeah, but Falks missed that chance. Why is he stalking me on the ferry and then breaking into my boat? Why didn't he just finish the job when he had the chance?"

Smitty's shoulders stiffened. They sloped down from his linebacker neck, Chris noticed, as if worn down by a yoke of suffering. "Change of plans. Scintella found out Natalie called you. That's why Falks called your cell. To let you know he knows."

"Shit." Chris scrubbed her hands over her face. "Then she's in even more danger."

"Maybe, maybe not," Smitty said to the window. "From your description, Falks was searching for something. You must have something he wants."

Chris gave a short laugh in spite of herself. "You've seen this boat and what I drive. I don't have anything of value."

"Has Natalie sent you anything?" Smitty asked. "A box, a letter?"

"Nothing lately." Nothing that had arrived yet, anyway. She straightened. "I'm supposed to get a package of clothes from her in a few days."

"Clothes?"

Chris shrugged. "She likes giving me designer clothes."

Smitty grunted. "Expensive hobby."

"She can afford it." Chris irritably swept her feet from the sofa to the floor and grabbed her coffee cup. Damn shakes were back. And she had work to do. But she still had questions. "So do you think Jerome's ticked off about an Italian dress?"

"Maybe she's sending you something valuable—like a document. Something incriminating." Garza glanced at Smitty. "You know the way Scintella works. Could he have left a paper trail and his wife got hold of something?"

"Maybe," Smitty conceded. "He's not the brightest bulb in the candelabra."

"Natalie could have dug something up to use against him," Chris mused. "She's scared, but she understands power." She had, after all, wrapped their grandfather around her little finger.

Garza grunted. "Scintella's not the kind of man you want to manipulate."

Chris tried to tamp down the fresh fear rising through her stomach. "What if Falks wasn't sent by Scintella? What if he's just a random stalker?"

"He's Scintella's man." Smitty crossed his lean, muscled arms. "I'll be here 24/7."

"But what does that mean for my sister?" Fear pierced her chest, making it hard to breathe. "If Jerome knows…"

Garza's scar throbbed red above his ear. "Anything could happen, Ms. Hampton." His gaze, when it met hers, lay heavy with the weight of his experience. He finds missing people, she remembered. How many had he found dead? How many mothers and fathers and brothers and sisters had he been forced to face?

Natalie could die, his gaze said. But it said more than that. Natalie could already be dead.

"I have to call her. She gave me a special number where I could reach her."

Chris grabbed her cell from the table but before she could hit the speed dial, Garza said, "What reason are you going to give her for calling?"

Chris paused. He had a point. Why would she call in the middle of the night? Just to chat? Because she couldn't sleep? The penalty for making Jerome even more suspicious was too high to pay just to assuage her anxiety.

"I'll wait," Chris said through her frustration. "Until morning."

"Don't mention the package," Garza ordered. "If she's managed to ship something on the sly, let's not tip off Scintella."

"This is going to turn into a waiting game, isn't it?" Chris asked. "Waiting to call Natalie, waiting for the package, waiting to get under way."

Garza's half smile was sympathetic. "I'm sorry. It doesn't get easier. But you have plenty to do in the meantime."

"McLellan will arrive on Monday morning," Smitty added.

"Can he help us work?" Chris asked, dragging her attention back to the task in front of her. First things first.

Smitty abruptly grinned his charming, lopsided grin. "You'll see for yourself."

"I hope so. We've got to launch in thirteen days," she said, feeling her nerves prick the skin, itching to get things done, and done fast. "Time's wasting."

Outside, faint peach light colored the sky, and the resident green monk parrots, so social, so busy, had already begun to chatter up the dawn.

Late Monday afternoon, Chris lay on a catwalk stretched inches over oily bilge water, a rough-drawn map of *Obsession*'s hull in one hand and a flashlight in the other. She didn't much care for poking around in the bilge, but necessity was a mother and there was no getting around it. Every through-hull—every hole in the boat that fed water into or out of the boat, through the hull—needed to be watertight. The last thing she needed was a hose to give way at sea.

She'd already suffered one setback. Bright and early this morning, Dave had had to confess the air compressor on his spray-painting equipment had failed. No hull painting, he'd said, until the new compressor came in on Thursday morning. And the other boatyards were booked up because it was prime boating season. It was one of the ironies of pleasure boating: no one wanted to fix up their boats until it was weather-fit to use them, which meant they lost half the season to repairs.

But not repairs like the kind she was going to have to do now.

At least Natalie had called yesterday. Three minutes away from the bodyguard she called Igor was all Natalie could grab. While in a public pay toilet, no less. The disposable cell phones she'd bought were extremely handy. Chris just prayed she didn't get caught with one.

First things first.

The bilge's overhead lamps cast dim vee's along the catwalk. *Glad I'm not claustrophobic,* she thought as she shimmied on her stomach a little farther forward toward the hardest-to-reach through-hull fitting. Damp mustiness filled her nostrils, made her skin clammy despite the growing morning heat. Around her, color-coded wiring and grimy hoses snaked along the hull. A few feet of belly-crawling brought her even with the fitting she was looking for.

The through-hull, placed several feet away on the starboard side, looked pretty rough from the catwalk. The flashlight picked out minute cracks in the hose that fed seawater into the engines' cooling systems. The clamps securing the hose in place showed specks of rust, too. Chris wiggled off the catwalk and balanced herself over the bilge to get close to the fitting. One good yank and the clamp snapped. Another yank and the hose popped off the through-hull barb. She looked at the crumbling heavy-duty rubber. Were all the hoses this bad?

"Captain Chris?"

A man's deep voice drifted through *Obsession's* dimly lit bowels.

Her stomach clenched until she realized Eugene Falks wouldn't be casually calling her name. No, this had to be a workman or something. She'd seen the revolver Smitty wore in his shoulder holster this morning and the way his gaze constantly flicked from door to window while he tore out the salon carpet. Nobody was going to get past Smitty upstairs while she lay prone down here.

She leaned against the hull wall to lever herself back onto the catwalk. Nearly there, her hand slipped from the hull and plunged into the bilge. The flashlight clattered, then splashed next to her and went out.

"Dammit." She fished the dead flashlight out of the filthy bilge water, trying not to use her imagination when her fingers touched solid, shifting objects near the bottom. God only knew what was down there.

"Chris?"

The man was close by, inside the engine room, and still calling her name. She crawled backward to the open crawl space door. Going ass-first into the engine room wouldn't be much of a greeting for the workman, but what the hey. He could learn to call before showing up.

She wriggled her butt through the hatch, got to her knees, straightened and said sharply, "What is it?"

The first thing she saw was an astonishing pair of gray eyes, very pale irises rimmed with a much darker slate. The man squatted about a foot from the hatch. They were nearly nose to nose, and his gaze pumped every ounce of blood in her body straight to her core.

She registered all of this at once: he hadn't asked permission to board her yacht, he was in his late thirties, he wore expensive Italian leather shoes, she was smeared with grease and oil, he had thick black hair, her right hand was now bleeding, he smelled wonderful.

Not your average Galveston boat monkey schlepping down to a job.

"Special Agent McLellan?" she asked.

"Connor." His remarkable eyes gleamed at her, kicking her pulse into high gear.

"Smitty said you'd show up today."

"He told me you'd had some excitement." His voice resounded through the engine room. "He also showed me around a little upstairs."

Chris got to her feet, then closed the bilge hatch. "*Obsession*'s not much to look at right now," she said as she looked around for a shop rag to wipe off with, "but she's built like a tank."

"I noticed."

She glanced up to find him staring at Hortense. "You won't have to worry about the engines. Detroits were made for tough lives. Some built back in the fifties and sixties are still powering shrimpers and tow boats. Hell," she said, running the dirty cloth over her arm, "these old ladies will outlive me."

"I don't doubt it."

"Come on upstairs. I'm ready to look at some daylight."

He followed her out of the port engine room into the lower deck passageway. "Will all this need to be fixed, too?" He waved a hand at the crumbling wall panels.

"Eventually. Hold your ears." She shoved the engine room door closed and winced at the metal-on-metal shriek. "Sorry about that. Out of WD-40. The two aft staterooms here were actually in decent shape when I got her, very livable. Mine's on your right. The one on the left needs a little work."

She opened her door to flash him a glimpse of her queen-size bed and wall of drawers. The mariner's compass quilt stretched across the bed's foot. Two frilly, decorative pillows, a nod less to traditional femininity than to homeyness, lay propped up against the real ones.

He stepped closer, caught the door as she was about to close it. "Very nice," he said, leaning in.

Chris suddenly realized just how big he was, how his shoulders filled the narrow space they stood in. What was she thinking, showing him her private space? She stepped back to cue McLellan to do the same, then closed the door when he let go. "You and Smitty can fight over the other big cabin."

She headed for the stairs, tapping doors as she passed them. "Engine rooms, starboard and port. Laundrette. Crew cabin, for the loser." She turned right up the steps to the upper passageway. When he reached the hall, she pointed to a forward door. "Another crew cabin, smaller than the one below. And behind it, the office."

She stood at the edge of the salon, looked at the disaster that was once merely a fashion-challenged salon. All of the ratty brown Naugahyde furniture had been shoved onto the aft deck, waiting for a landfill run. The good furniture—the mahogany tables, the brass lamps, a mahogany bench seat with a hand-embroidered cushion—sat on old blankets in the galley. A shirtless Smitty was hoisting a roll of torn and ugly carpet onto his bare shoulder.

"How's the flooring?" she asked.

Smitty grinned under his rime of dirt. "Solid as a rock. Marine planking. Thirty years old and still has the battleship gray primer." He headed toward the aft door with his filthy carpet mangle, but paused long enough to say to McLellan, "Change your clothes, boy. You gonna git yo' ass in gear for a change."

McLellan raised a brow, unruffled in his crisp white

dress shirt and dark slacks. He looked pointedly at the brown carpet strips hanging over Smitty's bare chest like a furry vest. "Staple some of that to your chest and you'll stop having woman problems," he remarked mildly.

"Hey," Smitty called from the aft deck, "don't go south with the mouth, pretty boy."

McLellan just shrugged.

"Have a seat." Chris waved at the bench seat as she threaded her way through the tables to the galley sink. "I'll wash up and be right with you."

"Smitty said there's a lot of work to be done." McLellan came to stand by the island counter that separated the galley from the salon. "He told me you were very resourceful." He paused.

She glanced up at him and found his gaze thoughtful, considering. And admiring as it slid from her chin to her collarbone, then lower. She realized suddenly the threadbare tank top and satin demi-bra she wore for hot and dirty boat work showed almost as much as they concealed.

Then he murmured, "I see there was much he didn't say." He went on, "For one thing, I didn't expect *Obsession* to be so..." He trailed off, looking around the profoundly empty salon, as though he expected to find his vocabulary there.

Chris dried off while she waited for him to finish.

He didn't. Instead he asked, "What does she weigh?"

"About a hundred thousand pounds."

"Stout lady," he said, nearly under his breath.

"She was built in the days when fiberglass was new and the boatyards were afraid of underbuilding. Her hull's about twice as thick as it needs to be."

"And a classic design." He nodded to himself, obviously pleased, and turned from the galley to the salon.

His masculine grace as he strode away reminded her of the world her grandfather had lived in with his antiques gallery, his art, his clothes, his money. The world she didn't belong in and never would.

Smitty might not look like a DEA agent, but neither did McLellan. This one at least had the air of command, but not the militaristic bearing she associated with state troopers. Different breed, she guessed. A rich one, given the way he dressed. She wondered which of them was the boss and decided on McLellan, who apparently didn't have a nickname. And didn't need one.

As she joined him in the salon's center, he turned to her. "This boat's very beautiful."

"She will be."

"Is everything on schedule?" His gaze sharpened as it roamed over the cracked windows, dingy wall panels and bare floor.

"So far. The boatyard can do the big jobs, but not all of it. My timetable says we need to splash next Friday. That means everybody pitches in." She eyed the impeccable crease in his slacks. "If you're up to it."

McLellan shoved his hands into his pockets, relaxed and clearly at home. "I'm up to it. Always glad to learn something new."

Chris paused, trying to figure out how to say what she needed to say. "Thank you for letting me be a part of this."

His eyes darkened slightly. "Against my better judgment, but Falks's attack on you tells me you're the key to this mission. It'll be dangerous but we'll keep you safe." He looked at Chris for a long, somber moment, as if he could see past her tough facade as easily as he could see past the salon's water-stained wall panels to the strong framework beneath. Then he said softly, "We'll bring your sister home."

Sudden tears threatened but she blinked them back, turned slightly to study the stout and faithful flooring. She'd concentrated for the past five days on the effort, the plan. Keeping the schedule. It was all she'd allow herself to think about. Never beyond that. Never to what if Jerome finds out, or what if he sends more goons to stop them, or what if Jerome skips the island and goes straight to South America?

Or, heaven forbid, what if he's already killed Natalie?

Chapter 4

Tuesday morning, Chris looked at the big cardboard box sitting on the galley's counter—the international postage coupons, the Natalie-typical hypertaped edges, the thick black block letters routing the box to CHRISTINA HAMPTON. Chris fingered a box corner, surprised her hands were so steady.

"Is that it?" Smitty asked from behind her.

She nodded. She smelled him before she saw him, all sawdust and machine oil from cutting wall panels to shape. He rinsed his hands in the galley sink while she plucked the craft knife from her back pocket and slit the packing tape.

The top flared open. A foam peanut popped out, clung to the cardboard. A sea of peanuts covered whatever lay inside.

"Moment of truth," McLellan said, stripping the gloves from his hands as he joined them. His bare arms bore angry scratches and grime smears. "Let's see what she sent you."

Chris hesitated. *Don't be stupid. She didn't ship you a poisonous snake.* She plunged in up to her wrists. A heavy, gift-wrapped box surfaced first. Chris hefted it, then set it carefully on the counter.

"Here's an envelope," Smitty said. He plucked the creamy letter from the peanut barrage and handed it over. Simple enough note. Chris read it aloud.

Dearest Chris,

I know you told me not to spend anything on you, but I also remember how you complained about that awful plastic or whatever compass you have on the helm. I don't think you can keep this one outside, but it'd make a great table centerpiece (that's a hint). I had it blessed by Father Xavier here in Rome, so maybe it'll be accurate for you.

The rest is just for you and whatever you do, don't wear these anywhere but parties! If I hear you've been trotting around the boat in these, I'll be furious.

I miss you. I'll call when I have a chance.
Lots of love,
Natalie

"The compass sounds promising," Smitty remarked when Chris finished.

"Too obvious." McLellan took the letter and scanned it. "If Scintella's monitoring her mail and gifts, he checked the compass."

Chris ripped through the gift paper and sliced the box open. She peeled off two layers of bubble wrap, then caught her breath.

An antique brass box nestled in more bubble wrap, its round top gleaming a dull greenish-gold. She carefully lifted the heavy top to reveal a gorgeous instrument with what looked like a vellum inlay of the compass points beneath a glass cover. North was designated by an elaborate star rather than the traditional diamond point. East's diamond had a smaller star painted on top of it.

Smitty whistled. "She wasn't kiddin' when she said *antique.*"

"How old is it?" McLellan leaned over the counter to look inside the box.

"Maybe eighteenth century," Chris replied. "Probably Italian." She set the top aside so she could remove the compass itself from the box. On the clean Corian counter, the instrument looked ancient. Arcane.

Smitty folded his dust-covered arms. "Needs cleaning."

"I'll do that on the trip." Chris traced the compass housing's greenish edge with her thumb, then looked at the black smear on her skin. "Brasso and two hours should do it. It's pretty tarnished."

"Does it open?" McLellan asked.

"Yeah, it does. It's gimballed so it can stay upright when the ship's under way." She pointed at the rods that held the compass in the center of its brass base. "It comes off those." She carefully lifted the compass from the rods and out of the base, then turned it upside down to display the small latches holding its bottom in place. "Compasses have to be calibrated so the dial sits properly and you don't think north is north-northwest or something."

"Do they fall out of true very often?"

"Go electronic," Smitty said.

Chris smiled. "Electronic compasses need calibration, too, every time you change the batteries." She eased the latches open and the bottom casing slipped off. Inside, two small adjustment screws protruded. "Turn these to reseat the dial."

McLellan examined the bottom cap while she played with the adjustment. When she held out her hand for the bottom to put it back on the compass, he gave it to her, then picked up the housing.

"Heavy," he muttered. He turned it upside down and ran his fingers inside it.

"Anything?" Smitty asked.

"Nothing obvious. Where's a flashlight?"

Smitty trotted off to the passageway where the rechargeable flashlight was plugged into a wall socket.

Chris peered into the housing. "You think she scratched his Swiss bank account number in there?"

The faintest smile flashed across McLellan's lips. "Smart-ass."

Smitty snapped on the flashlight and handed it to McLellan, who pointed it down into the cylinder. After a moment, he switched the light off. "No bank account numbers," he announced. "No treasure maps, no secret codes, no blueprints for WMD."

"Let's check the rest." Chris was already pulling plastic-wrapped bundles from the box. "She might have hidden a note or something."

While she dug through the clothes—why would Natalie ever assume Chris would wear a dress that short?—Smitty and McLellan pawed the peanuts out and examined the box itself. A few minutes later, a heap of expensive silk and satin lay on the counter and the box had been reduced to a jigsaw puzzle.

"Nothing here, either," Chris said, shoving a lacy, black merry widow deep under the pile. "None of the original store wrap had been touched and none of the items had anything sewn into the linings or hems."

"Long shot, anyway," McLellan replied. "Then maybe what Falks was looking for is already aboard. What was the last thing Natalie sent to you?"

Chris waved her hand at the gorgeous silk she would never have a reason to wear. "Just clothes like this."

"You don't party?" Smitty's smile held a hint of a leer. "Wanna start?"

McLellan scowled. "Has she ever sent you anything else?"

"No."

"If Falks is looking for something on this boat, it's on this boat." McLellan leaned his hip against the counter and surveyed the salon.

"We've taken the place apart," Smitty said. "We've got carpet torn up, wall panels taken down. Chris has been all over the engine rooms. Hell, if anything new shows up, she's gonna know it. My bet is it hasn't arrived yet."

"Possibly." McLellan turned again to face them, his handsome face like stone. "We have to be ready if Falks's mission changes again. That means we both stay aboard from now on. Wherever she goes, you or I go with her," he ordered Smitty.

"Why?" Smitty protested.

Chris squared her shoulders, suppressing the sudden fear that spiked through her chest. "Because if there's nothing to find, the next time Falks comes back, he won't be here to find anything. Am I right?"

McLellan reluctantly met her stare. "It would be like Scintella to send Falks here to teach Natalie a lesson. Given the boat race…" He let the sentence drift between them for a moment. "We won't let him hurt you."

"Just hold him off until we leave," Chris retorted. "Once we're at sea, I'll be fine."

* * *

We're sunk, Chris thought on Thursday afternoon. She slowly threaded the Chevy through the dry-docked boats toward *Obsession.* Smitty sat in the passenger seat, amiably waving at the workers and shouting to them in Spanish.

Chris glared at the boatyard office as she passed. Dave was a nice guy, she gave him that. A nice guy with a good heart and a mild manner but zero business sense and no inkling about customer service.

But then who the hell *did* in the marine services industry?

The carpet had shown up, but the carpet layers hadn't. She hadn't seen hide nor hair of the marine plumber. The service place supposedly supplying the new air compressor had called Dave bright and early this morning to say it'd be another two business days before it arrived. Monday, Dave had told her.

Monday.

Even if the new compressor actually did miraculously appear on Monday and the spray gun was in working order first thing Tuesday morning, the yard would have time to get only one primer coat and one topcoat on before launch on Friday morning. Unless the boatyard workers also ended up allergic to boats. Or work. Or both. And now it was too late to move *Obsession* to another yard for the work.

Anything else. It could have been *anything* but the hull painting.

And that wasn't her only trouble.

There was McLellan.

In the three days he'd been working with her, she'd idly fantasized about throwing him into the gulf several times, and just yesterday gave it some serious thought. A landlubber who didn't know what he was doing was one thing; a landlubber who insisted on quoting boating magazine articles on maintenance and upkeep ad nauseam was a nuisance. Everything that came out of his mouth started with, "I read in last month's *PassageMaker*..." or "There was an article in *Good Old Boat*..."

"I've spent the last year talking in excruciating depth to old salts who've worked on the water for decades," she'd finally said after having a brief vision of grabbing his ankles and levering him over the aft deck railing. "Not to mention taking this vessel out myself and working my ass off to earn my captain's license. I think we've got it covered."

"There's nothing wrong with trying something new," he'd retorted.

"I have a plan. Just stick to it, okay? And please stop talking to those kids. You're just encouraging them to hang out and steal something."

She had to admit, he did throw himself into each chore she gave him. Tear out the salon headliner? No problem. Strip all the intricate mahogany trim in the lower deck passageway? Sure thing. When she'd left that morning for what she hoped was the last landfill run, he'd been gung ho about polishing the hull.

If *Obsession* couldn't be painted, she could at least look as if someone had *tried* to remove the old rust stain runnels marring her sides. That rust, the byproduct of corroding screws in the chromed aluminum rub rail, had probably penetrated the gelcoat. There was absolutely no way *Obsession* could be turned into a showroom boat without a paint job.

She threw the Chevy into Park and stomped on the parking brake.

"I'll double-check the paint sprayer status," Smitty said as he swung out.

"Good luck." Chris peered out the windshield, squinting into the sun hovering behind the yacht.

McLellan was up a ladder, stripped to the waist, traces of sunscreen smeared on his wide shoulders and back. He wore a baseball cap backwards, a water-soaked towel packed between the cap and his skull and hanging onto his neck. His wet jeans clung to his butt and thighs. One of those damn kids was holding the hose spray on the hull, the droplets spilling in a waterfall of chalky white liquid down the side of *Obsession*'s hull. And what was that in McLellan's hand?

Sandpaper?

He wasn't polishing the hull. He was ruining it.

"What the hell do you think you're doing to my boat?" she demanded as she bolted out of the pickup. "Stop! Right there! Don't move!"

McLellan twisted on the ladder to grin down at her. "I saw this great article in *Cruising World*—"

"The hull's supposed to be polished. *Polished,* not ground to freakin' powder." Chris clamped her hands into fists to keep from grabbing the ladder to shake him down. "You're ruining the gelcoat and we don't have time to paint over it!"

"No, I'm not. I did some research last night. *Obsession* has a special kind of gelcoat that you can sand down—"

"We have a plan. We have a schedule. This is my sister we're talking about and you want to go farting around with some cockeyed magazine article? You can pull this stunt on your own boat, dammit, on your time. Not mine."

McLellan carefully folded his sandpaper square and tucked it into his jeans back pocket. He said something in Spanish to the kid, who turned off the hose and walked over to stand in the yard's warehouse shade. McLellan backed down a couple of ladder steps, then jumped the last four, landing easily. His chest, scattered with black hair, flexed powerfully as he took a deep breath. Under his sweaty baseball cap, his stony face and gray eyes looked remote and dangerous.

"Too late," he said in a voice like flint. "I've already ruined the stern."

"Shit."

Chris stalked around behind *Obsession,* aware of McLellan following her, then caught her breath when she saw her reflection in the eggshell-colored fiberglass. The old, busted prefab swim platform had been removed, so there was nothing above the yacht's waterline but crystal clear shine, unmarred even by polishing swirls. The stern mirrored the trees and buildings behind it. Hell, she could have put on mascara in that gleam. She ran her hand along the hull's surface. Slick as glass. Gorgeous.

They just might make it after all.

"She looks like she's been painted," Chris said, turning then to look wonderingly at McLellan.

He glared at her in silence.

"It's good work," she said, unwavering, "but you had no right to experiment on my vessel. You didn't ask my permission."

"You wanted the yacht to look good—"

"You could have ruined her, made her worse than before." Chris swept her fingers again across the glossy fiberglass, then turned to face him. "You could have done enough damage that we'd have to stay in New Orleans long enough to have her painted there. That would have cut into our time getting down to Isladonata."

"Dave could have put on the primer here and we'd get the top coat in New Orleans—"

"Top coats need to go on in less than twelve hours after the primers, otherwise they won't bond," she pointed out. "You have to understand something. Aboard this vessel,

I'm the captain. I'm the one in charge. This is my sister's life at stake and I'm deadly serious about making this thing work."

Muscles in his jaw and cheek flexed beneath his sweat-slick skin. "So am I."

"That means you learn to take direction." She drew herself up to her full height—still a good half foot shorter than his—and lifted her chin. "You don't take direction on a vessel at sea and you endanger not just yourself but everybody else."

"It's just some fiberglass polishing—"

"It's about remembering who's in charge," she snapped. She'd seen his type before. McLellan needed to know—and accept—how the land lay. "My boat, my project," she said. "Look, I'm glad your experiment turned out well. We'll keep doing it your way. That's not the issue."

She took a deep, calming breath, then laid it on the line. "But if you can't figure out how to listen to me, how to do what I tell you to do, you're not going anywhere on this vessel."

His eyes snapped fire but before he could reply, she added, "Once this boat leaves shore, I'm responsible for you. Morally and legally. If you do something that seems right to you even though I said not to do it, and you end up hurt or killed, it's my responsibility. Period. Admiralty law."

She fell silent and waited for him to jump her case again. He studied her for a few long moments, then nodded curtly once. Maybe even a DEA head honcho could take orders.

"It looks great." She reached up almost against her will to stroke the yacht's hull. "You've done a great job."

"*We've* done a great job." He nodded slightly to the boy, all baggy jeans and T-shirt, standing in the shade. "But thanks."

"Now show me how to do it," she said, "so I can get started on the other side."

Chris took several steps back from *Obsession* the following Wednesday evening and marveled. What a difference two weeks and several thousand dollars could make.

McLellan's trick with the gelcoat sanding had saved a substantial chunk of change and showed that *Obsession*'s builders had been a class act. The hull and coach house alike mirrored everything around them. The yacht's new window frames and high-impact glass would prevent water from leaking down the newly restored salon walls and pooling on the bare floor still awaiting its carpet. The new stainless steel railings and the rub rail shone like freshly minted coins.

"She looks good, doesn't she?" McLellan said as he joined Chris in the boatyard, wiping his paint-smeared hands with a towel that smelled faintly of thinner.

"She's what I always thought she'd look like," Chris replied, tugging her blond hair from its ponytail. "Beautiful."

"Yes, she is." McLellan's mouth curved in a half smile as he watched Chris finger-comb the strands. "You got your new prop finally."

"Yeah, that's a load off my mind."

Chris walked around to the stern, McLellan following, to look at the massive four-bladed bronze propeller. She reached out and fingered one of the blades, then grasped it and pulled down. The prop turned heavily.

"Remind me not to swim while the engines are running," McLellan remarked.

"Slice and dice," she agreed. "The swim platform's here, by the way. It'll be ready for mounting in the morning."

"We're nearly ready to go."

The suppressed eagerness in his voice made her glance at him as they walked up to the bow. He'd taken seriously to boating, even to spending an hour each evening with her reviewing the charts while Smitty sanded down mahogany trim strips in preparation for varnishing. He wasn't particularly mechanical, but he was a fast learner. More than once she'd caught him practicing his knot tying when he had a few spare minutes. McLellan was as ready to go as a landlubber who'd never been to sea could be.

"Yeah. *Obsession*'s got everything she needs to take us to New Orleans."

"So do we get to splash a day early?" He tossed his towel into a drum labeled FIRE HAZARD WASTE.

"I'd like to. We need to go over the sailing plans tonight when Garza gets here." She started up the ladder to the aft deck, McLellan following.

"We should talk about what happens when we get to the island."

"You mean when you guys go storming in, guns blazing?"

A scowl darkened his face as he swung onto the deck. "How we're going to fake our way through security."

She drew her hair back into its usual ponytail, then looked him up and down, noting how his T-shirt snugged his chest and wondering where he kept his firearm. "You're going to need a first mate's uniform," she remarked.

He shook his head. "That's Smitty's job," he said, watching his partner clamber up to join them. "I'm just a lazy passenger."

"Hey, Smitty," Chris teased, "your buddy doesn't think he's going to help out on this cruise."

"Aarr," Smitty growled and hooked an arm around Chris's shoulder. "You work for your grog on this ship, matie."

McLellan was not amused. "Someone's got to look like they're supposed to be going to this island."

Chris surveyed McLellan again. "You've got a point. How good are you at smooth talking your way into places you shouldn't be?"

"Ask his last girlfriend," Smitty said in his normal voice. "You got that engine room floor painted yet?"

McLellan scowled. "Done."

"I thought you were going to do that."

Smitty stuck his hand out past Chris so they could both see his uneven, grease-laden nails. "I did some of it. But I have to watch my manicure. I'm aspirin' to become a model like pretty boy over here."

Normally McLellan took Smitty's ribbing about his looks with good humor, but now his eyes were cold steel and his jaw locked. Smitty dropped his arm from Chris's shoulder and said, "Want a cold one?"

"Love one."

Inside, Smitty poured beer into chilled mugs while Chris and McLellan spread a navigational chart over the dinette table.

"Garza was right behind me," Smitty said as he set a mug in front of her.

"Good God, Smitty, did you leave him out there on his own?" McLellan snapped.

"He's a grown man." Smitty raised his voice as McLellan headed out to the aft deck. "He doesn't like being coddled." He slid into the horseshoe-shaped bench next to

Chris. "Wants to save the world whether it wants to be saved or not."

"I'm not sure helping a friend up a ladder's the same as saving him," she remarked.

Smitty grunted and sipped his beer. "His soft spot's got him in trouble more than once."

"I guess that's a liability in your line of work."

"Damn right it is. That kind of shit'll get you killed eventually."

Chris, acutely conscious of Smitty's muscular arm and very male scent, regarded him seriously for the first time. His wrist, she noticed, was tattooed with a rattlesnake. "So compassion is a weakness."

"Look," Smitty said, warming up to what Chris suspected was going to be a well-practiced monologue, "they talk about victims in the drug war but from the way I see it, there's only people getting what they ask for. The addicts, the pushers, the middlemen, the commandos, the guys out in the fields growing coca down in South America—they all make a choice. When guys like me and McLellan show up, all they wanna do is kill us because we're going to mess up the status quo. Nobody wants anything different. A bleedin' heart for one of these guys gets you dead. Period. I don't care how personal it is."

Personal? What about her sister? "And Scintella?"

"He doesn't get an excuse. Everybody else can say, 'Look at me, I'm an addict.' Or they'll say, 'I'm in deep and if I try to leave they'll kill me.' But he's the bad boy at the top of the heap. All he has to worry about is the guy on the rung below him, trying to drag him down."

Which meant Natalie was in a kind of danger Chris hadn't thought of. How often did the families of men like Scintella get caught in the crossfire? Made examples of?

Chris swallowed hard and was grateful when she heard Garza and McLellan on the aft deck. Get her mind back on business and she'd be fine.

Garza's forehead shone with sweat and he leaned heavily on his cane for the short walk through the salon to the dinette. McLellan held a bar stool steady at the dinette's head. Dressed in Dockers and a Race to Vera Cruz T-shirt, Garza resembled a yuppie sailor more than a private eye.

Chris watched him brace himself against the dinette and hoist himself onto the stool. "Should we have arranged to meet somewhere else?"

"No, not at all." Garza wiped his forehead with his handkerchief. "The yacht's clean, right?"

Smitty nodded. "Ran over it with a can of Raid."

"For bugs?" Chris capped and uncapped her pen.

"It was another reason Falks could have been aboard." McLellan slid into the dinette at Garza's right hand. "Slim chance, but there's no point in taking it."

His quiet confidence stilled her nerves. She nodded and breathed deep. Smitty's little diatribe had made her jumpy. *Don't live in the future,* she reminded herself. *Do what you have to do right now. And don't borrow trouble.* Chris put down her pen.

"Need more light?" she asked. She got up to flip the dinette switch and the little lamp suspended over the table burped on, casting a feeble ambient glow.

"Mood lighting's good, but I don't plan on seducing you until these guys are gone," Smitty remarked. "How about that salon lamp behind me?"

Chris snapped the switch. "Got another one down."

"I'm working on the wiring when we're under way," Smitty said. "Can't go blind on this trip."

"I bet it's a bad relay."

"I bet you're right, darlin'."

Chris unplugged a tabletop lamp and perched it on the counter behind Garza, then aimed its shaded beam toward the table and took the outside seat next to Smitty again. *Think sailing,* she ordered herself. *Don't think about guns and Natalie and how much trouble she's in.*

Before her nerves could kick in again, she turned the chart so north pointed at McLellan and south pointed at Smitty. Setting a clear glass paperweight on the southeast corner between Garza and herself, she said, "You can see this group of islands here." She gestured toward a little band of dots below Florida. "From what Natalie told me last time we talked, I think this is where Jerome Scintella's resort must be."

"Do your cruising friends know anything about it?" Garza asked.

She shook her head. "There's no reference to Isladonata anywhere. Not on any map or chart I've found, not on the cruising newsgroups, not the Internet, nowhere."

Garza nodded thoughtfully. "I haven't come up with anything, either."

"From what Natalie said, the island's been inhabited and used as a resort for some time even if it doesn't show up on charts by the name Isladonata."

"A code name, then." McLellan placed both palms on the two nearest corners. His fingers were both beautiful and strong, splayed over the paper like a concert pianist's. Her own hands, she noticed, still had oil ground into the pores even after her shower.

"Possibly," Chris replied. "Nat described it as a wealthy boys' club. Lots of gambling and high-class prostitutes. Scintella's going there for a business meeting."

The men were silent for a moment, studying the chart's

named and unnamed islands, then McLellan said, "Could she tell you anything about the security arrangements?"

Chris shook her head. "Nothing about the island itself. She did say Jerome has personal bodyguards who travel with them, and that everywhere they've gone he's had more waiting for him."

"Local hires," Smitty guessed.

Garza nodded. "Family connections. The Scintellas have been around a while. Lots of friends in lots of places."

Was Scintella that powerful and well-connected? Chris had thought that he was just another thug with money, but Garza made him sound like someone out of *The Godfather.* She shuddered.

Smitty put his arm over her shoulders. "Hey, we're here. Falks shows up, I take care of him. And I don't care who he works for or what he's doing."

I have no business doing this.

Chris stared at the chart's swirling lines—here's where the water gets shallow, here's a ship channel, here are all the markers of direction and distance and safe travel. Old World charts had had vast stretches of blue water labeled, "Ther Be Dragynes Here," but this was now, the twenty-first century. The only *dragynes* she had to contend with were the one trying to hurt her and the one out there somewhere who might hurt Natalie.

But it was uncharted waters, all of it.

Smitty gently tipped her chin toward him and smiled. "Hey. I mean it."

She searched his gaze and found nothing to be afraid of. Just a warm fondness. In spite of her fear of Falks, her fear for Natalie, she felt comforted. She quirked a smile, the best she could do, and Smitty patted her arm. "So what's our trip look like, *mon capitaine?*"

Chris swallowed hard as Smitty released her, then said, "We'll take it in two legs. The first will be our shakedown cruise from here to New Orleans."

McLellan's deep voice, sounding slightly strained, made her look at him. "Where we see how well the yacht is holding up."

"She'll hold up fine, but yes, it's where we work out the kinks. You'll get to experience the yacht in action."

"Ten bucks says you toss your cookies at the first four-foot swell, pretty boy."

McLellan turned his scowl on Smitty. "Twenty says I don't and *you* scrub the bilge with a toothbrush."

"Ah." Smitty shook his head. "Goin' south with the mouth again." He winked at Chris. "But you're on."

"We'll pick up two agents in New Orleans," McLellan said.

"Who?" Chris let her frustration flare in her voice. "Why haven't you mentioned this before?"

"You thought Smitty and I would storm a heavily armed private island on our own?"

The lack of sarcasm in McLellan's tone made Chris feel even more stupid and naive. "I like to have a plan," Chris snapped. "I'm a civilian and I don't know how stuff like this is supposed to go down. A little forewarning of *your* plans is appreciated."

McLellan's scowl deepened. "That's why I'm telling you now."

"You'll like Jacquie," Smitty remarked. "Tough babe."

If Smitty intended to make her feel better about this new information, he misjudged her. "If she'll help us get Natalie out, I don't care who she is. So you'll have four agents going to Isladonata. Is there anything *else* I need to know?"

"That's it," McLellan said tightly.

It wasn't, she knew. He had that look: the defiant, dare-me gaze that meant he was bluffing. There was still something going on underneath these plans, but she didn't have a clue how to get to it. Not without jeopardizing her role in the trip. She let her expression say what she wouldn't: *I don't trust you.* McLellan's already chiseled face hardened further.

She turned to Garza. "Are you coming, too?"

He cocked an eyebrow at her. "I'd be ballast. No, I'm going to stay here and be the investigator, build a case against Falks if I can."

"Even if the DEA can't figure out who he is?" Smitty's skepticism echoed in his rapidly drumming fingers.

Garza smiled. "There's more than one way to skin a cat. So the second leg is from New Orleans to Isladonata?"

Chris nodded. "I want to keep the shakedown to the ICW. The Intracoastal Waterway runs along the coast and is used for commercial shipping. Traffic's manageable during the day and at night we'll moor or anchor in protected inlets and coves. But from New Orleans to Isladonata, we'll be on open water." She traced the route, skirting the Florida coast in an arc toward the band of islands south of the mainland. "Even if we have a mechanical failure on that leg, we should be able to reach the coast without too much trouble."

"And how do we figure out which island is the right one?" McLellan asked.

"Natalie told me this morning she may be close to getting more information," Chris said, remembering the hushed excitement of Nat's voice, the relief they'd both felt to be *doing* something, *getting* somewhere.

"How?" Garza asked.

"Igor—the bodyguard—doesn't hang around when she's with Jerome. She got Jerome drunk last night and searched his clothes while…anyway, he's started wearing a key on a chain around his neck and she thinks it unlocks his briefcase. He keeps his travel diary there."

"Lat-longs?" Smitty asked.

Chris nodded. "I hope so. If she can get those coordinates, we're good."

McLellan gazed steadily at her and she suddenly realized how broad his shoulders were. How distant his gray eyes could seem in this inadequate light. "You sound very sure we'll succeed, Christina."

At her name—her real name, the name she'd been given before she was adopted and had become someone else—she met his gaze. Had *Obsession* been in the water, she would have been conscious of the subtle hum of a bilge pump running or the splash of water that signaled a functioning air-conditioning unit. As it was, she was cognizant of the absence of those sounds. She could almost feel the massive Detroits hunkered down in their engine rooms, waiting to go.

She would get to Natalie one way or another, and her best chance was taking this boat. Even if McLellan was keeping something from her. Even if Jerome Scintella had bodyguards and money and connections with dangerous people.

She lifted her chin, met McLellan's gaze head-on. "This is my sister's life. I'll make it."

Chapter 5

Best laid plans, Chris thought in the growing darkness on the flybridge. *Obsession*'s bow sliced through a swell. First day out and wouldn't you know it? A tanker spill and the subsequent cleanup in the ICW had driven *Obsession* from the ditch, through Johnson's Cut and out into the open Gulf of Mexico after all.

And given the southwesterly wind coming at a good clip over the water, the shakedown cruise was going to be a real boneshaker. That was the gulf for you. It was either smooth as glass or trying to kill you. There just didn't seem to be much of an in-between.

Chris turned the wheel to adjust course slightly. They had another three hours to reach the next cut back into the ICW. Rolling swells lifted *Obsession*'s stern, then slid beneath and dropped the yacht in a sickening slow-motion roller-coaster action.

She wondered idly whether McLellan was locked in the forward head spilling his excellently cooked dinner—and where had he learned to cook like that?—or if Smitty was hunkered down in the bilge, toothbrush in hand. Warm wind stroked her back. If the weather picked up a little more, she'd be forced into the pilothouse, but for now, the edginess, the wildness of it, thrilled her. Gave her something to think about besides Natalie and *dragynes*.

She checked the radar. The display showed no moving body for two or three sweeps, then a blip maybe half the size of *Obsession*. A thirty-foot fishing boat, maybe. A blue-water sailboat. Maybe one of the over-engined, testosterone-fueled Cigarette boats sometimes used to smuggle illegal goods into the lower forty-eight. Someone else forced out of the ICW by the spill.

Not necessarily Eugene Falks.

But if it was Eugene Falks, she had a surprise waiting for him. Not a fire extinguisher trick this time. Her grip tightened on the wheel. No, this time it'd be a Ruger 9mm.

The radar arm swept again. Nothing. Whoever it was stayed just out of range.

She shook off the thought. No sense in scaring herself. Wasn't that what Gus had said just before they'd left him at the dock? And the other important thing: *If you run into trouble, if you need anything, you give old Gus a call, you hear me? Nobody messes with my favorite girl.*

Until now, she hadn't had much time to scare herself. After this morning's launch, Smitty had been his usual playful, almost affectionate self. McLellan had kicked around the yacht like a kid in a candy store, examining everything, asking questions a mile a minute. They'd joked and chatted and teased her by turns until it felt like a good-natured assault. What were they trying to do, nice her to death?

She thought about McLellan's trips forward and aft, his eyes' gleam as he recognized the practical application of his book learning. He'd stood for almost an hour at the bow, watching the yacht slice the waves. She hadn't seen genuine excitement like that in a long time. Hadn't felt it herself, either.

It *was* exciting to finally be under way, in a sound vessel, *her* vessel. *I'm coming to get you, Natalie,* she'd thought more than once, and each time her heart had surged at seeing her sister again.

The helm compass's glow showed *Obsession* on the correct heading. No oil rigs or other standing obstacles dotted their immediate path. She wondered how bad commercial shipping traffic was backed up in the ditch while Parks and Wildlife cleaned up the mess. *Obsession* hemmed in with a bunch of barges wasn't an image she wanted to contemplate. The old girl was a strong boat, but Chris respected both the water and a larger, heavier vessel. Either could crush the yacht to splinters of fiberglass.

One hand on the wheel, she leaned over the chart table again to double-check Smitty's notations from his six-hour stint at the helm. As she studied the charts, she heard nothing but the wind filling her ears, smelled nothing but clean air growing cooler with the threat of storms. She raised her head to look out over the black water, at the fluttering path of light leading to the fingernail moon just lifting above the horizon. The gulf heaved long, slow waves against the yacht. Beneath the surface, she sensed, the water roiled and churned, always moving, never satisfied with stillness. Suddenly the pitching waves seemed to be all part of one huge being, separate from it and tied to it and within it all at the same time.

"We say the sea is lonely," McLellan said as he joined her at the helm.

She smiled as she straightened and met his relaxed, open gaze. "William Meredith," she replied. "'The Open Sea'."

His delighted grin warmed her. "Beautiful opening to a poem about drowned people, isn't it?"

"I thought it was about being glad to be alive."

"That, too." His deep voice softened into an almost intimate tone, as though the connection—quotation and poem—was deeper than merely intellectual.

She slipped back behind the wheel and perched on the captain's chair as *Obsession* heaved up over another rolling wave. "Not feeling sick?"

"Stomach of iron." McLellan shrugged. The gesture opened his windbreaker enough to let her see the pitted grip of the gun strapped under his arm. His T-shirt clung to his ribcage and she wondered suddenly how hard his muscles would feel under her hands.

She clutched the wheel instead. "I guess Smitty's on his knees in the bilge," she said lightly.

"Do you care where Smitty is?" McLellan leaned a palm against the console to face her.

She caught a whiff of his clean scent before the wind snatched it away. *Smitty who?* She swallowed. "Have you talked to Garza since we left?"

"My cell died once we got away from Lafayette. I'll check in when we get close to a big city again."

"You can use the satellite phone. It's old technology and goes on the blink sometimes, but you might get through. I'm going to replace it."

"Did you find the one you want in that New Orleans catalog?"

"Yes." It'd be a nice chunk of change from the DEA

"rent" she had left, but she definitely wanted to get that phone before they headed for Isladonata. Just in case.

"I'll dig through my magazines," he offered, "and see what the reviews say about it." He shot her a jaunty grin. "I know what you think of my articles but—"

"You made a believer out of me with the gelcoat trick," she said with a little laugh. "If you can save me some cash with a good alternative, by all means do so."

"Damn fine job you've done," he remarked. He leaned his hip against the console to brace himself against the yacht's movement. She felt him studying her and met his gaze. This close, in the eerie green instrument lighting, his eyes were nothing resembling remote. His humor had fled, replaced by something—an intensity—she couldn't name.

"You're an amazing woman," he said abruptly. "Knowing what you want, going after it."

"It's my sister's life," she replied quietly.

McLellan's rueful smile looked haunted. "Family ties." He turned his head and Chris saw his noble—there was no other way of putting it—profile, a shadow of stubble making him look rugged rather than polished. "This is personal for me."

Chris remembered Smitty's derisive tone: *A bleedin' heart for one of these guys gets you dead. I don't care how personal it is.* "In what way?"

He was silent for a long moment. Waves collapsed over each other, pushing and crashing. "My brother got involved with a local drug dealer."

"How old was he?"

"Nineteen. He knew better. He got into selling, hooked up with some dangerous people." A sharp gust blew his windbreaker's collar up against his throat. "It was the power, I guess. That's what he wanted. That and the money."

Chris could understand that. Not for herself, but wasn't that exactly what had enticed Natalie into the trouble she was in now? Jerome and his private jet. Jerome and his ready wad of cash. Jerome and his hundred-thousand-dollar sports car. Jerome and the private London wedding. The Jerome Chris had seen only from a distance and never met.

"My brother made a series of bad decisions and at the end of the day there was nothing I could do to save him. Antonio and I spent three months trying to track him down. When we found him…" His jaw tightened, then he said, "It's not easy to watch police divers drag your little brother's body out of the water, knowing that maybe if you'd said something differently, maybe shown him a different path, he'd be alive and married and playing with his kids right now."

Chris said nothing as she automatically scanned the instrument panel, looking for warning signals while she thought about what he'd said. How many times had she lain awake at night since Natalie's phone call, wondering if she'd said or done something to drive Nat to marry someone like Jerome? Chris knew exactly what McLellan had felt. Might still feel.

"What happened to him?" she asked softly.

"He pissed off the wrong man."

When McLellan didn't seem willing to elaborate, she said, "Did you catch him?"

"No." He braced one hand on the back of her chair, briefly brushed her shoulder, as *Obsession* climbed a swell. "Part of me wants to kill the bastard."

She said nothing.

If Natalie ended up dead—and here Chris felt her stomach clutch hard—would she want to look down the Ruger's sight at Jerome Scintella the way McLellan wanted to look at the man who killed his brother? Her gut went liquid with dread.

She glanced at him, saw the guilt in his clenched jaw, in the character lines around his eyes. Heard it in his voice as he said, in almost a whisper, "I don't intend to let your sister suffer the same fate." He raised a hand as though to touch her, but didn't. "Or you."

She let out a long breath, realizing how easy she found it to relate to this man and how much she wanted to believe what he said about keeping her safe. When he leaned closer, she tried not to think about how good he smelled and how good his arms would feel around her.

Then he smiled. "You're strong. Like I was a few years ago. Dedicated. Ambitious. Professional."

"You're not those things now?"

"I do my job. I go home with a clear conscience, knowing I've done the right thing." His gaze lingered on her mouth, slipped to the open neck of her shirt, then flicked back to her eyes. "But I'm not sure that's fulfilling anymore."

"What could be more fulfilling than chasing bad guys?"

"It's not that cut-and-dried." He exhaled slowly. "I want to do things differently. Not live in such a dark place."

They weren't talking about his DEA work anymore, but Chris wasn't sure where he was headed. His conversation shifted beneath her feet like the waves beneath *Obsession*'s hull, and she felt suddenly more at ease with him than she ever had on the open water. More alive.

"I should try to sleep. I'm laying carpet tomorrow." He shoved away from the helm console, away from her, then paused. "I haven't had a day this good in a long time," he said softly. "Thank you."

She smiled a little, pleased and frustrated that she felt pleased. Then she met his gaze and the frustration died. He leaned in and she lifted her chin ever so slightly and then his firm lips were on hers. Her breath stopped. His fingertips lightly touched her chin, then slid along her jaw, and the fleeting thought his lips might follow weakened her knees. The boat rocked up and over a rolling wave; they swayed with the movement, balanced together, in a strengthening kiss that baffled her senses and absolved her of all thought. There was only his scent, the sensuous slide of his lips against hers, his warm breath on her cheek, his arm slipping around her waist. When she opened her eyes, there was his cheekbone, lifted by the dim light into masculine marble.

Ther be Dragynes here.

She leaned back to break the kiss but McLellan's hand held her still for the instant it took to sweep her lower lip with the tip of his tongue. She gasped. He pressed a kiss against the corner of her mouth and lingered. Catching her scent, she realized. The thought excited her darkly.

"Christina," he murmured into her ear and her name sounded like music—

The yacht lurched to starboard, throwing him against the helm console. A crack and boom echoed up from the boat's hull, then a distinct metallic thunk sounded from the stern. Cursing, Chris yanked the throttles into Neutral. A hot fist of dread clutched her stomach.

"Dammit," she muttered. *What'd we hit?* She flicked the searchlight switch. Its beam laced the water, skimming over churning foam.

"What the hell was that?" McLellan leaned over the railing to scan the darkness.

She ignored him, irritated she'd been provoked into carelessness. If her boat had been hulled because McLellan was messing with her, she'd take it out of his hide. If the Coast Guard could reach them in time.

For a couple of tense minutes she swept the searchlight steadily over the water to the yacht's port side. Nothing but black waves, cresting white in the strengthening, howling wind. In the far distance, the utter blackness of the shoreline loomed.

Feet pounded the flybridge steps behind them. "What happened?" Smitty called, buttoning his cutoff shorts as he joined them.

"We hit something I didn't see," she snapped, leveling an angry glance at McLellan. "Man the searchlight," she told Smitty, then quickly marked their position on the waterproof chart.

When she turned, Smitty had swung the light to starboard, illuminating only the open gulf as it swept toward them. Then he pivoted to shine on their wake and picked up the angular black crisscrosses of a pipe grid thrusting through the waves.

"Shit," Chris muttered.

"What the hell is it?" McLellan asked.

Smitty whistled. "Oil rig debris. That'll take a bite out."

"Oil companies don't have to clean that up?"

Smitty shook his head as he played the light over the pipes, rusted and jagged with weather. "They do, but this could have broken loose in the last hurricane."

"I think it hit a prop," Chris said. "Maybe a rudder."

"Dammit."

An amber light flashed on the console. It was the aft bilge pump, in the lowest part of the boat. She counted while the light shone and the pump ran, a good five seconds. If *Obsession* was taking on water, it wasn't much. Yet.

Chris killed the engines, heard the sudden absence of

exhaust roar. "We're far enough offshore we can drift for a few minutes. I'm going to go down and have a look around. You guys prep the inflatable in case we need it. The spare gas can for the inflatable's outboard is in the lazarette."

"The lazarette's the one place on this tub I haven't been yet," Smitty said, grabbing hold of the railing as a wave shoved the yacht's nose to port.

Chris watched the bilge pump light flicker on again. "The hatch is in the aft deck floor, toward the very back of the boat. The gas can's within reach."

"Gotcha." He looked at McLellan. "You get it while I keep watch up here."

"Right."

Chris made her way toward the starboard engine room, trailing one hand on the lower passageway's gutted wall to help keep her balance as the yacht began to pitch side to side. Without the engines running and in gear, the yacht lacked the ability to point her nose into the waves. For a few minutes at least, they'd be at the mercy of the on-coming storm. The tossing had already knocked Smitty's broom from the passageway corner where he'd parked it so that it lay across the floor. She kicked it out of the way and swung the port engine room door open.

The thick odor of hot metal hijacked her breath. Hortense, mute now but radiating heat and faint exhaust fumes, hunched in the room's center. Chris's first thought was that the hull had been punctured, but the bilge pump hadn't run fast enough and only one amber light out of five had shown. That meant the water wasn't rising fast enough to suggest a hull breach.

No, she bet the rig pipes had struck a propeller, which was the lowest part of the boat. If that was the case, the stuffing box—the point where the prop shaft came through the hull—was leaking more than it should. All stuffing boxes were designed to leak anyway because the prop shaft had to turn in order to make the propeller turn. It was only a few drips a minute, nothing that would overwhelm even a single bilge pump. But if the shaft had been knocked out of alignment with the engine, the stuffing box might have been damaged and the water might now be flowing in at a dangerous rate.

Chris grabbed a flashlight and a wrench from the tool chest, stuck the wrench into her back pocket. A misaligned prop shaft could do irreparable harm to an engine. If an engine shaft had been knocked out of alignment, *Obsession* would have to limp into New Orleans on the remaining engine, losing them a day on their schedule.

I don't have time for this, Chris reminded her Creator as she yanked open the hatch that led aft, toward the stern and the stuffing boxes. She wriggled down the catwalk, played the flashlight beam over quickly rising bilge water. A subtle whirring reassured her; the closest midships bilge pump was sucking water from the hold and spewing it outside. The pump shut off automatically when the water level dropped below the trigger point.

She finally reached the stuffing boxes, both out of reach from the catwalk. The yacht heaved up and over another wave, throwing her off balance. Helluva time for the waves to pick up some chop. *Give me a break,* she prayed irreverently. *Just a few minutes of calm, okay?* The boat dropped a sickening foot before slamming into the trough and ramming her against a bulkhead.

Fine. I'll handle it on my own.

She braced herself and aimed the flashlight's beam at the distant starboard stuffing box. A single drop winked in the light, then another. It looked good. Water slapped and beat the fiberglass hull, but underneath the hollow-sounding booms and whacks, she could hear the flat crack of water on water. She shifted the flashlight from one hand to the other, then shone the beam on the port stuffing box.

A cascade spewed from the box like a faucet left half-open.

There you are. Chris glanced at the water level in the bilge. A little high, but when the pump kicked back on, it'd drop again.

She thought about the general problem for a moment. She wouldn't be able to tell if the prop shaft was still aligned until she started the engines again. And while she believed the bilge pumps could keep up with the incoming flow, she didn't like taking that chance. The flashlight beam dipped toward the hull. The roiling, oily water had risen past its normal point, nothing but clean crosshatch fiberglass above it.

Chris held her breath and tried to hear past the riotous clap of water on the hull. No whirring. She shimmied back to the bilge pump that had been running a moment before and lifted the float switch to prompt the pump to run. Nothing happened. She cursed, wriggled back to the stuffing box. Even with four pumps still good, she didn't like leaving this veritable water faucet running full bore.

She fished the wrench out of her back pocket and reached far out from the catwalk for the stuffing box's packing gland. She'd have to tighten that gland nut to slow the incoming flow. Even stretched full out, she was a good foot from the nut. The prop shaft, a solid steel pipe about two inches thick, gleamed greasily and blocked the only area where she could get to the stuffing box.

"Nobody told me when I inherited this boat I needed to be two feet tall with arms six feet long," she muttered.

She held her breath and snaked under the prop shaft, grazing her back and side on it. Too damn close. The hot oil smell was almost overwhelming. *Concentrate.* She angled her body so her feet braced against the catwalk and her shoulders rested on the hull. With a resigned sigh, she lowered her butt into the cold bilge water. She propped the flashlight between her shoulder and ear like a phone to aim it at the packing gland. A wave hit, banged her shoulder and threw her upper arm against the prop shaft.

Note to self: Take up yoga.

Turning her shoulders slightly, she could reach the packing gland nut *and* work the wrench. Just great if you didn't mind pressing your cheek to a greasy prop shaft that was still hot from spinning at a few thousand RPMs. Or dropping your ass down into an oily bilge.

Chris fought to get the wrench into place while the gulf waves hammered *Obsession*'s hull. A couple of wrench turns was all she needed, just enough to slow the water flow without stopping it completely. She got the first turn okay.

Just one more and I'm outta here.

She heard the distinct click of Hortense's starter, then the engine roared. *Shit.* Her upper arm was jerked toward the prop shaft. Chris instinctively threw herself backward, away from the spinning shaft. Her head banged the hull. The flashlight splashed into the bilge. Her torn sleeve, caught around the shaft, spun wildly before being slung away. The flashlight's beam, green and watery, winked out.

Oh God.

In the distance, light glinted on pipes and edged the wooden catwalk. Near her, total blackness and hot, humming metal. In her mind's eye, she saw her ponytail whipping around the shaft like thread on a spool, dragging her into the steel bar. It would crush her skull like a Christmas pecan.

No·one knew she was this far down in the hold.

She could yell, but they'd never hear her over the noisy Detroits. And she hadn't had silencers put on the exhaust system yet so the aft exhaust pipes' rumble would muffle her screams.

The yacht lurched. She braced harder against the hull. Trying not to move forward, trying not to feel the hot air blowing off the spinning prop shaft two inches from her nose, she felt around in the bilge for the flashlight. The smooth cylinder filled her hand like a lifeline.

Smitty better remember his Morse code. Careful not to raise the dead flashlight too high, she tapped on the hull: three quick taps, three taps with a second between them, three quick taps.

Nothing.

She tried again, then again. Still nothing. Was the bilge water rising? She stopped tapping to reach her shaking hand under the packing gland. After a moment's cautious searching, she found it. Water gushed through the gland onto her palm. Were none of the bilge pumps running? Catching back a sob, she tried the SOS code again, striking the hull harder. A single lock of hair escaped from her ponytail and slid down her neck.

Please, no, she prayed. It was so damned dark. So hot and dark.

Bilge water licked up, soaking her shirt midriff. Yes, the water was definitely gaining on her. She molded her back more firmly to the hull as the yacht rolled up and over another wave. *Get a grip,* she told herself between sobs. *You're not dead yet. If all else fails, you can stay right here until they figure out they need to stop the engines.*

Right. Until the water rises so high you drown.

Chris took a deep breath, then froze as a wave of nausea

rolled over her. Exhaust fumes seeped into the tight crawl space, filling it.

"Can you cut me some slack here?" she yelled, then instantly regretted it when the dizziness hit.

If I stay here, I'll die.

She couldn't go over the prop shaft, but maybe she could go under it. She gingerly ran her hands along the fiberglass as far as she could reach, feeling for the exact shape of the hull. There was just room to slide her body down into the water, along the bottom of the boat, and out the other side. She carefully wet her hair, plastered it to her head. Just in case.

She took a shallow breath and slipped into the bilge's rising seawater. Under water, the engine's roar was a nightmarish, alien grumble. Above her, the shaft spun, threw air onto her nose. Oily liquid licked over her lips, teased her skin. Half-dizzy, she eased beneath the prop shaft.

Her hand found the catwalk. Clutching her ponytail with her other hand, she levered herself out of the bilge water and into safety. She hauled herself onto the catwalk, heaving for breath and trying not to cry.

Chris coughed a couple of times. This wasn't just diesel fumes. It was exhaust fumes, fumes that should have been ejected from the boat's stern just like car exhaust from a road vehicle. She had to get out before they choked her, killed her.

And I didn't swim through a stinking bilge to die now.

She worked one foot onto the catwalk. The other caught on something in the bilge, then she got it loose. On shaking hands and knees, she backed toward the hatch just like she'd always done when she came below. The familiar way. As she got closer to the engine room, the catwalk lightened with the stray beams from the overhead lighting system shining through the hatch.

Then she was in the engine room and could stand. At her first deep inhale, the exhaust fumes nearly choked her.

Shit.

She had to get out, to get above, into the space and fresh air and some kind of bright light. Queasy, dizzy, she reached for the engine room door.

It was locked.

Chapter 6

"McLellan! Smitty! Down here! Let me out!" Chris yelled, banging on the door with her fist until her hand ached.

She pressed her oily ear to the steel and listened. Nothing but the metallic clatter of Hortense patiently chugging along.

If both men were on the flybridge, they'd never hear her.

She turned the door's L-shaped handle and shoved. The door wasn't locked because the handle turned. No, it was stuck. Or blocked.

Her mind flashed on the broom she'd kicked aside in the passageway. Had the yacht's motion shifted it, caused it to wedge against the door?

She pounded the steel door twice, more from frustration than panic. "Dammit," she muttered, then coughed when she inhaled.

She irritably kicked the door, then reeled back, fighting dizziness. She dropped onto the tool chest, knocking a stray screwdriver into the floor. *Don't be stupid. Don't waste your energy. Think.*

No crawl spaces between this engine room and Claire's. No hatches up into the office above. Why wasn't the extractor fan working? Without it, there was no way of venting the exhaust fumes, which shouldn't be in the engine room in the first place. The acrid, cloying stench irritated her eyes, made her stomach roll as badly as the yacht.

She blinked rapidly to clear the tears away. Oily water eased in runnels down her arms. She ran one greasy hand through her hair to get it back out of her face. Hortense rumbled and rattled, never missing a stroke. Chris's gaze snapped suddenly to Hortense's massive bulk. *I'm an idiot.*

Abruptly she stood, grabbed the emergency stop lever on the top of the engine and pulled.

Hortense obediently chugged to a halt.

Chris had to sit down again. The room reeled around her; the yacht's careening up and over waves turned her stomach. If she puked now she'd probably pass out from the blood rush to her head. She swallowed, held on. Coughing, she leaned her head on the wall behind her and stared at the join of floor and wall, trying to stay conscious.

Across the passageway, Claire continued her grumbling for what felt like all night. Night. Yes, it was night and way past her bedtime. Footsteps pounding on the staircase jolted her from a doze. A man shouted something she couldn't understand. A snapping sound, then the door swung open.

"Christina!"

McLellan's strong arms went around her and lifted her. Floor, shoulder, cologne, shirt, wall, ceiling. She closed her eyes and concentrated on not throwing up. By the time she opened her eyes again she could see stars beyond the aft deck's ceiling and a cool, fresh wind hit her full-on. McLellan had propped her in a deck chair and was reaching in the fridge for a bottled water. *Obsession* lolled in the waves, Claire vibrating comfortingly deep in the hull.

McLellan swabbed her face with a towel doused in icy water.

"Damn," she muttered, then started coughing.

His strong hand supported her head until the spasms faded. "That was close," he murmured.

She leaned her head on the chair's back. "You have no idea."

"Need a drink?"

"Something to settle my stomach."

She closed her eyes. The fridge snicked open and the seal broke on a plastic bottle's cap.

"Here."

He held the soda to her lips and she drank gratefully. There was nothing in the world like a cold Coke Classic going down hard and fast. It worked wonders on the human body and attitude. At least the darkness had quit crowding on the edges of her vision as her stomach latched onto the soft drink.

"Hang on," he warned, pulling the bottle away. "Don't make yourself sick."

The wind, tinged with Claire's exhaust, blew over the rail and weakened her knees. Behind the fumes, she could smell the metallic scent of rain. The storm she'd seen on the weather fax earlier, headed their way. She just wanted to lie in this chair and feel cold rain on her skin. And breathe.

When McLellan dabbed her cheek with the towel, she said, "I'm okay. Really." Her voice sounded like it'd been sanded down to the bone.

"You don't look okay." His voice was firm, steady. He

kept wiping her face, and she realized she felt comforted. "What happened? Why are you wet?"

"I was tightening a packing gland when the engines started."

His puzzled frown said he didn't understand, so she shook her head, the explanation caught in her aching throat. "There's an exhaust leak somewhere in the engine room."

"How the hell did the broom get wedged against the door?"

"It was lying in the floor and I kicked it out of the way. It must have rolled back in the wave action."

He refolded the towel to a clean spot and passed it over her lips, held it there. She met his gaze, intense in the darkness. He hadn't turned on the overhead light, she realized. There was nothing but starlight shining on them, and the dim glow of a galley lamp.

He drew the towel slowly down her jaw, down her neck. He frowned when his gaze wandered to her torn sleeve.

"The prop shaft caught it when the engine started." Her voice scraped and trembled.

He pressed her oily hand against his cheek. "Promise me." His warm breath on her wrist felt like a caress. "Promise me you won't go down there alone again."

She didn't answer. For this moment, she felt safe. If he hadn't found her, she'd have either suffocated in the fumes or drowned in the bilge—

"The bilge pumps," she said, her brain finally starting to fire on more than one cylinder. "The bilge pumps weren't running."

"Damn." He pressed the towel into her palm and headed through the salon.

She struggled out of the chair to follow him across the salon's steady gray planking, then the galley's tile, then the teak and holly strips of the pilothouse. The steel railing of the stairs leading up to the flybridge chilled her hands. Her fingers felt hot, like sunburn. McLellan's back, just in front of her, was a mile away. He turned his head and cursed, then wrapped his arm around her.

"Why didn't you stay put?" he growled as he guided her to the flybridge's bench seat.

"Good Lord, Chris, what happened?" Smitty asked, eyes wide.

"Bilge pumps," McLellan barked. "Are they running?"

Smitty switched each pump on manually. In turn, the amber lights above the switches flickered on. "Yeah, everything's good. Hortense quit all of a sudden—"

"I pulled the plug," Chris said. "I was working on the stuffing box when you started her."

In the eerie green instrument lighting, Chris saw Smitty's face go still. "Holy shit." He abandoned the wheel to sit next to her, take her hands. "I'm sorry."

"Why the hell did you start the engines?" God, her voice sounded rough.

"The depth meter went crazy. I had to keep us from running aground. I thought you were just sticking your head in, not climbing around down there." He squeezed her fingers. "I'm sorry, Chris," he said as he pulled her into his embrace.

She felt helpless to do anything more than wait for him to let her go. Her muscles had long since given in to shock and fatigue, her throat still felt like a scratching pad, and she tasted chemicals. Beneath his shirt, Smitty's heart beat clear and strong.

"I'm okay," she protested.

First things first.

"Are we away from the shoals now?" she asked, pulling

away. She stared at his white shirt. She'd imprinted it, like a crime scene outline.

"Yeah," he was saying. "It was the weirdest thing. The GPS hit a dead spot and then all of a sudden the depth meter started screaming. I had to get us off the shelf or whatever the hell was down there."

Her brain, bleary as it still was, recognized the dead spot phenomenon. The itinerant cruisers had mentioned it to her when she talked about traveling near the ICW—an area where GPS devices sometimes lost contact with the satellite. Rumor had it the Navy and Coast Guard occasionally tested a GPS-blocking device around that area, and it blocked satellite transmissions for several miles, even into the gulf.

"Don't start Hortense again," she said. "There's an exhaust leak."

"We should haul ass for a doctor," McLellan said from the helm where he held the wheel.

"No, I'll be fine after a while."

"How long were you breathing carbon monoxide?" he demanded.

"I don't know. Just a few minutes maybe. There's not much carbon monoxide from diesel."

"It was a fog in the entire lower passageway. What makes you think you're okay?"

"Look, just give it until we get to New Orleans. I've not lost motor function or my ability to speak. I'll get a checkup when we land."

"Probably a day late, though," Smitty said grimly.

"We can make it up on the run south. As long as the bilge pumps keep working, we'll be fine." Chris hesitated. "I'll be fine."

McLellan's face was cut stone in the dim light but he said nothing.

She pushed the stray lock of hair back from her fore-head. The lock that would have killed her if it'd wrapped around the prop shaft in the dark. How long would it have taken them to find her body?

"I'm going to shave myself bald," she said to no one in particular.

"Don't you dare," McLellan said softly, his frown clearing a little. "Come on. You can't shower and sleep in your cabin with the stench in the passageway. Fumes everywhere. You take a shower in the guest bathroom and I'll make up the upper crew bed for you. Smitty can handle the boat."

"I've still got two hours on my shift."

"I got it," Smitty said. "Least I can do after almost killing you."

McLellan shot Smitty a hard glance and Chris felt Smitty stiffen. "Come on, Christina."

She took McLellan's hands and let him pull her to her feet. His arm went around her as he guided her to the stairs.

"I'll go first," he said, "in case you fall."

"I'm not a total invalid," she insisted. "I don't need help."

His skeptical look annoyed her even more, but she didn't have the energy to argue. She was just tired and shaky, not on the verge of collapse. Still, it was nice to have his arm around her as they navigated through the pilothouse into the galley, then into the upper passageway to the guest head. His arm felt just like she'd thought it would, just as it had around her earlier.

"What do you want to sleep in?" he asked, leaning in the forepeak bathroom's doorway as she turned on the shower. "Do you have a nightgown or something?"

She caught sight of herself in the mirror. She looked like a refugee from a forced labor lube and tune. Black grease and oil smeared her hair and face. Her shirt hung awkwardly on her frame; the ripped sleeve had taken part of the side seam with it and her bra showed there. Her cheek and the bridge of her nose sported a light red streak, like a faint burn, but from what she didn't know and couldn't remember.

No wonder he thought she was going to pass out on him.

Something to sleep in. Something soft and comforting. She nodded to him. "Top right-hand drawer. A T-shirt and the gray sweat pants."

He closed the door, leaving her alone in a space that was suddenly too small. She braced her hands against both walls to steady herself. *How long am I going to be shaky?* She stripped off her nasty shorts, then pulled off what was left of her shirt, dropped them in a slimy heap on the floor.

She closed the frosted shower door behind her and leaned into the warm spray. The new water heater was doing its job, she noted absently. The shampoo she'd put in this bathroom for Natalie's return, a wildflower scent, smelled wonderful.

A rush of cool air over the shower door startled her. Outside, she saw a figure draping a towel over the bare rod, then laying pale garments on the toilet seat. He paused, as if waiting for something or thinking about speaking. Then the bathroom door clicked closed.

She shivered. McLellan couldn't see her through the frosted glass but she felt exposed. Bare. Vulnerable. She ran her hand through her wet hair, down over her taut breast. *Be honest.* She felt aroused, knowing he was just out there while she was just in here.

Stop it. It's just been a long time.

But it was more than that. She'd nearly died. She wanted to feel the weight of him on her, keeping her covered up, safe from everything that threatened to hurt her. She needed comfort, raw and physical, to remind her she was alive.

She twisted the shower knobs to Off and opened the door. Cold air struck her like the back of a hand. She hurriedly toweled off and slipped into the oversize T-shirt and comfortable track suit pants. *Better,* she thought, then caught sight of herself in the slowly defogging mirror. Her eyes were still red-rimmed, irritated with the fumes, she told herself, and it made her irises that much bluer. Preternaturally blue. She opened the door.

The smell of hot chocolate wafted in her direction and her knees weakened again. Perfect. McLellan stood at the drying rack in the galley, putting away the dinner plates.

"Hope you made enough for two." She perched on a galley stool, feeling a bit stronger from just the shower and the smell of chocolate.

McLellan grinned and tossed his drying towel over his shoulder. "Comin' up." He poured her a cup. "How many marshmallows?"

"I didn't know we had marshmallows."

"Because you didn't do the shopping, Captain. I did."

"I like having a galley wench," she teased, then stopped short as her gut clenched at the normalcy. *No tears. Not now.* "Three, please."

He handed her the sweet-doctored mug. "How are you feeling?"

"Better." She forced a smile as she sipped the best cup of hot chocolate she'd ever tasted. "This is certainly helping."

His eyes narrowed. "You had a helluva close call."

"Two or three times over, when you think about it." She put a death grip on her mug. "Guess I have a few lives left."

"I've been there a couple of times myself," he said as he settled onto a stool next to her. His gaze, which could be so gray, so distant, studied her so intently she wanted to squirm. "My line of work is dangerous, but at least I expect it to be."

"Have you been shot?"

"Once, yes."

"How long were you in the hospital?"

"How long do you think you can avoid talking about how you feel?"

When she didn't answer, he leaned close. "You didn't promise me."

She carefully sipped her chocolate. "Promise you what?"

"That you won't go into the engine room alone again."

She faced him then, meeting his gaze squarely. "If you'd been with me tonight, we'd both have died."

A muscle in his jaw flexed briefly. "I went down there while you were in the shower. You left a trail of oil all the way to the stuffing box. There was a handprint on the hull." His eyes darkened, but with what emotion she couldn't say. "Promise me, Christina."

"I can't—"

"You can do whatever you want once we get you and your sister home," he said irritably. "But until then, I don't want you down there alone. I want someone with you so this doesn't happen again."

"It was a freak accident."

"I saw the prop shaft." He swung off his stool and paced into the galley. "I understand now what it could have done to you." His hands fisted as he strode back to her, then abruptly he let go to take her face in his hands and kiss her hard.

Yes. His anger made him rough with her, made his lips and tongue demanding. *Yes, this. Exactly this.* He threaded his fingers through her hair, licked the soft spot just under her ear. His shoulders, solid under her hands, flexed as he palmed her breast through her smooth cotton shirt. It had been so long. *Connor,* she thought, and didn't know if she said his name aloud.

He abruptly pulled away. "I'm sorry." He stroked her drying hair, then shook his head. His fingers trembled slightly as he let her go. "I'm out of line."

"Don't worry about it." She wanted to tell him to kiss her again, but he was right. This was business. They had to concentrate on Natalie first. This…temptation…would distract her. Make her wish for something that would just get in the way of saving her sister.

And the last time he'd kissed her, *Obsession* had come close to being hulled. She didn't believe in signs, but maybe it was time to start.

Chris clamped down on her awakened and unanswered need, tried not to feel the heat pooling in her core. "I should get some sleep," she said, then before McLellan could reply, she fled from her bar stool into a strange and lonely bed.

"Chris! I'm so glad I reached you on this damned phone!" Natalie's voice sounded harsh over the international connection the following evening. Her words were nearly overwhelmed by a pulsing, pounding background beat.

"Are you okay?" Chris surveyed the early evening sky, which lay clouded and brooding above the flybridge where she stood. "Is something wrong?"

"No!" Natalie shouted. "I've got news."

Sound casual, Chris reminded herself as she settled into the captain's chair and propped her legs on the helm console. Jerome might be listening, even in the middle of a party. "What kind of news?" she asked.

Sound dropout cut in, coming back only on the word, "Igor."

"What did you say?" Chris asked.

"I said I've got a new bodyguard. Igor's been canned."

"How'd you manage that?" Chris's throat throbbed with her quickened pulse.

"I told Jerome Igor made a move on me."

"Did he?"

"Of course not! But it got rid of Igor."

No doubt at the expense of the man's life, Chris thought. "That's a dangerous game, Natalie."

"Why shouldn't I use Jerome's paranoia against him? Now he thinks I'm a good little wife and he's given me more leash to play on." Her laugh trilled, incongruous with the seriousness of the situation. "But you could say I've found a guardian angel."

Chris's fear spun quickly into annoyance. Did Natalie not understand how treacherous this was? "What are you talking about?"

"Jerome let me get a new bodyguard. His name's Gabriel and he's helping me do things. I still have to use these damned disposable phones to call you, but at least I can call you without taking my life in my hands."

Chris forgot about being annoyed. "So you can tell me where you are now?" Good God, that would solve everything. "Do you know where you'll be over the next couple of days? I know some people, we can get you out—"

"No! Jerome's still keeping me in the dark." Natalie paused while the music lagged and a DJ shouted something in another language. Then she said, "I'm still stuck, Chris. Gabriel's nicer, but he's still Jerome's employee. Not mine."

And possibly had been told to give Natalie just enough leash to hang herself. Chris scrubbed her face with her hand. "I don't know, Nat. Maybe it would have been better to keep Igor."

"Why?"

"Better the devil you know."

"I disagree. Gabriel has possibilities."

Possibilities. That was how Natalie always character-ized a man she intended to sleep with.

"God, Natalie—"

"It's okay. I'm careful," Natalie insisted, just as she always had when she'd skated on thin ice.

Chris half envied her blissfully ignorant confidence; it had to be easier on the nerves than her own ponderous planning and worrying.

"But here's the best part," Natalie continued. "I got into Jerome's briefcase this morning. I think I've got the lat-longs for the island."

The lat-longs?

But then, if Natalie had been working her feminine magic on the bodyguard... As Chris had told Smitty and Garza, her sister understood power.

"What are they?" Chris asked hurriedly as she shot out of the captain's chair. *Don't go dead,* she begged the terrible phone connection. She grabbed a ballpoint pen from the side table and scribbled the numbers on the back cover of McLellan's *Yachting* magazine as Natalie rattled them off. They looked right, but she wouldn't know for sure until she plugged them into a GPS. And even then, they could be wrong.

She'd just have to take them at their word. Not as if she had a choice.

"And exactly when are you going be on the island?" Chris asked.

"In a few days, I think. But I don't know if we're going straight to Isladonata or if we're going to stop in New York first."

If they stopped in New York, the DEA could catch them coming through Customs, Chris thought. Maybe she wouldn't have to take *Obsession* to Isladonata. Maybe it would all be over, that simply.

"When will you know?" she asked.

"I'll try to find out and call you again tomorrow. All I know for sure is that we'll be on the island next weekend."

"Then I'll plan to be there."

Natalie sighed. "You always have a plan." Then as drums started pounding, she shouted, "I'd better go!"

Chris barely had time to say goodbye before the phone clicked. She settled back on the bench seat, watching the sky darken and calculating the timetable. Anticipate the worst, she ordered herself. Assume Jerome Scintella stayed out of New York, which a smart man who knew he was also a wanted man would.

After a day of normal bilge pump activity and no sign of more leaks, *Obsession* lay at anchor off the ICW tonight. They simply couldn't take the chance of traveling the busy ICW at night on only one engine. They'd limp into New Orleans tomorrow, a full day behind schedule despite their one day head start. Once safely there, they would see about the hull damage. Hortense's exhaust leak would have to be pinpointed. Chris hoped to hell it'd be a scratch-and-patch job. They didn't have time for a complete exhaust system replacement. The window for snatching Natalie back from Jerome Scintella had already shortened enough to make Chris nervous.

Chris intended to have a look at the exhaust system when McLellan and Smitty went ashore in New Orleans. If they would let her be alone in New Orleans. They thought they were supposed to protect her from Eugene Falks, but the cadaver wouldn't have followed her across the gulf, would he?

Falks hadn't found what he had been looking for, she

reminded herself. Whatever the hell that was. And she was still alive. So yes, it was possible he'd followed them, even though she'd kept an eye on the radar today, which had betrayed no sign of their being tailed.

Maybe she'd ask Natalie about Falks when she called tomorrow. If Nat knew the man's name, they'd know for sure whether Falks worked for Scintella. And if so, maybe why he'd attacked Chris.

Or would even asking the question put Natalie in more trouble, as Garza had suggested? Chris's need to know wrestled with the dread of causing her sister to put herself in more danger. Chris trusted this Gabriel about as far as she could throw him. Natalie so easily took people at their word, especially when they offered something she wanted. Her guardian angel might turn out to have a much darker side.

"I wish you'd chosen better," Chris told her sister aloud. Had Natalie taken the time to get to know her husband instead of being ruled by hormones, she might have discovered Jerome's paranoia. Or that he was a drug smuggler.

Now the only thing between Natalie and death was Chris. Just like the only thing between Natalie and the consequences of her earlier bad decisions—cars, relationships—had been Chris. The woman just didn't think of the future.

Yes, Chris admitted, she herself always had a plan, every piece painstakingly laid out in order. The only problem with this trip was that the pieces weren't cooperating.

She'd lost a full day on the schedule, the yacht required repairs and she'd have to check the lat-longs Natalie had given her to see if they were correct. God only knew if they'd be able to bluff their way onto the island and whether they'd get themselves gunned down in the process. Or sunk.

On impulse, she reached into the helm's cabinet to pull out a handheld Global Positioning System device. Might as well find out if the lat-longs were good. She plugged in the numbers. The display flickered, then showed her a definite dot on a large scale map, south of Key West. Chris zoomed in. The dot quickly became an oval-shaped island with an inlet cut into the south side. So the island did exist, and the lat-longs were valid. Or appeared to be. It could be a setup, just some random island out there with a crew of men waiting to gun them down when they arrived.

But what if the lat-longs were correct? What would happen if she did manage to bring Natalie home in one piece? If McLellan and Smitty failed to capture Jerome again, would he come after his wife? Would he send hired men out to track her down and bring her back? Would she and Natalie have to leave town? How would they live? She hadn't thought beyond the immediate rescue, getting Natalie away safe. Now, the future's black maw yawned before her, a place where no light penetrated and no light escaped.

She watched the cumulus clouds that hovered in the west darken into gray. The storm was catching up, inexorable and haunting. A cool gust of wind, laden with the steely scent of distant rain, swept over her cheeks. Finally, as the sky faded into true night, she wept.

Chapter 7

Dawn broke over the Harborside Marina channel as Chris turned *Obsession* into it. She throttled back for the channel's no-wake zone. Predawn mist lay thick across the water. Two ghostly fishermen bobbed in a flat-bottomed boat near the reeds, their poles extended out both sides like spider legs. She took one hand off the wheel to wave. The men gawked, flashed waist-high waves, and got back to the serious work of drowning worms.

Obsession passed the first red channel marker, her bow shouldering aside the brown-green water. Smitty and McLellan stood together down on the foredeck, Smitty in his shorts and muscle T-shirt leaning on the bow rail with his bare foot propped up on the bowsprit, McLellan in classic white linen slacks and navy golf shirt. Occasionally Smitty motioned to the anchor or to the cleat where he tied off the port bowline, but Chris couldn't hear what they were saying. From the back they looked like Robinson Crusoe and Cary Grant discussing the vagaries of the yachting life.

Chris's gaze slid off to the marina's breakwater, where the last herons of night were lifting from the bright wooden posts, long legs trailing like snapped kite strings. A flash of movement caught her eye. She scanned the far, reedy bank until she found it: a seagull sitting quietly in the water. The bird suddenly struggled, rose half a foot into the air, then collapsed. Fishing line maybe. *All tangled up,* Chris thought. *I know how you feel. I'll be back for you, girlfriend.*

Below her, McLellan pointed at the approaching breakwater while Smitty made up-and-down wave motions with his hands, then cupped his hands in the shape of a boat's hull and demonstrated a bow cutting water. McLellan had turned into a full-fledged boat geek, spending most of the past two days under way poking around the yacht, asking questions, generally making a nuisance of himself.

Nuisance. She'd always assumed that DEA agents kept to themselves, cleaned their guns and generally didn't show an interest in anything but firepower and arrest techniques. McLellan was very different.

Christina, he'd breathed against her cheek.

Her core warmed several degrees. *Note to self: Acquire flameproof chastity belt.*

Mist scattered in front of *Obsession*'s bow as they reached the last channel marker heading into the marina. For the first time in three days, the boat parted the liquid mirror behind a breakwater, gliding effortlessly. Even Claire sounded subdued, muffled by the light fog. A lone cormorant surfaced well ahead, its black-feathered body riding low in the water as it surveyed the scene, then dove again, wings stroking it deep underwater for its breakfast. Chris gathered the waters around New Orleans were making a comeback after last year's devastating hurricane.

She picked up the VHF mic. "Harborside, this is *Obsession*. Over."

"*Obsession*, I gotcha," the radio blared. "Head straight on down yer left there, Cap'n. Slip 43 will be to yer right toward the end, over."

"Slip 43, over."

"I got yer diver, too. He'll be down at eight t' have a look atcha hull."

"And a mechanic?"

"He's booked this mornin' but'll be out after dinner."

Dinner? She started to object, then remembered. *Dinner* meant *lunch* in these parts. She grinned as she said, "Thank you, sir. I see you've got some new pilings and docks."

"Ya," the harbormaster replied. "All this was built back up 'bout a month ago. We glad to see ya."

"I'm glad to be here. *Obsession* out." She put the mic down and fished a headset out of the console cabinet. "Good morning, Smitty," she said when she had it on.

"Howdy, ma'am." Smitty gave her a thumbs-up from the foredeck where he'd donned a matching headset for taking orders and giving her piloting feedback.

"Slip 43."

"Yep."

She drew the yacht alongside the open slip. Kind of a tight fit, she noted, but doable, even for a girl *Obsession*'s size. The trick was using the engines instead of the wheel to pivot the boat. Given she didn't have Hortense to work with, it'd be a little trickier. She spun the wheel hard to port and tapped Claire forward. *Obsession* obediently pivoted her nose to the left. Then Chris rapidly spun the wheel to starboard while she shifted Claire into reverse. The yacht's stern started to pull over to the right. Chris continued to jimmy the wheel and engine until the yacht was backed neatly into the slip.

When she looked down, she spotted McLellan on the deck helping Smitty with the lines, fore and aft. *So now he wants to be a first mate.* Smitty came back to the foredeck in plain view.

"Through with the engine?" she asked, and he slashed his hand across his throat.

Chris killed Claire, then removed the engine keys from the ignition and pocketed them. After stripping off her headset, she set about her normal duties: turned off the instruments, recorded the journey data in the log, and calculated fuel usage for the two engines and the generator. Claire had really sucked down the diesel during the trip, but given the detour outside the ICW they'd had to take and the accident that had taken Hortense out of action, the gallons per hour were acceptable, within what she'd expect for one engine at cruising speed.

She was putting the canvas console cover over the helm when her core fired up and she knew McLellan had joined her on the flybridge.

"I know you don't need any help, so I won't offer." He dropped onto the bench next to the console. "I'd just be in the way."

She tossed a shy smile his way. "Thanks for *thinking* about offering."

"My pleasure. Since I can't help putting the boat to bed, maybe I can help with something else."

"What's that?" Chris fastened the last cover snap.

"Let me get you a hotel room in town tonight."

She reached out to polish a smudge off the stainless

steel throttle lever on the console next to her. Was he propositioning her? "I appreciate the gesture but it's not necessary."

"You deserve a break. It was a rough night." His eyes registered only a calm anticipation. Nothing more or less.

"I'm fine," she said quietly. "The excitement's over and done with."

He leaned forward, propping his elbows on his knees. "You deserve a chance to relax. I'll take you out to dinner. It's the least you could do since you won't let me get you a doctor."

She glanced at her still-reddish knuckles. Friction burn, probably. That close to getting her hand chewed off by the propeller shaft. "I'm okay."

"You're not okay, dammit, you were almost killed," he snapped, straightening. "You breathed in so much smoke you nearly passed out."

"It turned out fi—"

"You got lucky." He irritably stood and took two steps away, then turned back. "Good God, woman, don't you let anyone help?"

"If I thought you could help, yes, I'd let you," she answered. "It's all said and done. I don't know why you're making this an issue."

"I need you to get us to that godforsaken island." He shoved his hands into his pockets. "You're the one who knows this boat inside out. I've watched you pilot for the past three days. Smitty was impressed as hell that you backed the yacht into the slip just now on only one engine. We could get by without you, but we'd look like a bunch of amateurs even if we didn't trash the boat in the process."

"Smitty could pilot—"

"Smitty's got a high opinion of himself but even he

admits he sucks in close quarters. You just kissed the dock with a hundred tons of boat. He'd ram it into the next state."

Competence. Yes, that's what he'd appreciate most in her. That's why they needed to keep their distance, to concentrate on the job at hand.

First things first.

"Don't worry," she replied. "I'll perform when it's time."

"Christina." He opened his mouth, then closed it, eyes darkening. "Do you want breakfast up here?"

She nodded, trying not to feel bereft as his lips pressed into a line, shutting her out. Those firm lips she remembered so well, capturing her while the wild wind filled her ears and emptied her mind. Rough and demanding on her after she'd nearly died, his hand hot on her breast. Since that moment two nights ago, he hadn't tried to touch her. But his expression now provoked a loneliness she hadn't felt in a long time.

Chris studied McLellan's broad back as he headed for the stairs to the pilothouse. He could be as dangerous as Jerome Scintella, she thought, just on the right side of the law. Magnetic, challenging, rough around the edges.

Carries a gun. Gets shot in the line of duty. Chases much better-funded bad guys who wield small armies. Would never take a desk job or, from remarks Smitty had made, settle down. Wanted to take his vengeance on his brother's murderer.

In his own way, McLellan was a *dragyne,* too. At least to her.

But they needed to be a team. She needed to trust his judgment just as he needed to trust hers. They'd never do that as long as they were both being pigheaded.

Even if it did mean chancing a piece of her heart.

"Connor."

He paused at the stairs and turned his head to look at her.

She stroked the throttle absently, thinking about best laid plans and the chances you took sometimes to get things right, even when it seemed like a terrible risk.

"Why don't you join me for breakfast?" she asked. She shifted the throttles full forward. "Then we can talk about dinner."

"The water's thicker than usual this morning," the diver said. He stood on *Obsession's* new teak swim platform and fitted his diving mask's strap around his head.

"Is it still bad after the spills last year?"

He shrugged. "Couldn't go in for a long time, but it's cleared up some. I'll feel around for a while, see what I can find." He leaned over to the dock and switched on the air compressor, adjusted the mask over his face, then unceremoniously dropped from the platform.

Chris leaned over the aft rail, watching the diver's flippers flutter the water, bubbles hurling themselves to the surface.

"I wouldn't have that guy's job for the world," Smitty said over the compressor's rhythmic clatter. "I saw what swims down there once and I ain't goin' back."

"I thought you got wet occasionally, ex-Coastie."

"Yeah, but out there where it's safe." He nodded toward the gulf. "Too many stories about two-headed turtles around the coast. Especially after the brew kicked up by hurricane Katrina." He shuddered dramatically. "McLellan's looking for two-headed birds."

"Bird watching?"

"Up on the bow." Smitty leaned his shoulder against hers and smiled into her eyes. "He's got a sissy streak a mile wide, darlin'. Keep that in mind when he gives you the bedroom eyes, okay?"

"You mean like the bedroom eyes you're giving me now?"

He heaved a sigh. "Guilty as charged. I wear my heart on my sleeve. But only for you." He batted his baby blues at her. "I'm a real man, baby."

"I'll take that under advisement."

"But you don't believe me."

Before Chris could answer, the diver surfaced, blowing thick, broad bubbles in the green water. He stripped off his mask and swept his hand back over his platinum-tipped brown hair. "There's a gouge in the hull, but it doesn't feel deep. I'll get a light down there and have a look."

"How are the props?"

He shrugged. "You got some dings and a bent blade where the rig hit. Lowest part of the boat, props always hit first."

"And the prop shaft?" Chris asked. "She took on a lot of water after we hit. I need to know if it's out of alignment."

The diver blew water off his nose and considered. "Let me get a look." He hoisted himself easily onto the swim platform and dug through his gear bag, coming up with a battery-powered waterproof lamp. "Be right back." A splash, and he was gone.

"The gouge will be expensive," Chris mused.

"Depends on the length and depth," Smitty said. "Maybe it'll just be a scratch and can wait until we get back."

When we get back, Natalie will be home and Obsession *will be totally restored. Just in time to run from Jerome Scintella.*

"Hey," Smitty said, looping his arm over her shoulders. "We're gonna get your sister, okay? Don't ever doubt that."

She nodded. "I'm just worried about what'll happen when I get her home."

"How do you mean?"

"What if Jerome comes after us? He's a drug smuggler—"

Smitty burst out laughing, his light tenor echoing under the aft deck roof. "Sweetheart," he said through a chuckle, "they ain't comin' after you."

"Natalie thinks he will."

"That's one little problem that'll take care of itself." At her startled glance, Smitty said, "He's going to be in prison, darlin', put there by yours truly. Besides, it won't be worth his while to off her. Too risky. I don't care how good she is in bed."

Chris opened her mouth to reply but he went on, "Look, you know and I know that your sister is a good woman. But guys like Scintella see their women as just this side of property. She causes trouble, he'll be glad to see the back of her as long as she doesn't make off with the family jewels."

"Wouldn't it make sense for us to change her name or something?"

He shrugged. "Records are pretty open. You'd have to put her in the witness protection program or something like that—"

He broke off as the diver exploded from the water.

"The hull's okay!" the diver called. He shimmied onto the platform with a seal's ease, leaned over, and shut off the compressor. "What you've got is a surface gouge, nothing serious. The fiberglass is how thick on the bow? Half-inch?"

"Three-quarter," Chris replied.

The diver shook his head. "This is cosmetic. I took a little longer this time and checked the rest of the hull. You've got dings here and there. The prop is definitely bent, but the shaft looks straight as an arrow."

"Can I see?"

The diver stared. "You mean you want to go down?"

"You said it was safe enough these days, right?"

The diver scratched his ring-pierced eyebrow with his forefinger and frowned. "Never had anybody want to do that, but okeydokey."

The cool water soothed her sun-warmed skin as she slipped beneath the boat. The diver, using snorkeling gear while she had the compressor, shone his searchlight on the gouge. She ran her fingers, yellow-green in this water, over the wound. It wasn't deep. She could barely feel the glass matting beneath. No worse than scraping a concrete piling. *Good girl.* Chris patted *Obsession*'s hull as if she were a huge and placid sea mammal.

The diver motioned her aft, pointing out chips where the rig pipes had passed under the hull. Then he splashed the light across the prop, one of its blades twisted and another bent almost in half. But the shaft, from what she could see with his big light, looked straight. That was a minor miracle. She'd know for sure when she started Hortense and felt for vibration. She ran her thumb over the bronze blade, then shuddered. The water was cooler than she liked for an extended dunking. Her royal blue racing wet suit, meant to be used above the surface, didn't cut it for long. She stroked for the surface and climbed onto the swim platform.

Smitty and McLellan leaned on the railing above her, gazing down. McLellan had changed into shorts and had one foot propped on the lower rail. His thighs and calves looked like a triathlete's and were covered with fine black hair.

"Should we give her a towel or just enjoy the view?" Smitty remarked.

Chris glared at him through the diving mask and tried

not to be aware of McLellan's evaluation of her cleavage, or lack thereof, in the half-unzipped wet suit.

"What's the verdict?" McLellan asked as Smitty shoved away from the railing.

She tugged off the mask and laid it on the teak platform for the diver. "I think it's okay. The prop's mangled and will have to be replaced. That's a quick haul, just a couple of hours in the sling. After that we can start Hortense and see how she behaves. If she vibrates we'll need to get the prop shaft realigned, but it looks good so far."

"I like the sound of that." Smitty dropped a folded towel on her head. "Three days and nights here to finish up the amazing restoration and then showtime."

Chris shook out the oversize towel and rubbed her arms. "We need to talk about Isladonata tonight."

"Can't," McLellan said. "I'm taking you to dinner."

"Hey, you makin' moves on my woman?" Smitty growled.

McLellan grinned. "Just making up for a bad trip. The lady deserves a night on the town."

She armored herself with the towel. He was being way too nice. And that T-shirt was just too damn tight over his shoulders. "Smitty can come if he wants."

"No, he can't." McLellan clapped Smitty on the shoulder. "He's going to be scrubbing the bilge with a toothbrush, aren't you, champ?"

"The hell I am," Smitty shot back. "Bring me back some jambalaya, will ya? Consolation prize for the night shift."

"Night shift?" Chris asked. "You guys are serious about guarding me, aren't you?"

"Ma'am, it is our pleasure and duty," Smitty said.

"Then I guess if I want to take a sail," she said, nodding toward the little wooden sailing tender sitting upside down on the flybridge, "I'll have to take one of you with me."

"Afraid so."

Chris sighed. "Then who's going?"

"Why, I'd like a sail with a pretty little thang like you." Smitty's eyes twinkled.

McLellan's glare could've melted stone. "I'll go."

"What?" Smitty spread his hands like the unarmed man he wasn't. "Why shouldn't I?"

"Whoever's going," she said as she headed inside, "uncover the tender while I change and get my tool bag."

In her cabin, Chris changed into shorts and a tank top, pausing long enough to comb out her wet hair properly and tie it back. When she got back up top, McLellan had already neatly folded the sailing tender's canvas cover. In the midmorning sunlight, the little boat's gleaming varnish was almost too bright to look at.

"What are we up to?" he asked, abandoning his thoughtful caress of the gunwale.

"A rescue mission. Help me launch this."

They lowered the wooden tender by the rooftop crane. It took only a few minutes to rig the little mast and boom. Chris dropped her tool bag under the tiller seat and settled in. McLellan sat on the windward side, out of the way of the boom. The tender bobbed precariously with the mismatched weight of her cargo. She needed the wind to balance her.

"Raise her," Chris said.

McLellan's hands worked quickly on the main halyard, lifting the sail up the mast, stretching the sail taut and cleating off the line. He moved easily, showing how his few days on *Obsession*—dropping and raising the anchor, working the lines—had sunk in.

They eased away from *Obsession*, McLellan keeping

watch for marina traffic until they gained the channel and headed out toward the open water of Lake Pontchartrain. As they passed out of the marina's wind shadow, the tender picked up speed and put her shoulder in, knifing through the green water of the basin. The wind gusted, pitching the tender hard over, where she liked to be. Chris directed McLellan to lean far out to keep the tender at a good angle, his feet hooked under the coaming on the opposite side. She adjusted the main sheet and pulled the tiller to bring the little boat closer to the wind.

The tender was really flying now, skimming across waves and dappling sunlight, occasionally throwing a bow wave onto McLellan's face and chest. Every time it did, he looked back at Chris and grinned. She found herself irrationally pleased by his boyish joy. Sailing a tender was such a little thing.

Then the shoreline was coming up fast and they had to tack.

"Prepare to come about," Chris said. "We're going to switch sides."

"Right."

"Helm a-lee." Chris pushed the tiller away.

McLellan scrambled under the boom to take up his position on the other side. Chris ducked as the boom swung over her head. The tender paused as she pivoted, sail snapping violently in the changing wind.

"Drop the sail," Chris said.

McLellan hesitated only a second, then nimbly uncleated the halyard and let the sail drop. The tender stilled, moved only by wind on her hull.

"What's this about?" he asked with a smile. "Testing my ability to take orders?"

Chris ignored the gentle gibe. "It was right around

here." She scanned the bank. "I saw her on the way in this morning."

Seconds later, she found what she was looking for. A few yards away, a seagull sitting in the water near the shore picked up as though to fly, but rose only a few inches before collapsing back.

"Fishing line?"

"Probably. I couldn't tell when we came in." Chris pulled a pair of leather gloves out of her tool bag and tossed them to him. "You hold her and I'll cut her loose."

"Won't we scare her?" McLellan worked one hand into a glove.

"Better we scare her for a few minutes than her starve to death."

Chris eased the tender slowly nearer the gull. As they got closer, the gull struggled, then subsided.

"She's exhausted," McLellan said.

"There's no telling how long she's been caught here. Are you just going to use the one glove?"

"I'll offer her that hand to bite. If I'm going to hold her, I'd rather do it with my bare hand. I can almost reach her now."

"Catch her feet if you can."

McLellan leaned over as the tender drew close. He delicately grasped the bird's feet. The gull's wings swept up, fighting. His gloved hand grabbed the fishing line and pulled it out of the water so Chris could slice through it with a knife. McLellan brought the bird into the tender. It struggled, its head snaking from side to side, its beak snapping.

McLellan held his gloved hand in front of the gull's beak. It bit his forefinger and held.

"Are you okay?" Chris sorted through the mass of fishing line hooked around the gull's neck and back.

"Sure. She just needs to chew on me for a while."

"There must be five yards of line here."

It took Chris a few minutes to cut up the line and draw the pieces through the soft gray feathers. Twice while she was working, the gull flapped its wings feebly to escape. Chris wondered if McLellan's fingers were too tight on the gull's paper-thin legs, but after each struggle the bird settled back onto his hand. She looked up to gauge McLellan's mood. He seemed perfectly content to let the gull bite him while she untangled things. More than that, his narrowed eyes and thoughtful expression suggested he was studying the bird.

Of course. Smitty said he liked them. "Are you a birder?" she asked.

He smiled. "Not until now. What's this one, do you think?"

"Bonaparte's gull."

"It's not like the noisy ones I saw in Galveston."

Noisy could only mean the ubiquitous black-headed gulls that perched on pilings all over the marina from dawn till dusk. When they weren't trying to steal fish from the terns. "Those are laughing gulls."

"Yes, they do laugh."

"That's the last bit. Hold her another minute and let me do a check."

Chris carefully unfolded each gray-and-white wing in turn, studying the lay of the feathers. "Do you see anything I missed?"

He lifted the gull to look under its neck. "I think you got it all. There was one bit lashed around her throat."

"Yeah, I got that one first. I think she's done."

McLellan held the bird for another moment, its feet still between his bare fingers, its belly nestled almost against his palm, its beak firmly gripping his gloved forefinger.

Then he raised both hands as if to toss the gull into the air, as if it were a raptor.

The gull arced its wings for balance but didn't move.

"She won't let go of my finger."

"Let go of her feet. She won't stop biting until she's free."

He spread his fingers from the gull's legs. The bird hovered, wings wafting gently, impossibly light, then it opened its beak and rose effortlessly into air.

They watched the gull arc steadily over the marsh. Sun glinted across dewy tall grasses and speckled the green water. Rich brine tinted the wind, which was starting to kick up with the day's heat.

McLellan stared at the bank, his expression thoughtful. *He's gone away,* Chris thought. Wherever he was, he looked like any other man, *dragyne* or not. More than that, he looked vulnerable, his face relaxed.

"That was great," he said softly, looking after the bird. Then he turned and met her gaze, his eyes gentle and clear, accessible.

"It's good karma."

He reached out with his bare hand. She impulsively gripped it. He leaned forward, kissed her knuckles, then turned her hand to place his lips lightly against her palm. A thrill shot up her spine.

"Thank you," he said, not releasing her.

She steadied her voice. "For what?"

"For letting me do this with you." Heat rimmed his eyes and his slow smile.

"It's not a big deal."

"Not to you, maybe." He slowly released her hand, his fingers trailing lightly across her palm, and looked off toward the marsh. "It's been a long time since I've done anything that good. That simple."

Chris studied his profile, clean and bright against the rippling green water. "When was that?"

He stripped off the glove and looked at his hands. "A long time ago."

"Since your brother died?" she asked, half-afraid of what he'd say.

His eyes darkened, haunted even in the sunshine. "Was murdered. Threw his life away."

"You couldn't have changed him," she said gently. "No more than I could have convinced Natalie not to do any of the stupid things she did."

"Was she in trouble a lot?"

"Her fair share. Shoplifting once. It was a mystery. Our grandfather was wealthy and gave her anything she wanted. It seemed like fun to her, I guess. A challenge."

"Did she get caught?"

"She did a few hours of community service when she was fourteen, yeah."

His half smile held more than a tinge of sadness. "Sean was into a little more than shoplifting."

"Did you know?"

"I saw the signs but they didn't register. Stupid of me, but I was in denial. Not my brother. Not drugs." He raised his head to look over the reeds where the fishermen had long since packed up their bait and gone home for the day. The stiffening breeze ruffled his hair. "Certainly not selling them. When I figured out what he was doing, it was too late."

"You tried to get him out," she said softly.

"After the damage was done." His jaw flexed. "I know it was his choice. Antonio spent a good year pounding that into my thick skull. But I could have done more. I could have watched out for him better while he was growing up."

Chris absently adjusted the tiller to keep the sailing tender out of the reeds as the wind swept along the hull, pushing the little boat farther east. "Was he much younger than you?"

"Five years. But I left home when I was eighteen." A hard glint flashed in his eyes, then he said, "I wasn't as good a brother to him as you are a sister to Natalie." His lips pressed to a thin line, which Chris knew meant, *Let's not go there.*

"Are you making it up to him now?"

His gaze snapped to her face. "Yes. But I'll be done soon."

I should be afraid, she thought as she studied his remote gray eyes. A man who could kill another human being suddenly sat here with her in this small vessel being blown lightly away from shore. Guilt and vengeance were bound up together in his face like the blood brothers they were. Her heart ached for him.

Then Connor abruptly smiled, the determined fury slipping from his expression, a shadow fleeing sunlight. "Being with you helps."

The smile she gave him in return felt shy, natural, right. "I don't see how."

"Priorities change." His gaze flicked to her lips, then back to her eyes. "Maybe it's time to get a new dream. Quit living in the past."

"You have to give up the old dream to embrace a new one."

He was silent a moment before he said, "Not always. Sometimes you get to have both."

"And sometimes realizing the old dream makes the new one impossible."

He stared at her, heat warring with something like regret or sadness. "We should go."

His words were as good as turning his back on her. Connor's complexity, his internal battle, made her wonder what he'd do if he ever caught up with his brother's murderer. If he'd be able to hold himself back, to choose justice over revenge.

And if he couldn't, would it change how attractive he was to her?

Questions for another time. Time for home. She turned the tiller, guided the sailboat into clear water. "Raise the sail."

Connor ran the sail up the mast. Chris nudged the little boat a hair to the east. The sail filled with a whooshing pop and the tender was off, heading more or less in the right direction.

Chris felt herself smiling like an idiot. The air smelled clear and bright, free of summer's cloying heat. The tender champed through a light chop, speeding along as if it didn't have a care in the world.

For this moment, this very second, she didn't, either. McLellan had helped her save a seagull. More than that, he'd revealed something of himself, helped her understand a little better who he was. Here she was, sailing her little boat and nearly, finally, ready to save her sister. Here was the tender, dipping her shoulder into the rippling waves. Her smile became a grin. McLellan, drenched by the spray, his soaked shirt clinging to his chest, turned his head to look at her. Then he gave a whooping cry and raised his arms, as though in victory.

Chapter 8

Chris latched the door wide open, then dragged a plastic crate filled with quarts of oil in front of it for good measure. Satisfied the door wasn't going to close on her, she turned to survey the port engine room.

The hatch leading into the hold was closed, just as it should be. All was well. She wouldn't be going down there again any time soon. No way, no how. A niggling doubt tweaked her gut—as if she were about to leave on a long trip and had forgotten to pack something important—but she ignored it, tore her gaze away. God, she was sweating ice.

Chris wiped her clammy temple on her sleeve. Back to business. Hortense's exhaust leak.

"Well, old girl, let's see where it hurts."

Chris unlatched the tool chest lid and paused. Was that her screwdriver lodged between the chest and the wall? She leaned over to pick it up. *What the—?*

A small black box, no bigger than a pack of cards, sat shiny and new on the floor. She'd bolted the tool chest to the floor herself when she'd first taken custody of *Obsession,* and it hadn't been here then. Wires ran from the box along the wall to disappear behind the water heater.

"What the hell are you?"

The black box didn't reply.

"You're not much help," she told it.

The flashlight showed the two wires, red and green, snaking up the hull behind the water heater. Red and green. If they sucked electricity from the 12-volt system, they should have been black and white. Was it a transponder? Dave's guys from the boatyard wouldn't have installed it, would they?

She could almost hear Dave's voice now: "If it ain't on the work order, we don't do it."

A small fear sprouted in her stomach. Before her mind could kick into high gear imagining things, she shook her head. *Get a grip. Trace the wires. Find out what this thing is. Get the guys.*

Chris dislodged her screwdriver from behind the tool chest. Her mental map of the boat's layout told her the wires would run behind the office wall so she headed upstairs. The salon was empty.

"Smitty?" she called.

Normally he came running like a puppy, but not this time. McLellan had headed into town to make his hotel arrangements.

She was on her own. *Just don't disturb anything,* she told herself. She slid the office door open. Inside, her charter logs, maintenance records and electronics manuals filled the bookshelf above the desk that bore her laptop. The inkjet printer sat on its little table, strapped down against the threats of waves. Her purse slumped beside the laptop, her cell phone stuck headfirst into the outside pocket. Drawn curtains cast the room into dimness.

She yanked back the heavy curtain to get more light. The decorative wall panel below the window was like all the others in the boat, screwed into a wooden frame set inside the hull's fiberglass. She settled cross-legged on the floor and got to work with the screwdriver. A couple of minutes later, the panel dropped loose. She set it aside.

The wires were there, behind the wooden framing, red and green against the fiberglass. They ended in bare tails just below the window. A transponder. These wires had been broadcasting *Obsession*'s position to someone—*Who? Why?*—across the open gulf. The tails were held in position with duct tape, of all things. A temporary solution at best.

Someone had been in a hurry.

Was this what Falks had been doing aboard *Obsession* that night? And why? Why would he need to know where—

The small fist of fear in her stomach opened and grabbed a double handful of her insides.

Where *Obsession* was. Where *she* was.

No, that couldn't be right. It wasn't Falks. She would have heard him open the engine room door that night he attacked her.

Someone else had planted it. An accomplice?

Whatever it was for—whoever it was for—she wasn't going to touch these wires. She'd show it to McLellan and Smitty when they got back. She thought back to the boat she'd continually spotted following them to New Orleans. This time of year, sure, there'd be plenty of traffic as sailors took advantage of the good weather to make their journeys east and west. And when *Obsession* had been forced from the ICW to travel into the gulf, it made sense that whatever boat was behind them would do the same to avoid the tanker accident.

"Problems?" Smitty asked from the doorway.

"Maybe. Take a look at this."

He hunkered down next to her, his aftershave, spicy and clean, closing the space between them. Chris filled him in on the transponder she'd found and pointed out the antenna tails. "You think someone's following us?"

His normally open face settled into hard lines and for the first time Chris saw the authority figure, the man of law, in his expression. "Let's take a look at the transponder."

In the engine room, he knelt next to the tool chest and studied the black box for several long moments. "Care to make a guess who put it in here?"

"I don't know. I only saw it a few minutes ago."

"Do you think Falks could have installed it the night he broke in?"

She shook her head. "I hadn't oiled the engine room door. Opening it would have woken me up, no question."

"And Dave?"

"I can call him but I don't think he or his guys did it."

"Not even if Falks paid him to?"

Chris caught her breath. "Dave's a friend. I can't imagine him taking money to do something like this."

"But one of his men could have planted it."

"I don't see how." Chris's mind flickered through days of boat chores. "Most of their work was outside and we were working inside. Wouldn't one of us have noticed a workman being where he shouldn't?"

"Good point." Smitty stood, his jaw clenched. "Then we've got a problem."

"What do you mean?" she asked, afraid to ask.

"Sit down." He steered her to sit on the tool chest and

went down on one knee in front of her. "Has McLellan told you what we're doing?"

"You've been in all the conversations I have." Fingers of dread started caressing her stomach. McLellan's brooding silences. Her conviction there was something he wasn't telling her about. "What else is going on?"

Smitty rested his hands on her knees, like a parent comforting a child. "The reason we haven't been able to catch Jerome Scintella is because we have a mole somewhere in the department."

He paused to let her take that in, then continued, "Someone keeps telling Scintella when we're gonna show up. Normally we'd send a huge team out on a mission like this. Twenty, thirty guys. More if Scintella's as heavily armed as we think he is."

"So you're using only four agents—"

"Because these are the four we know we can trust." His grip tightened. "But maybe there's actually only three."

Chris didn't realize she was holding her breath until she let it go in one long, slow exhale. "You think McLellan planted the transponder?"

Smitty's eyes closed. "God, I hope not." His head bowed, showing her his glossy blonde hair. "I've worked with him for years. Trusted him." His shoulders hunched. "Shit."

Chris tentatively put a hand on his shoulder. "You don't know for sure," she said, refusing to accept the theory Smitty was offering. "Why would he do it?"

"It makes sense." Smitty rubbed his face with his hand. When he lifted his head to meet her gaze, his eyes were a little red. "It makes too much goddamn sense." The lines of his face went sharp with anger, with hurt. "You've seen the way the guy dresses. We don't make that kinda money. Nowhere near."

"Maybe he inherited…" Her protest died as Smitty shook his head.

"He used to be like the rest of us, busting our asses to make ends meet. After a couple of years he started showing up in nice clothes, nice shoes. I just never thought—"

"Okay, so he saved his money and has good taste," Chris argued. "It doesn't prove anything."

Smitty's voice was rough when he said, "He's already made a move on you, hasn't he?"

The fingers of dread clutched her heart and her face went hot. *Christina,* McLellan had said. She swallowed. Nodded, unable to speak.

Smitty shrugged off her hand and stood as though he wanted to get away from her, not look at her. "I need to talk to Garza. Get him investigating McLellan's background. See if his bank account says what I think it says."

Chris got hold of herself well enough to say, "But he hates drugs. What about his brother? He was killed by a drug dealer—"

"What?"

"He told me his brother was murdered."

Smitty frowned. "His brother died, but he wasn't murdered."

"McLellan said he was shot by a dealer who wouldn't let him leave the business."

Smitty shook his head, brow still furrowed. "That's not true. Sean was drunk off his ass. Him and his buddies were playing around with a gun. Coroner's report said he'd shot himself in the head. End of story."

Chris closed her eyes. How could she reconcile what Smitty was telling her with what McLellan had said? "So how did he end up in the water?"

"You're nineteen years old and your buddy accidentally

kills himself. You've already been in trouble with the law. What do you do?" Smitty shrugged. "You weight his body down, toss him in the water and hope he doesn't wash up."

"But he did wash up."

"I know," Smitty said quietly. "I was there." He knelt in front of her again and took her hands. "I hate like hell it happened to the kid. But it had nothing to do with a drug dealer."

The fingers of dread grabbed a double handful of her stomach. "Then why did McLellan lie to me?"

His snort was short, sharp. Cynical. "It's a good tactic. You're trying to save your sister so he tells you a story about a brother. Makes an emotional connection with you. Followed by what? A physical connection?"

Chris tried to breathe, let her mind play through all the interactions she'd had with Connor McLellan. The haunted look in his gorgeous eyes, his reluctance to share his past, the sense she had that he wasn't telling her everything. His desire to know all there was to know about the yacht. Because he was making plans for it? To hijack it? Maybe he wanted to keep her aboard because if he hired a man to pilot *Obsession* to the island, he'd have more trouble subduing that man than a woman who trusted him. She shuddered.

But there was also his kindness, his care of her the night of the accident. His continued demands she see a doctor. Those kisses. His hand moving on her body.

"He's always been good in vice," Smitty said softly. "Don't see why he couldn't go the other way with it."

Chris stiffened. The thought of McLellan seducing women in the line of duty made her feel…dirty. Used.

Smitty tightened his grip on her hand and she clutched his strong fingers like a drowning woman. When his arms went around her, she let herself ease into his embrace. Let herself rest, just for a moment. Every line of his body was taut, strung tight. Smitty's hands gripped her sides.

Who was telling the truth? Same facts—a young man shot dead and pulled from the water—but different stories about how he got there. Smitty could be the mole. Or not. McLellan could be the mole. Or not. It all depended on who was telling the truth.

Then a thought occurred to her and the words she had to say felt like lead on her tongue. "He painted the engine room floor."

Smitty released her abruptly and sat back on his haunches. His eyes, sparking with fury, scanned the crisp, white floor marred only by smeared oily footprints. "So he had plenty of time to install the transponder. He could have run the wiring any time we were out looking for spares."

"He planted a tracking device in case what? We got away from him?"

"So Scintella will know where you are."

Chris's stomach churned, hot and heaving. "I'm dead, aren't I? No matter what I do, Natalie and I are dead."

"No, don't think like that." Smitty grabbed her arms and gave her a little shake, his expression fearful, almost desperate. "Listen. I'll call Garza, get him working on this." As she watched, he gained control over his facial features as if putting on a mask. The lawman was back, ready for the job. "Can you be casual with McLellan? We can't scare him off. This'll be my chance to arrest the mole, get him out of the agency. Do that and we have a shot at Scintella." His fist clenched. "Finally."

Chris thought of McLellan's apparent joy in the seagull, the sailing. If she kept that in her mind—if she used those images to temper her emotional responses to him—she might be able to do it. "Being nice to him isn't like trusting him."

Smitty rose and she stood with him. "If you find anything else," he ordered, "let me know. We might be able to build a case here, and I don't want anything to slip through the cracks." His concern shone in his blue eyes. "And for God's sake, Chris, be careful with him. Can you get out of doing dinner with him tonight?"

She shrugged. "I don't know. He wants me to meet the other two agents."

Smitty frowned, apparently considering, then nodded. "You'll be safe with Russ and Jacquie. They're stand-up. Besides, he doesn't dare show his hand. He needs to stay deep in the DEA, feeding information to Scintella. He won't jeopardize his position." He turned to go, but paused and reached back to cup her cheek. "Stay strong, pretty lady. I won't let anything happen to you."

Chris nodded. McLellan had said that to her more than once. Full of promises, these men. But Smitty smiled when he said it, with what looked like genuine affection, then left her alone in the engine room.

It was too much to take in all at once. She sat down on the tool chest again and lowered her head into her hands. Best laid plans shot to hell. And back. In spades.

One good thing: both men needed her. There was plenty of time between now and the arrival at Isladonata for Garza to do his research and for Smitty to pinpoint exactly what McLellan had been up to.

Unless it was Smitty up to no good. His story sounded plausible but it was all one man's word against another's. She couldn't know anything for sure right now.

How easy it would be to give up. Just throw in the towel and go home, let the DEA—if that's who these guys really were—sort out its mess on its own.

Lost at sea. That's how she felt. Totally lost.

She raised her head and looked around the engine room. This place she knew. Claire hunched, quiet and still warm from her run. The faulty extractor fan Smitty had repaired while they were underway this morning hummed briskly.

How could so much metal and diesel fuel and electrical wiring feel like home? There was a certainty to it, she mused, not like people. A machine worked or didn't in predictable ways. Mysteries could be solved with some logical thinking because everything was right there in front of you to see. Hell, she'd torn down and rebuilt both engines herself.

But this thing with McLellan... She hadn't imagined the pain in his expression or in the way he carried himself when he talked about his brother's death. That had been real. And why *should* he tell her about a mole? That was DEA business, not hers.

It just upped the ante for her, though, didn't it? What she didn't know could hurt her. No wonder McLellan walked around looking haunted. Well, keeping things secret could do that to you.

By contrast, Smitty was an open book, a straightforward guy with every emotion and thought visible right there on his sleeve.

"Where's Smitty?" McLellan demanded from the doorway.

"Talking to the boatyard manager, I think."

"Do you need any help with anything?"

She shrugged and clenched her hands together to still the trembling. "No. I'm just trying to figure out the best way to finish the last of the work."

He stared hard at her. Chris felt her chest tighten. Did he somehow know what she'd been doing? That she knew about the transponder?

"You're not supposed to be down here alone," he said.

She nearly let out the breath she'd been holding, then stood and gestured to the makeshift door stop. "I'm okay."

McLellan's scowl deepened. "We had a deal."

"No we didn't. You just thought because you wanted me to promise that I had promised."

"Dammit, Christina." He took a step toward her, then stopped himself. "Cooperate with me on this," he said in a low voice.

"We're tied up at the dock," she retorted. "I think the engine room is safe." *At least on its own. When no one but me is in it.*

He said nothing to that, only glared for a few seconds, then turned on his heel and left.

What's up with him? she wondered as she closed the cabinet drawer. Then voices raised in anger above her head got her attention. McLellan was seriously pissed off. Smitty's tenor came back at him, equally angry.

She shuddered involuntarily. The few times she'd heard her father fight with Granddad, she'd hidden under her bedcovers. When you were eight, adult anger, all that horrible energy, was terrifying. Still was, in a way.

She tiptoed to the stair bottom. No need to strain to hear.

"You weren't supposed to leave her alone," McLellan snapped.

"Hey, I went to arrange repairs, okay?" Smitty responded hotly. "She's not going to get into any trouble in ten minutes."

Quick, hard steps, as if McLellan was pacing. "Anything can happen in ten minutes and you know it."

Smitty made a disgusted noise. "We're supposed to be *partners* in this thing. Do you trust me or not?"

Chris backed away from the stairs. Who was playing the

good guy in that little drama? And how would she ever be able to tell?

What if McLellan was the mole?

Ignoring the bolt of regret that shot through her, she slipped back into the engine room. She could do her part and make sure the device actually was a transponder. Kneeling next to the tool chest, she made two quick slashes with a craft knife through the block of white sealant securing the box to the floor. Her fingernails just fit inside the slash. She pulled up gently. The box rose slightly as the remaining sealant flexed and gave. Perfect. She'd be able to cut the transponder loose later, maybe park it someplace where it'd confuse whoever was following them.

A satisfied smile welled up in her soul. Oh, if it came right down to it, she could cause a helluva lot of confusion.

Chapter 9

Late that afternoon, Chris tossed her bath towel on a chair and stretched in the cool AC. After a day of screwing in wall panels and putting up mahogany trim, it felt good to be in her cabin. Alone. Away from the two men she should never have taken aboard.

She'd have been better off coming on her own. Taking on a pair of DEA agents might have seemed like a good idea two weeks ago, but it was sucking now. With every turn of the screwdriver, she'd wondered who to trust, who not to trust. One of the two men living on her boat was a liar. Possibly a mole. Possibly a killer. She'd call Gus tonight from the hotel.

In the meantime, she at least had this cabin to hide away in. A room of one's own, she thought and mentally saluted Virginia. Virginia Woolf, who'd loaded her dress pockets with stones and walked into a river.

Maybe not a good role model for a seafaring woman.

Chris collapsed face down on her bed and sighed. Her shoulders ached. Her back ached. Her fingers cramped from clutching a screwdriver.

But God, *Obsession* looked good. And she'd talked to Natalie again, felt a little more confident every day that went by with her sister still calling her. As long as they were able to maintain contact, they might both stay alive.

Chris rolled onto her back, reveling in the box fan's relatively cool air blowing over her clean, damp body. Sinfully wonderful, that's how it felt. Her tired mind wandered over other things that felt wonderful: hot showers in winter, the fur of that Russian Blue cat her grandfather had had for so long, the black silk robe Natalie sent her last year.

She levered herself, exhausted muscles and all, from the bed and opened the hanging locker. Natalie's gifts hung neatly in their protective plastic bags. Little black dresses Chris had never worn, chic linen pant suits meant for attending posh birthday parties and visiting art exhibits. Chris reached to the shelf above and drew down the black merry widow Natalie had sent, shook it out to look at it.

"She must have high hopes for my love life," Chris murmured.

More likely, Natalie was judging Chris by her own yardstick. Natalie had never lacked for anything, including men panting after her. Chris had never had that kind of attention lavished on her. And she certainly had never had a reason to wear anything like this.

On impulse, Chris slipped into the lingerie. It clung and gripped and hugged parts of her that hadn't been treated that way in a long, long time. She turned to the full-length mirror on her cabin door and froze.

That wasn't her. But it was, long and lean and curvy all at the same time. Her sun-streaked hair, now dry, flowed over her shoulders in soft waves, bright against the black lace. Chris turned from side to side, checking out the lay of this strange new land. She looked…

Powerful.

Hell, in a merry widow, any woman would. Pure sex. That's what this little scrap of material was about. Put it on in half a minute and get it ripped off in even less time.

Chris shivered. It had been a *very* long time.

She dug through the half-dozen shoeboxes in the hanging locker until she found what she was looking for: the black high heels Natalie had given her years ago. Chris slipped them on and walked slowly back to the mirror. The height made her legs longer and slimmer. When she turned, she had to catch herself on the bed corner. Damn heels. But she could see why men liked them. Or liked what they did to the female form.

She'd just never seen why on her own body before. Her fingers traced the line of her jaw, down her neck, over the lace and silk barely covering her breasts. Down her sides, over her slender hips, which no longer looked so boyish, to the line of lace dipping toward the cleft of her legs. How easy it would be to command a man to get on his knees before her, to let his hands stroke her thighs, to watch him pull aside the silk and lace to lean forward and put his mouth—

The image of McLellan's dark head poised between her thighs startled her. *Not him.*

Yes, him.

McLellan wanted her. She knew it in her bones. Men were so mechanical. So automated. See the cute girl, get a raging hard-on. Could she use that knowledge—his weakness—against him? Could she force herself to be seductive, if only to distract a man who might be her enemy? To tempt him into believing he controlled her?

If it meant her survival, yes, she could. If it meant Natalie would be safe, yes, she could.

The thought of Natalie made her smile despite herself. Natalie had understood from the age of seven her power over men. How many evenings had Chris waited patiently while Nat, already adept at style and color, applied Chris's makeup before a date? Natalie's pinky had stuck out at a precise angle while she penciled eyeliner with a master painter's skill, her tongue tucked firmly in the corner of her mouth while she daubed blush onto Chris's cheeks.

Chris awkwardly stepped out of the heels to put them back in their box, then paused. There, in the closet's back corner, sat the metal box she'd put there two days before *Obsession* had left Galveston.

Chris pulled it out and sat cross-legged on the floor to look at its smooth surface. After a moment, she opened the nightstand drawer without getting up and plucked a small key taped under the drawer's bottom. She unlocked the box.

Inside, the Ruger 9mm lay, black and expressionless, in its foam cutout.

If I'd had this the night Eugene Falks broke in, I wouldn't be worried about him now.

It was one reason she'd not bought a gun until now. Without touching it, she could remember the cool steel in her hands, the gunpowder's musky scent with its curious, tangy afterbite, the controlled leap when she squeezed the trigger. The handgun course wasn't required for her captain's license, but she'd heard so many cruisers debate the pros and cons of firearms aboard that she'd taken a six-week course, just to see for herself. In all her range hours, she'd never missed a target. And standing there, firing round after round, she'd known suddenly just how easy it would be to solve the problem of fear with a single bullet, a crook of her finger. *Come here,* the gesture said. *Come here and die.* The sense of power. The seduction of control.

It'd been the reason she hadn't bought one before. But after Falks, after her conversation with Smitty…

She studied the Ruger's gorgeous lines for a moment, then took it from its foam bed. So real. A little heavy for her, but the action was smooth as silk, the kick reassuringly solid. She pulled back the slide. Empty chamber. She ejected the magazine. A full ten rounds.

Chris slapped the magazine back into the gun. After a moment's thought, she racked the slide to load the chamber. She stood to put the gun in the nightstand drawer, then caught sight of herself in the mirror.

The sex goddess was packing.

She smiled a small smile, enjoyed the moment, before she laid the Ruger in the drawer. The gun's box and the merry widow—her secret weapons—went back in the closet.

The nightstand loomed heavy with threat beside her. Would she be able to use the Ruger if it came to it?

She saw again Eugene Falks's single eye staring at her in the shaft of light.

Yes. She'd be able to use it.

In a heartbeat.

From Chris's first glance around The Blue Note, the French Quarter restaurant had two kinds of patrons: serious blues lovers and serious lovers. The blues lovers clumped around small tables near a low stage where a band played a jazz tune so cool she had trouble following the music. The lovers paired up in high-backed booths and sat together on the same wide bench, a single dim lamp suspended over the table and the lovers' hands busy beneath it.

"Classy joint," she remarked dryly as the maître d'

showed her and McLellan to the last corner booth. She drew her jacket closer over one of Natalie's ubiquitous little black dresses, conscious of McLellan's warm hand on her waist.

He waited for her to sit down, then slid into the seat across from her. "I'm glad it survived Katrina. It's my favorite."

Given the restaurant's clear division of clientele, for which? she wondered. The music or the making out? Or for making connections with Scintella?

Then again, she thought later, cutting into a delicately seared piece of sea bass, it might just be the food. The steaming sauce, a luscious combination of crab, cream and peppers, set off the fish's tang perfectly. Heaven on a plate.

"You look like you're enjoying that."

"It's almost as good as your cooking."

Had she laid it on a little thick? She glanced up and found his gaze riveted to her open jacket top. Before she could call him on his gawking, he said, "I think you should take that jacket off."

"Brazen lech," she returned. God, it was hard not to shudder. But with revulsion or excitement? She didn't speculate. She set her wine glass down carefully on the white linen tablecloth. "You've been hitting on me one way or another since we left Galveston—"

"I'm sorry about that."

"I don't think you are." She studied him in the dim light. "You're a handsome man. You're charming and clearly used to getting your way with women. If you were sorry, you wouldn't keep saying provocative things."

His sudden grin proved all three of her points. "And here I thought you were complaining about my groping."

"That's next on the list." She didn't smile.

His teasing humor faded until his expression settled

into stone. He paused while the waiter removed their plates, then he leaned forward to grasp her hand. "I'll be honest with you."

She let her fingers rest in his, trying to ignore her heart's pounding. "About what?" she asked lightly.

He abruptly released her. "I'm attracted to you."

Her heart's pounding became almost painful, like a thumb throbbing under too tight a bandage. "And there's a problem with that?"

"Hell, yes, there's a problem." He tossed his napkin onto the table as if the situation irritated him. "I'm on a mission. I can't do my job if I'm hot and bothered over you."

"I guess that *would* be a problem." She deliberately imagined him on the phone with Scintella as she tried to get control over whatever emotion was making it hard to breathe.

His scowl deepened. He reached for her again, then stopped himself and grabbed his dessert spoon instead. While he turned it over in his hand, he said almost angrily, "Let's have this conversation in Galveston, when we can do something about it."

"Assuming we both make it back to Galveston."

He glanced at her, then studied the spoon again. "I'll get you home, Christina. The question is whether you'll have the time. You'll be busy with your sister, getting your charter business up and running. I'll—" He trailed off as his gaze went to the front door, which was out of Chris's field of vision. His eyes suddenly lit up, pleased.

"Excuse me," he murmured as he left the booth without a backward glance.

Chris swallowed hard, then leaned partly out of the booth to see what had pulled him away from his declaration of lust for her. She watched him stride purposefully toward the door, then pull Halle Berry toward him and kiss her warmly on the lips.

Chris turned back to her excellent glass of wine, relieved by disgust. It figured. If he was as free with his "affections" as Smitty had implied, he'd mug down on any pretty woman, no matter which side of the law she walked.

But it took the pressure off, she suddenly realized. His gesture toward this other woman reminded her who he was and what he wanted to do—and she didn't want to jump into the sack, much less a relationship, with a crony of Jerome Scintella's no matter how good his hands had felt on her that night. She took a deep breath. Regaining perspective was always a good thing.

I'm after Natalie and nothing else.

Then McLellan leaned into the booth, a warm, open grin on his face. He smelled faintly of the woman's perfume, something musky and sensual. "Christina, this is Jacquie Adair and Russ LeBlanc. This is Christina Hampton."

The good guys had arrived. Chris let go of a faint sigh of relief and shook hands with the perfect Jacquie, faintly surprised by the friendly warmth radiating from the woman. Another agent who didn't look like one.

"I'm so pleased to meet you," Jacquie said. She flashed a brilliant smile as she slid gracefully—while wearing a long, slinky dress—into the booth across from Chris.

"*Mon dieu,* so am I," Russ murmured.

Chris shook his broad, powerful hand. Definitely cop material. She smiled into his alert, hazel eyes and took in his severe haircut, the character lines around his eyes, and his almost military bearing. In his dark suit, he reminded her, of all people, of Antonio Garza.

"Have a seat." McLellan sat next to Chris and draped his arm across the bench back behind her.

While Russ and Jacquie ordered drinks and McLellan rearranged his and Chris's wineglasses, Chris studied them. Russ and Jacquie had the easy familiarity of a married couple. Chris would have gauged them to be opposites: her gorgeous and cultured and elegant, him plain and earthy and matter-of-fact. They sat near each other, but there wasn't the same physical affection she'd briefly seen between Jacquie and McLellan.

Had McLellan and Jacquie been lovers? Were they still?

"How's it going?" Russ asked McLellan once the waiter was gone.

Jacquie's voice was all whiskey and smoke as she added, "I didn't think we'd see you again."

Chris tossed a sidelong glance at McLellan. "Did they kick you out of town last time you were here?"

"I left in a hurry, but it was for a good reason." His fingers lightly touched her shoulder, then he leaned in to say in a low tone, "I'll tell you later."

"Are we havin' dessert, *chère?*" Russ asked Jacquie.

"Death by chocolate, as soon as possible," she said at the same time as Russ. They laughed and Russ raised his hand to flag down the waiter again.

"What's your boat?" Jacquie asked.

Surprised by this abrupt entry into business, Chris said, "She's a custom design. Nineteen sixty-six."

"A classic," McLellan remarked, pride emanating from his voice. "Gorgeous yacht."

"Think it'll fool the island security?" Russ asked.

"I'm counting on it." Chris ran her finger over the rim of her wineglass. "I'm not leaving my sister with that madman."

No one said anything for a long moment. The band had picked up a slow blues tune—one that made "woe-is-me" sound like seduction—that throbbed in the walls while the harmonica's raspy notes cut through the cigarette smoke that hung over the tables. McLellan's body radiated tension and Chris struggled not to be overwhelmed by the dark mood suddenly enveloping them.

"We'll get her back," McLellan said. "We'll do what we can."

"I know the risks." Chris turned to take him on, will for will. "I know there's a good chance this might go down wrong and people will end up hurt. Natalie could be one of them."

"So could you," Jacquie said quietly, her brown eyes liquid with concern.

Chris swirled her wineglass. "If Scintella's the badass everyone thinks he is, why are there only four of you?"

The three DEA agents exchanged glances. At some signal Chris didn't notice, McLellan said, "We think someone close to the Scintella case is feeding him information about our plans to catch him. He's slipped away from us twice."

"The only way he could have done that is if he has someone on the inside," Russ added. "We've been conducting an internal investigation but haven't turned up anything yet."

"We'll get him." Jacquie tipped her drink toward her as though trying to read some sign left in the glass's bottom. "The mole's got to show his hand sometime."

McLellan nodded. "He will." He seemed to want to say more, but didn't.

Silence descended on the table as the waiter delivered Jacquie's demise in the form of a richly layered and lathered chocolate cake. Russ sipped his whiskey and soda. Jacquie buried her fork to the hilt into the dessert.

After a single bite Jacquie said, "This is spectacular." She handed Chris one of the extra dessert forks the waiter had brought. "Try it."

Chris forked a smooth, creamy serving. At the first taste, Chris realized heaven on a plate was nothing. This was beyond heaven. The chocolate shot straight to whatever part of her brain registered ecstasy. "Good Lord," she said. She turned the fork upside down and drew it slowly from her mouth until she realized McLellan was watching with more than a passing interest. "That was really good."

"Have another," McLellan encouraged. "I'm sure Jacquie won't mind."

"No, I won't," Jacquie said, pushing the plate closer to Chris. "If I have any more I'll pass out right here."

"How are the renovations coming?" Russ asked.

"Everything's done except for having the wall panels in the lower passageway replaced and a wiring problem in the salon," Chris answered. "I'm checking out some engine trouble we had, but I'm hoping it'll be a scratch-and-patch job."

Russ nodded, as if familiar with the term. Even Jacquie seemed undaunted by boating language. Of course, Chris reflected, if you live on a coast, chances are you've been on a boat at some point.

She savored the last bite she'd allowed herself and wondered how far she should push McLellan. Hell, it was Natalie's life at stake and she needed to know how bad things could get on Isladonata. "When are you guys coming aboard?"

"Tomorrow," Russ replied. "Got my jammies packed and everything."

"I checked the lat-longs my sister gave me. Isladonata's inside U.S. waters." She glanced at McLellan. "Are you planning on hooking up with the Coast Guard?"

"Already done."

"And you're not afraid word will get back to the DEA?

I mean, if the mole is paying attention, won't he know what you're doing?"

McLellan's fingers rested gently on her shoulder. She wished she'd left her jacket on. It might have suppressed the raw heat that flared in her skin at his touch, the heat that went ice-cold when she thought of the transponder. "It's okay. I've got it handled."

I wish I could believe you.

Jacquie leaned slightly toward Russ, giving him a nice view of her lovely cleavage. "Let's go. I haven't packed my jammies yet."

"Want some help?" His gaze wandered lazily from Jacquie's chest up to her eyes.

"You know better than that, white boy."

Russ rolled his eyes. "Does she always put me in my place or what?" He winked at Chris, telling her the play between him and his partner was just that. "See y'all tomorra."

"How long have they been flirting heavily?" Chris asked, giving up and dipping her fork once more into the luscious dessert as Russ and Jacquie walked away.

"Years. You're going to OD on that," McLellan said in a low voice.

"If I'm lucky I will."

He let his arm drop around her waist and leaned close. "Looks nice."

She raised a brow at him, hoping her skepticism would persuade them both she didn't feel the hot thrill spiking up and down her spine at his touch. "You're laying it on a little thick."

McLellan's rueful half smile admitted defeat, then he leaned in and let his lips brush her ear. "Christina." He paused, leaned back. "Dammit."

"What?"

"Pager." He fished it out of his jacket's breast pocket and glanced at the screen. "Smitty. Will you be okay while I use the phone?"

"You don't have your cell?"

"Battery's dead and I didn't get a chance to replace it today." He caught her chin in his hand and lightly kissed her cheek. "I'll be right back."

She watched him stride off toward the anteroom where the phone bank was, thinking no man should look that good in slacks and a Hugo Boss jacket that snugged his shoulders. Hugo Boss, which according to Smitty, a DEA agent shouldn't be able to afford. Never mind. She had death to keep her occupied. She dug the fork into the slim remainder of Jacquie's dessert.

"Mind if I join you, Ms. Hampton?"

She glanced up, then froze when Eugene Falks slid into the booth.

Chapter 10

"Don't." Falks propped his foot against the seat next to Chris, blocking her way, before she could bolt. "Not if you want to see your sister again."

Chris warily settled back. Falks's ghoulish face shone under the dim overhead lamplight like a nightmare, his black shirt a stark frame beneath his sharp, white chin.

His mouth thinned into what might have been a smile. "I'm sure she'd be very upset if anything bad happened to you."

"What do you want from me now?" she asked. Her throat, once rich with chocolate and sweet wine, now felt like sandpaper when she swallowed.

His breath whistled through his teeth as he inhaled. "Mind if I smoke?"

Without waiting for her answer, he stroked a wooden match into flame and lit a long, thin cigarette. He slipped the matchbox into his shirt pocket.

"It's a shame, really," Falks said slowly around picking a stray tobacco fragment from his tongue. "Your sister is such a pretty woman." He squinted at her. "You must take after your mother."

Chris fought back the panic threatening to rise up and drown her. "Why are you stalking me?" She licked her lips, tried to breathe.

"For shame, Ms. Hampton. I'm not a stalker." He put one bony fingertip into the ashtray and dragged it toward him. "Your sister tells you all her secrets, doesn't she?"

She swallowed. "Not necessarily. My sister's a grown woman—"

"—so she does whatever she wants and then calls you in to help her fix things after she's screwed them up," Falks finished. "Common among siblings. And you're not through saving her yet, are you?" His wide, pale eyes narrowed. "I can't let you do that."

"Is that why you tried to kill me?"

"Not kill you. Put you out of commission."

"Why not just kill me?"

"Mrs. Scintella would have suffered some distress over that event. Mr. Scintella didn't want to give her an excuse to make more trouble than she already has."

"But you were searching my yacht when you broke in."

"Of course I was." He cast a pitying look at her. "You can't expect us to ignore Mrs. Scintella's little deception."

"What are you talking about?" Chris clamped her hands on the bench seat as if it were a tossing ship's deck. *This must be a nightmare,* she thought. *It can't be real.*

Falks blew a thin stream of smoke that clogged her already tight throat and stung her eyes. No, it wasn't a dream or her imagination.

"Let me be blunt. If you and your sister believe you can

deceive Jerome Scintella, you're playing a game you won't survive." He raised a whiskery brow at her. "She merely has to give the money back."

"What money?"

"Don't waste my time, Ms. Hampton. Chris, isn't it?" Falks squinted at her again, his expression almost meditative. "You're an attractive woman. It'd be a shame to have to kill you."

"I don't understand—"

"Bullshit."

Falks's mild, vaguely genteel manner sharpened into a hardened, steely edge. He leaned forward, his cigarette ash teetering precariously and casting up a thin spiral of smoke. Chris could see his yellowed teeth between parted lips and the faint pink around his eyes. From the fire extinguisher spray? she wondered abstractedly as she instinctively drew back, out of biting range. *McLellan.* She had to stall until McLellan came back.

"If you're telling me she stole money from her husband, I don't believe it."

"She made a mistake," Falks snapped. "Her husband is willing to forgive her if she admits her error. This time."

"What error is that?" Chris retorted. "Wanting to live her own life without being watched? Wanting to live in peace without wondering when he's going to hit her next? She doesn't need his money. She has her own."

"I don't see that their domestic issues are your business."

"She's my sister. That makes them my business."

Falks's sneer crinkled his face like old dough. "Hence my little get-acquainted gesture."

"Yeah, big man tries to run me down in a powerboat."

"Maybe I like dancing with pretty girls."

"Even when they spit in your face?" She deliberately

stared at the pinkish skin of his temples. "Leave me the hell alone."

"Not until you give me the money your sister took."

"She's not a thief. Jerome's delusional."

"Delusional?" Falks stared at her, then burst out laughing, a hitching, craggy, horrible sound like a dry-heave retch. He plucked a business card from his breast pocket and slid it across the table to her. His long fingers lingered, almost caressing, on the card. "You will bring the money to this address."

She looked at the card, which was blank but for the street address painstakingly scripted in a spidery, old lady's handwriting. Then beneath that, *Noon.* "Why do you think I have it?"

"I know, Ms. Hampton, because I know everything. I know how much money is in her private account and how she spends it. I know where she shops, who she calls, who she e-mails and when she goes to bed at night. I know she's lately taken to fucking her bodyguard. I know she very recently sent you a box filled with lingerie you'll likely never wear." His gaze flicked to Chris's bare shoulders, groped her breasts. "Unfortunate." He blinked twice. "I know her accomplice intercepted a courier package meant for her husband and put it in a box addressed to you."

"You've got it wrong."

Falks leaned back and spread his hands. "Unlikely."

"Maybe it hasn't arrived yet."

"The shipping company assured me it's in your possession. Now either you can get it for me, or I and some of my rowdier colleagues can come take it from you. They quite enjoy boat rides." He flicked the cigarette absently with his fingers. "Not to mention the smell of burning fiberglass."

Chris's fear edged into anger. Touch *Obsession,* touch her home, and she'd take it out of his hide.

Falks's pale eyes crinkled at the corners. "Do me a favor. Ask your sister if she'll consider changing her mind about leaving her husband." He tapped ash into the tray's center with a single fluid motion, like a master painter effortlessly daubing light onto canvas. "Then ask her if she believes she can afford to be so stupid, especially when her husband has…access…to those closest to her."

Chris's heart banged her chest wall. *Where the hell is McLellan?* "I'm sorry my sister ever got involved with him."

"I'm sure many people feel the same way, but there they are, involved with him." He drew on his cigarette, his eyes slits in his skull. "Some of them got in over their heads. And a few of them have stayed there, I'm sorry to say."

Chris's blood ran cold.

Falks put his cigarette out and delicately balanced the stub on the tray's edge, aiming it at her. "Remind her that it just takes a little effort to reach out," his hand darted like a snake to snag her wrist, "and touch someone."

Chris stifled a scream as his bony fingers bit into her skin, squeezed her wrist bones. He smiled, dark lines beneath the craters of his eyes, his teeth bared like fangs. He smelled of tobacco and cold, damp stones.

"Tell your pretty boy about our conversation and your sister dies. Do you understand?"

She nodded.

"Be on time tomorrow, Ms. Hampton." Falks abruptly released her, allowed her to breathe again. He slid from the booth, then paused, his brows tipped up in what might have been concern. "Take care you aren't mugged on the way to our appointment. Thirty million dollars is a lot of cash to be carrying around."

Stunned, Chris watched him go and tried to breathe. Thirty million dollars? It was all too much to get her brain around. She picked up the business card. Noon. And she had no idea what time it was now because she wasn't wearing a watch. She stared at the cigarette butt, lying aimed at her like a gun.

She had to get back to *Obsession*. Tell Smitty and McLellan and get them to help her tear the yacht to pieces to find this thirty million dollars Falks was so confident she had. God. Where could it be? They'd already looked everywhere there was to look.

She glanced toward the phone room. The heavy door was just closing, then she saw a hand catch it and shove it open again. McLellan stepped out and held the door for an elderly black man to enter. Faint cigarette smoke scented the booth. She couldn't let McLellan know Falks had been there with her.

Then she stopped.

Falks had said not to tell McLellan he'd been there. Did that mean he and McLellan weren't connected via Scintella? Did Smitty have McLellan wrong? Could *Smitty* be the mole? But why would Smitty tell that story if it meant he'd implicate himself?

Unwilling to take any chances, Chris hurriedly tucked the business card in her purse, then got out of the booth. First things first. She had to get back to *Obsession*. If she had to tear the damned boat apart to find the money Jerome Scintella thought Natalie had taken from him, she would.

As she wound through the tables toward McLellan, she tried to breathe and relax her muscles. Stress, anxiety— hell, sheer panic—tied her up in knots inside, but she had to *look* okay. Just until she got back to *Obsession*.

"That didn't take long," she lied when she reached McLellan. "What did Smitty want?"

McLellan was distracted for a moment while he paid the bill at the bar, then curved his arm around her to guide her to the door. "He got a call from Garza and wanted to update me."

"Anything new?" Her voice sounded like she'd been strangled.

"Not really."

They stepped out onto the bustling Bourbon Street, where throngs enveloped the sidewalk and street. The smell of fried seafood and rich gumbo lingered in the night air and behind it, the tang of coming rain. In the distance up ahead, a party gained decibels as it spilled out of a club. New Orleans—irrepressible, iconic—was making a comeback.

"What time is it?" she asked.

His watch glinted in the street light. "Nearly eleven."

"No wonder I'm so tired." She smiled, and felt how feeble that smile was, how panicked she must look to him.

"Are you feeling okay?"

"Can we just go to the hotel?"

"You must be exhausted."

He whistled up a taxi for the short ride. When they got out, Chris tried to pay attention to the wrought iron railings, the bowing crepe myrtles, the freshly clipped and pungent grass of the hotel's courtyard, but images of Falks swelled inside her mind. Those pasty, ghoulish hands signed the register for their rooms. His pale eyes stared out from portraits hanging in the hallway. His stale breath wafted into her face when McLellan opened her room's door.

Chris looked around while McLellan methodically searched the room, checking the closet and bathroom, the balcony.

"Do you want the windows open?" he asked. "There's no way anyone could get in."

She nodded, and he opened them. He knew she liked

fresh air. And the storm that had followed them along the coast was coming, bringing its copper-penny smell with it.

McLellan grasped her upper arms with his warm, comforting hands and his gray eyes registered a gentle concern, almost protectiveness. He's not like Eugene Falks at all, she thought. Not a walking corpse. He'd saved her from the engine room and held her and made her feel safe. He wanted her to see a doctor. Loved to sail. She could trust him, couldn't she?

"What's wrong?" he asked.

"It just caught up with me," she blurted. "The whole thing with Natalie and the boat. I had everything planned and ready to go, but we hit that oil rig and the accident with the prop shaft and the exhaust and I don't know if Natalie's okay and then tonight I had a nice evening and met your friends and it seemed so *normal,* and then—"

And then she was pulled into his arms, against his hard chest. Chris slipped her hands under his jacket, needing his body's warmth, to feel the flesh and muscle on his bones beneath the soft cotton shirt, to smell his clean, masculine, living scent. After a moment, she heard him murmuring to her hair: *It's okay, love. I won't let anything happen to you, Christina.* His strong palms pressed her close, stroking her back until she was tempted to believe him.

She began to shake, shaking to pieces. Just like a bent prop. You're driving along and then something happens and the prop gets bent. You keep trying to go on and go forward but the timing's off, the balance is wrong, and then the engine shakes itself to pieces, trying to go and go.

"I can't keep going," she said against his shoulder. "I have to keep going."

"I know." He stroked her hair.

The scene played itself through her brain at high speed—

the fear, no, the terror, Falks's threats, his cold touch. Now here she was, McLellan's clean scent filling her nostrils, his hands strong on her waist and shoulder. She clung to him like a woman falling from cliffs or airplanes or sanity.

Get a grip, she thought, but when she reached, there was nothing to grab hold of.

Except him.

Nothing mattered except this, her mouth wet and demanding on his, her arms wrapped around him. Consumed. Yes, to consume and be consumed, to drown, lost in the heat and friction. To *feel* something—life, blood, breath, her back against the wall, her hands unzipping him, reaching in, grasping his hard length. Hearing him groan, feeling the cool air on her thighs, her dress pulled up, his hot hands searching, moving, parting her, stroking, *yes,* then pushing her hands away and levering against her.

This, she thought, *this.* Nothing but this physical sensation, her body, his body, moving together, driving and climbing, arching up and then over, over, until suddenly she broke, crashing headlong, rushing and rushing, mindless, thoughtless, hearing herself cry out his name. Then he gasped, "Christina," in her ear and drove deep, hands dragging at her hips as he shuddered against her, then finally giving out, spent, and slipping back down into the warmth that was them together.

His arms tightened around her as he breathed hard on her neck, almost tickling. She burrowed deeper into him, wanting to cover herself in his scent, her hands clutching his shirt, feeling the hard muscle beneath the soft fabric. He raised his head and kissed her.

McLellan's tongue flickered gently against her lips, tasting her again as if for the first time. His lips found their way to her neck, and his hand roamed down to cup her bottom and keep her close. When he finally lifted his head, she saw in his eyes the same vulnerability she'd glimpsed so often before, the same gentleness—that old-fashioned *regard*—rimmed with passion and lust, and for a split second she thought he loved her.

Oh God, she thought. *I can't do this now.* No matter how much she wanted him. No matter how badly she needed to feel him close.

Still, she captured his mouth again, giving as good as she got. Just another few minutes of his heat and strength filling her up, that's all, she told herself. Just a few minutes, here in the arms of this man who loved seagulls and boats, who maybe even loved her. In this safe refuge, in the midst of this horrible storm of confusion and fear.

Natalie. The money. Falks. The mole.

Chris pulled away. "So much for waiting till Galveston," she whispered, all her voice could manage.

He nuzzled her neck. "Extenuating circumstances."

"Or bad judgment."

He slowly drew back. She saw his face darken with hurt, then anger. He abruptly released her, leaving her body feeling cold without him to warm her. McLellan turned his back on her to zip up. She shimmied her dress back into place and steeled herself against the tears rising in her throat.

"Don't open the door to anyone but me," he snapped. "I'll knock at eight for breakfast."

Then he wrenched open her door and left.

Chris stared down at the antique compass sitting on the mahogany coffee table. Outside the salon's partially drawn curtains, night had settled down hard on the marina, mist falling around the piers' overhead lights. She checked her watch. Tomorrow's noon deadline didn't give her much time to search *Obsession*.

Now she ran her fingers carefully over every glossy centimeter of the brass compass. It was hopeless, she knew. The compass was clean and empty. Guileless. A clue to Jerome Scintella's missing thirty million dollars wasn't here.

Falks was wrong about the money and Natalie's part in it. Anything could have happened—the courier who was supposed to deliver the money to Scintella could have stolen it and framed Nat, or Scintella could be using this as an excuse to get rid of his wife.

But the point was, he *thought* he was right. And he was so convinced he was prepared to kill both Chris and Natalie if she didn't come up with the money.

Now, sitting cross-legged in the floor, Chris wiped her brow on her T-shirt sleeve and wondered where Smitty was. When she'd come aboard, she'd called for him, but there was no answer. After poking her head in every cabin except her locked one, she'd concluded he'd gone out.

McLellan hadn't followed her from the hotel as she'd expected. After he'd slammed her door, he'd stalked down the hallway to his adjoining room. While stripping off her dress, she'd heard his television blare. The door between their rooms remained closed. Chris ruthlessly clamped down on the pain she felt—the pain she'd caused—and concentrated on the task at hand.

She tugged the compass from its housing and looked inside. As empty as it had been the day it arrived. She reseated the compass on its gimbals and watched the beautiful dial orient itself.

Natalie was a dead woman. Chris was a dead woman.

She backed onto the sofa and sat quietly for a moment. No money. No nothing. Her gaze wandered over the salon's new windows, the freshly sewn curtains, the pretty beige carpet McLellan and Smitty had so carefully laid, the new galley appliances. So much work. All for nothing if she couldn't find Falks's thirty million dollars.

The brass compass, which she'd spent hours polishing until her hands blackened with tarnish and the metal gleamed golden, winked in the lamplight. No map, no compass, could possibly help her now. She didn't even know which direction to turn for help. The compass dial pointed, unwavering, south.

She'd always known what to do before, from the time they'd gotten lost playing settler—Chris pulling Natalie in their red wagon into the wilder trails of their grandfather's property—to her decision to keep living at the estate during most of college. Natalie hadn't wanted to live there alone with the old man, and though it'd been difficult to stay, Chris had. At least until she'd moved in with a boyfriend for one semester. But by then, Natalie had been getting old enough to have lots of friends and lots of things to do. Chris's presence in the mausoleum their grandfather called home had been less important, and the timing had been right.

But what was "right" now? As Chris closed the lid, she let tears of frustration tumble down her cheeks. New carpet smell filled her nostrils and churned her stomach. She tipped her head back, stretched her aching neck muscles.

There was no place aboard that much cash could possibly lie undetected. Chris had seen the yacht stripped to its bones and found nothing out of place, so there was no point in tearing down wall panels and sniffing around the bilges for bundles of bills. But Falks clearly believed the money was on the yacht and wouldn't take "it's not here, you idiot" for an answer.

If she wanted to save her sister, she needed to think outside the box.

She froze.

The box.

Chris scrambled off the sofa. The transponder was too small to house anything of value, but it might hold a clue. She ran down to Hortense's engine room. Inside, she grabbed the craft knife from the tool chest and ratcheted the blade out. She hacked through the remaining sealant that held the black box to the floor.

The box was a bit too large for a standard transponder—the size of a cigarette pack—but at the same time it was way too small to hold thirty million dollars. Still, it was her only hope. A key, a code, *something* could be concealed in it. The sealant creaked and snapped as it gave up its seal.

Chris held the smooth, rectangular box in her hands. Heavy. Was it still giving off a signal? Who was listening to it? She thought hard for a moment, then popped the wires out of the clips that secured them to the floor. No need to take a chance on letting the listener know she'd found out the box's purpose. She'd leave the wires connected to the device and doing their job.

She put the box on the workbench and studied it. Heavy-duty black plastic of some kind, built to be waterproof and withstand a pounding. She shook it like a child testing a Christmas present, but it offered no clues. A seam ran around the unwired end, as if it had a lid. Maybe she could pry it open. A long-necked screwdriver wedged into the seam, but no amount of levering cracked it. She'd have to cut it open.

Chris clamped the box onto the table so the lid hung off. She fished around in the tool chest until she found the jigsaw. It took her only a few seconds to load up a new blade, then plug the saw into the AC outlet.

Rattling her teeth as she held it, the jigsaw spewed thin shavings across the workbench and onto her arms. Suddenly the blade caught, hung in the thick plastic. She released the trigger and took a deep breath.

Calm down. Don't drive so hard. Easy does it.

She bent down and fit the blade in the cut, then pulled the trigger. The saw went more quickly this time, shearing through clean now that she gave the blade time to do its work. The plastic bent back from the pressure she applied until the box was open enough. The saw ground down to silence. Hands shaking, she set the jigsaw aside.

She gripped the lid's edge and bent it further away. The flashlight's beam shone into the darkness, illuminating the wires and electronic chip of a transponder that faithfully broadcast its location.

But there was nothing else. Nothing at all.

Fighting back tears of despair, she flipped the clamp open to release the black box from the work table. Why couldn't it have been filled with gold coins or a priceless artifact or something else suitably valuable? Anything she could fob off on Falks as being worth the money he insisted Natalie had stolen.

As she ran a bead of black quick-cure sealant around the box top she'd created, she tried to reconcile Falks's "facts" and what she knew to be true about her sister. Natalie had inherited nearly that much money from their grandfather, so it wasn't as if she needed it. That one shoplifting arrest when she was fourteen had netted Natalie the attention she'd so desperately wanted from their grandfather, and Nat had done her community service to pay for it. Theft and deception weren't Natalie's way.

Chris pressed the top into the sealant. She really needed to hold it down until the sealant set up, but she had to go talk to Smitty. Or if she couldn't find Smitty, McLellan.

The thought of waking McLellan and telling him about Falks made her stomach tighten. God, he'd be pissed she hadn't told him earlier. Unless, of course, he was on Jerome Scintella's payroll.

Don't go down that road, she ordered herself. Falks had warned her not to tell McLellan about his little after-dinner visit but maybe that was to make her trust the mole.

Or maybe Connor has always told you the truth.

"And maybe I was stupid to have sex with him tonight," she said aloud. Much as she'd needed it. Irritated by that thought, she turned the box on its head and reached for a wrench to weigh it down. And paused.

There, on the box's black bottom, just within the ridge of white sealant that had held the box to the floor, was a fingerprint. Smudged, but a fingerprint. She carefully pressed her own thumb on the box's clean top, held it for several seconds, then moved it. No print. Whoever had left his fingerprint had probably had residue of some kind on his hands when he mounted the box. She'd had that happen before, walked around all day sticking to every object she picked up because she'd gotten something on her fingers.

Something like drying paint.

She peeled back the top again and pointed the flashlight inside. The box's bottom was clear, nothing electronic attached to it. Good.

With more methodical patience than she'd had before, she reclamped the box and fired up the jigsaw. The blade bit slowly through the plastic, carved the bottom cleanly away without chewing up the wiring. It took only moments to apply the black sealant to the clean-cut edge and refasten the transponder to the floor, just as it had been. With it mounted in the shadows, behind the chest, whoever had put it there would have a hard time seeing it had been tampered with.

Chris put away her tools, then swept the shards and trimmings into the waste can. "A clean tool area is a happy tool area," she muttered, "especially when it hides what you've been up to."

Overhead in the salon, footsteps. Smitty was back. And from the sounds of it, moving furniture.

She tilted the fingerprinted box bottom to the overhead fluorescent light. The print shone and glittered like a badge. But whose was it? McLellan's? Smitty's?

Shit. She'd meant to call Gus from the hotel where she could have privacy but Falks's little visit had screwed her brains. Now that Smitty was back, he could easily overhear her conversation. That phone call would have to wait.

Inside her cabin, she carefully locked the door before going to her bed's head. Feeling along the headboard, she found the indentation she was looking for and pressed. A hidden hatch popped open.

Like many oceangoing sailors, one of *Obsession*'s previous owners had carried a firearm aboard. An American caught armed on someone else's coastline could find himself imprisoned in an unforgiving country, so some sailors created little cubbyholes to hide their weapons. Chris had once been aboard a luxury ocean-going sailboat whose master stateroom had a full-width false wall that concealed a small arsenal, including several long-range rifles and an Uzi.

Obsession's armory had just enough room for the plastic oblong carrying the precious fingerprint and one gun. She slotted the plastic piece into the cubbyhole.

Now, to deal with Falks.

She closed the hatch and headed up to the salon, taking the steps two at a time.

"Hey, Smitty, I—" Chris stopped short at the edge of the salon.

A man lay on his back across the mahogany table, his legs hanging off the aft end, his arms at disjointed angles. Blood dribbled from what should have been the man's head. Flecks of blood and what might have been bone or cartilage spattered the carpet, smeared his blond hair.

Buried in the man's face was the brass compass.

"Smitty." The word was so faint she was barely aware she said it. Was he breathing? Somehow still alive?

She ran to him, reached for his arm to check his pulse.

The man's hand was skeletal, flesh pulled taut over bare bone. The compass dial pointed south. Then she saw the biker boots, the white shirt splashed with blood.

Eugene Falks.

Chapter 11

"Good God, Chris, what have you done?"

Chris rose and turned to the aft door. Smitty had paused in the doorway, half out of his lightweight jacket. Behind him, McLellan's silhouette.

"I was checking for a pulse."

McLellan shoved past Smitty and strode to the dead man, felt his skin, glanced at the blood pooled on the carpet. "You check the flybridge," he barked to Smitty.

Then he turned his remote gaze on Chris. "Where were you just now?"

"In my cabin."

He grabbed her arm and pulled her to the stairs, drawing his gun from his shoulder holster as he went. She tried to wrench away but his grip didn't loosen. "Let go of me!"

McLellan didn't speak. He manhandled her through the lower passageway and into her cabin. After a cursory glance around the room and into her private bathroom, he shoved her onto the bed.

"Don't move!" he ordered.

"I didn't—"

"Stay put!" He slammed the door as he left.

What, was she under arrest in her own cabin? On her own yacht? She'd be damned if she just sat down and obeyed some swaggering man's orders. At the sound of McLellan's cabin door closing, Chris angrily jumped off the bed.

She had the doorknob half turned when she heard the starboard engine room door bang shut. In a moment, the port engine room clanged. Chris released the doorknob. Seconds later, the forepeak cabin door creaked open, then after a moment clicked closed. Her blood chilled.

He was looking for the killer.

Because Eugene Falks had been murdered during the few minutes it'd taken her to clean up the engine room work space and then stash the fingerprint in her hidey-hole. While she'd worked, over her head, a man had been murdered in her salon.

In her home.

McLellan's feet pounded back up the steps. Raised voices, heated arguing. McLellan and Smitty. Either of them could have done it, she realized. Either could've been close enough to the yacht to have killed Falks and left, then returned as if for the first time.

Chris slid her nightstand drawer open. The Ruger lay right where she'd put it, next to a handheld GPS she'd been playing with, plugging in the lat-longs Natalie had given her. On impulse, she opened the hidey-hole and tucked the Ruger inside next to the plastic square containing the fingerprint.

Had she not stopped to hide the print, she might have interrupted the murderer. He might have killed her, too.

She'd just closed up the hidden compartment when her cabin door opened. McLellan, fierce and inevitable as a thunderhead, strode in, shut the door, locked it. Her heart pounded. The man who'd held her so desperately just hours before wasn't here; this was someone else, etched with rage. She took a step back from him, out of reach.

McLellan paced the room twice, breathing hard, then stopped to glare at her. "What the hell do you think you're doing?"

"About what?"

"Don't bullshit me. What were you doing here tonight?"

"You think *I* killed Falks?"

His face went still. "You recognize the dead man?"

"I sprayed his face with a fire extinguisher at close range when he attacked me," she snarled. "Yes, I know the dead man."

"Not much left of his face now."

She shuddered. Falks's fingers, so long and bony, rose in her mind—clutching the cabinet's edge as he stalked her, clinging to the aft deck railing before he dropped to the ground, casually flicking ash from his cigarette. She should feel relief, she thought abstractedly, but all she felt was horror.

When the monster threatening you was murdered, what greater monster lurked behind him, waiting?

"I recognized his hands." Chris clamped her own hands together to keep them still. "I didn't kill him."

"Whether you did or didn't, we've got a helluva mess to clean up now." He raked his hand through his hair, not looking at her. "Russ and Jacquie are on their way over. We got lucky. Russ has some New Orleans contacts. They'll take care of the investigation."

"Investigation? If we have to wait for an investigation, we'll miss our window—"

"That's what I'm saying," McLellan said sharply. "They'll take care of it. Shit."

After a moment, she ventured, "Did you find the killer?"

He shook his head. "No evidence of forced entry. No broken windows." His set jaw told her everything she needed to know.

He thought she'd done it. He thought her capable of killing. Stabbed by that distrust, Chris resisted the urge to squirm or look away or even shift her weight. She held his gaze and thought about breathing, how each breath she took was another leading her on through this moment, where she still lived and Natalie was still relatively safe.

When he spoke again, his voice rasped, rough and angry, from his throat. "Why did you come back here?"

She willed her own voice to be strong. "When you were on the phone in the restaurant tonight, Falks approached me. He said Natalie had stolen thirty million dollars from Jerome and sent it to me. If I didn't produce it by noon, he'd kill me and burn my boat to the waterline."

His shocked stare raised her hopes high enough that his next words shattered them into shards of anger. "So you killed him instead of giving him the money?"

Son of a bitch! "No, I didn't!" Her fingernails bit into her palms, she clenched her fists so hard. "I came here to look for it even though it was useless. Natalie didn't steal Jerome's money. She didn't send me anything except that compass Falks is wearing on his face." Chris gestured toward Hortense as she said, "I was in the goddamned engine room trying to figure out what the hell a transponder was doing installed behind the tool chest while someone brained him. I heard footsteps up there and thought—"

"Wait a minute." McLellan raised a hand. "What are you talking about?"

She'd let that information slip. Now she couldn't go back. "Somebody installed a transponder. It's been broadcasting *Obsession*'s location for who knows how long."

She watched the wheels start turning in his head, the anguished look return to his angry eyes.

"I found it that night of the trip." There was no need to explain exactly which night. "I checked it this afternoon—yesterday. If Falks was tracking the signal, he had plenty of time to get to the marina and follow us to the restaurant." Chris made an effort to relax her hands, get herself under control. "He just had to wait for you to leave me alone."

"Why didn't you tell me, Christina?"

Startled by his soft tone, she met his gaze. In it, she found that hauntedness again, the fear he'd been too late. Or betrayed. "He said he'd kill Natalie if I did."

His short nod was his only answer. He unlocked the door and opened it. Upstairs, Chris could hear a woman's voice—perhaps Jacquie's—and more male voices. Out the porthole, she saw only the reflected light of nighttime New Orleans, not the flashing red and blue of cops or red and white of an ambulance. Russ's friends were apparently taking care of things, just as McLellan had said they would.

Only now McLellan didn't say anything as he quietly closed the door behind him and shot the bolt home.

"I brought you breakfast." Jacquie set a tray piled with still-steaming eggs on the little desk near the bed. Chris's stomach growled at the thick scent of fresh bacon cooked just as she liked it, but she didn't move from her chair.

Jacquie handed her a mug of fresh coffee. Chris peered into the cup. "Did he spit in it while he poured?"

Jacquie didn't even crack a smile. She settled on the foot of Chris's bed and crossed her long, shapely legs. Her white shorts shone starkly against her dark skin. Before she raised her own mug to take a sip, she said, "You've got the wrong idea."

"Do I?" Chris retorted. "McLellan thinks I killed Eugene Falks so I'm under house arrest. I think I've got exactly the right idea."

The blue gradient scarf Jacquie wore around her stylish bun touched her right shoulder when she cocked her head slightly. "We've got everything under control. Falks's body's been moved."

"I heard the steam cleaner going. Did the blood come out of the carpet?"

Jackie ignored her sarcasm. "We didn't find any evidence as to who actually killed him, but we're still looking."

"So you're keeping me locked up on my own boat because…" Chris paused to let Jacquie finish the sentence.

"Lots of reasons."

"Which you're not going to tell me."

"Chris." Jacquie leaned forward, her long fingers wrapped around her mug, her expression earnest. "It's not because we don't trust you."

"Right."

"I know you're probably used to doing things your own way, but let us handle this. It was different before Falks. Easier."

"I guess a corpse in my salon would liven things up a bit."

Jacquie frowned. "This attitude isn't helping."

Chris set her mug on the floor and leaned forward to put her elbows on her knees. "Then put yourself in my place and tell me what my attitude should be. A man who tries to run me down on the water and then attacks me on my own boat—in my home—shows up last night after our little dessert party. Thirty million dollars is planted somewhere on my vessel, he says, and if I don't find it and give it to him, he'll kill my sister." Chris sat straight, squared her shoulders. "So I come back here and while I'm investigating a transponder that was planted in my engine room without my knowledge, that same man gets himself murdered in my salon, practically over my head. You're all acting like *I'm* the problem, goddammit, and I'm tired of it."

Chris flung out of her chair and paced to the door, too angry to sit still. "I didn't ask for any of this to go down. Do me a favor. Give me one good reason why I should trust you or Russ or Smitty or McLellan after this." Her chin lifted. "Just one."

Jacquie met her gaze for what must have been a full thirty seconds before saying, "We're trying to do what's best."

"Then you're not trying hard enough."

"It's for your protection."

Stunned, Chris stared. "*My* protection."

"Yes. Yours." Jacquie stood, as calm and cool as if they were discussing her tennis club's new chef. "When word gets back to Scintella that Falks is dead, which it will, he'll likely send someone out for you."

"I didn't kill Falks!"

"You don't understand. It doesn't matter whether you did or not."

Suddenly Chris saw the hard-boiled agent in Jacquie's demeanor, the steel, the years, the strain all written in the fine lines around her eyes and tense corners of her mouth. A woman who'd seen more of life and death than she wanted, but was still around to talk about it.

And then came the realization, crashing down like a tidal wave, that Chris was in so far over her head she might never see the surface again. What had she been thinking when she agreed to this crazy trip? Snatching her sister from a paranoid husband had been dangerous enough, but once she found out he was a hardened drug smuggler wanted by the DEA, wouldn't it have made sense to back out and let the DEA handle everything?

Except they needed you.

Hell, she could have handed over her boat to McLellan and Smitty, let them sort everything out.

But the truth—and here Chris had to admit it—was that she'd never trusted them to get Natalie out alive, never trusted them to put Scintella second on their priority list. Never trusted them with her yacht, the only place in her life that had felt like home to her since her mother died.

And she certainly didn't trust them now. Not after the transponder. And the half-truths. And the things McLellan wasn't saying.

And the fact she suspected either McLellan or Smitty had killed Falks, perhaps to keep the cadaver from implicating him.

Breathe.

First things first.

She needed facts. Not "facts" from these agents who didn't want to tell her anything, but from an outside source. Someone she could trust to know what the hell he was doing and tell her the truth straight up.

Then she could make a plan. Then she could decide what to do.

"I need to make a phone call," Chris said.

"I see," Jacquie replied, though her expression suggested she didn't. Or didn't like what she saw. It was hard to tell, in the way it was always hard to tell with stylish, elegant people who could choose whether or not to give a clue what they were thinking.

"Now," Chris clarified.

Jacquie sighed. "You can make it from the upper passageway, can't you? The reception will be good enough there?"

It'd damn well better be, Chris thought, as she followed Jacquie out of her cell.

Because she wanted Gus Perkins, the one man she trusted, to hear every word she said.

"I have to leave," McLellan said after lunch later that day.

Chris tried to gauge the others' reactions where they sat around the dinette, boxing her in. McLellan stood at the table's head, arms crossed, unshaven and angry, a thundercloud in black, threatening them all with torrents and lightning and fury.

"What's going on?" Russ asked.

"Garza's on my case and I need to settle some things with him."

McLellan didn't look at her, but Chris knew where he laid the blame. Apparently Gus Perkins had heard her perfectly and, as she'd known he would, had raised a ruckus with his old HPD partner, Antonio Garza. Too bad McLellan didn't like being pushed into this particular corner, but he'd pushed her first.

And if he was actually the mole the DEA was looking for, maybe she'd just improved the odds of getting Natalie back in one piece.

"You have to go back to Galveston?" Smitty asked.

"Garza's threatened to go over my head and blow us out of the water. I need to be there to calm him down. I'll be back by the time *Obsession* leaves the dock tomorrow." McLellan unfolded his arms, and his shirt drew tight across his chest. "Jacquie, I want you with Ms. Hampton every minute. She's not to leave the yacht and should stay out of sight."

Chris couldn't let that order pass. "That'll make it difficult to finish the work that needs doing."

His remote gray eyes flickered briefly with annoyance. "Then track down the engine exhaust leak. Smitty can handle everything up top. Russ, what's the word from your buddies?"

Russ scrubbed a hand over his crew cut. "Falks is hanging out in the morgue for the time being. No prints off the compass, no fibers, nothing that points to the perp."

"Must have been a strong man to cave his face in," Jacquie remarked.

"Nope," Russ replied. "With an object that heavy, you can only rule out little old ladies and kids under twelve. The first hit knocked him out. The rest were just for fun."

"Or rage," Smitty muttered.

Chris felt the weight of their collective expectations fall on her shoulders. How close had she come to admitting to McLellan the kind of anger that could pound a man's face to pulp? She tensed her spine against a shudder. She could never kill a man. Not like that. Not when she could have simply pulled the Ruger's trigger.

In self-defense, for Natalie, she could use a gun. But not for anything or anyone else. Certainly not for money, no matter how much.

"My plane leaves in a couple of hours. You know what you need to do." McLellan glanced around at his team. "I'll keep in touch. *Obsession* needs to be in Key West by Wednesday at the latest. Smitty, keep us on schedule."

"Right."

As the agents shoved out of the dinette, Chris fisted her hand and wished she could slug Smitty. It was stupid to feel possessive about her yacht under the circumstances—she already had enough to worry about—but *Obsession* never strayed far from her mind. And Smitty, despite his Coast Guard experience, was enough of a boat cowboy to botch a delicate, cosmetic job. In all her sailing years, she'd only met two men who had the same eye for detail that she had. Smitty wasn't one of them.

Ironically, McLellan was.

"I need to talk to you," she said quietly as she slid out of the bench where McLellan stood.

"In your cabin."

He followed her downstairs. This time, he shut the door gently, didn't lock it. She turned, dreading the cold, accusing glare she knew she would face but steeling herself for it. But instead she found uncertainty, with something behind it that looked like yearning. Suddenly, here was the man who'd sailed with her, who'd held a seagull's delicate body in his bare hand. Here was the man who'd confessed his powerlessness over his brother's fate and rage at the monsters who'd killed him.

She took a steadying breath. "What do you think will happen to Natalie now that Falks is dead?"

"It's hard to say. Scintella's not going to chance killing Natalie until he gets his money back. Even to a guy like him, thirty mil isn't chump change. I think she's still safe."

Chris scrubbed her face with her hand. "But he might send someone else for his money. Someone we wouldn't recognize."

"Perhaps."

"Falks said Natalie was working with someone to steal the money from a courier. Does that sound possible? To do, I mean, if she were the kind of woman who'd steal from her husband."

"Anything's possible." At her frown, he added, "Look, I'll keep you safe. That's my first priority."

"If that were true," she said slowly, "I could never have left the hotel without you."

His jaw clenched hard, made a harsher line by the stubble on his cheeks. She wondered suddenly if this was what had happened to his brother, here one minute and gone the next because McLellan had lied to himself about his priorities. If that story was even true. The air-conditioning kicked on, spraying cool air around them.

"How long are you going to keep me a prisoner?"

"You're not a prisoner. But we'll keep you under wraps for as long as it takes."

"To do *what?*"

"Catch Jerome Scintella." His voice ground like whiskey over rocks. "You won't be safe until we have him in custody."

"What about my sister?"

"Natalie's a priority, too."

"One of these priorities has to come first."

"We can work together to get Natalie back."

"But that's not why you're here." Chris raised her chin, looked him in the eye. "You're working an old dream and to hell with anything and anyone else."

"You don't believe that. Not after what happened…after last night."

She shoved her hands in her jeans pockets. "We fucked once, okay?" She glanced away, at the bed where her quilt lay crumpled in a heap. "Don't pretend it meant more than it did."

Stark pain registered in the lines around his eyes. "That answered a few questions."

She was silent for a moment, then asked, "Why did you show up here last night?"

"I went to your room but you weren't there. So I called Smitty."

Why did you come to my room? she wanted to ask, but didn't. To seduce her? She suppressed the dark excitement that thought aroused. It was likely that what he'd just told her was merely a convenient tale to explain his presence aboard, when in fact he'd come to retrieve the thirty million dollars—wherever the hell it was—for himself. And found Falks. And killed him.

She shivered.

"Why do you ask?" he added.

"You were at the hotel and Smitty was gone. I thought I was alone here. At least until I thought I heard Smitty come back." He was silent for so long, she said, "You're going to miss your plane."

"Christina." McLellan's whole body seemed to radiate desire, a wish, a futile hope. "I need you to trust me. To be totally honest with me."

"The way you've been with me?" Her chin rose as she fought back sudden tears. "The way you told me from the beginning you're fighting a mole in your agency? That you normally take three or four times as many agents into a bust as you are now?" Her tired smile felt watery. "What part—of *anything* you've said to me—am I supposed to believe?"

He turned and left her cabin without a glance, without arguing with her or telling her she was wrong or asking her to reconsider. But that was for the best. She couldn't tell anymore what was truth and what was lie in his words.

All she knew was that with him gone, with Falks out of the picture, she could concentrate on what was next to be done on the yacht, her plan firmly restored, if perhaps modified. If she knew Gus, he'd bullied Antonio Garza into investigating McLellan; Garza would keep McLellan in Galveston until Gus was satisfied they'd caught the mole.

Then the plan would go back to normal. Chris would pilot *Obsession* to Isladonata, and the straight-up DEA agents aboard would capture Scintella, call in the Coast Guard, and Natalie would be saved. Everything would be okay.

It had to be.

Chapter 12

Chris knelt in the lazarette, the wide, deep storage locker beneath the aft deck's floor. She shoved aside the heavy-duty plastic five-gallon gas container that held the fuel for the inflatable's outboard and studied the wiring board bolted to the lazarette's wall. Much of the salon's lighting and electrical system ran back here, where a series of relay switches that governed who knew what—they weren't labeled or color-coded—did their work of turning on and shutting down electrical current to various unknown parts of the boat.

Even her long nap and impulsive crying jag after McLellan left hadn't prepared her to tackle this one. She wiped her sweaty face on her sleeve and tried not to think about how hot it was in this little crawl space. Or that Jacquie sat in a deck chair overhead, a little Beretta tucked in her shorts pocket.

The relay board stared back at her. Each wire, covered with its insulated black coating, mocked her: *Guess what I do!*

Sort of like this whole damned trip, she thought. Lots of confusing inputs and no obvious answers.

She shifted back on her haunches to ease the pain shooting through her knees from kneeling on the lazarette's wooden flooring. She knew only that whatever was going on with this mission looked less like a legitimate DEA operation and more like a clandestine one. But if it was secret, would the agency dare take on a civilian? Wouldn't that mean a security risk, no matter who the civilian was?

She tapped her screwdriver against her chin. First things first.

McLellan had saved her life in the engine room and seemed hell-bent on protecting her when he wasn't pissing her off with his attitude, holding her prisoner on her own boat or trying to charm her out of her pants.

Chris trailed her finger down one of the wires. No, McLellan wasn't involved. And she wasn't thinking that way just because she was a little sore from the rousing bout against the hotel room wall last night. It just didn't seem right for him. Didn't make sense. He was too much the man in charge. He'd have too much on the line if he were heading up some kind of special operation against Scintella and still playing the bad guy. Wouldn't something like that look suspicious after a while?

But that left only genial, charming, good ole boy Smitty, who was out on the dock sawing marine plywood into replacement wall panels for the lower passageway.

"How's it look?" Smitty called from overhead as if her thoughts had summoned him.

She glanced up to see him leaning over the open hatch. "Come see for yourself."

Smitty lowered himself into the lazarette beside her, bringing his musky working man scent with him. "Shit," he muttered after a minute's study of the relay board. "You didn't wire this up, did you?"

"You think I'd do work like this?"

He shook his head. "It'd take a full day just to figure this mess out, much less fix it."

"Looks like spaghetti right now."

"Yeah," he replied, "but by the time we're through, it'll look like a four-course meal."

Like the four-course meal they weren't going to eat tonight because McLellan wasn't on the yacht.

"I traced that bad salon switch to this relay board," Chris said.

"The one for the recessed lighting?"

"Yeah. Why don't you go flip it on and let's see what happens."

"Yes, ma'am." Smitty winked, then hoisted himself out of the lazarette. He took one step and disappeared from view. "Hey, girlie-girl," he said to Jacquie.

Could it be Smitty?

And the better question: *Why?*

While Chris waited, she eyed the heavy mechanical spares she'd bought and stored in the lazarette: the extra prop shaft it looked as if Hortense didn't need, bronze strainers for the fuel filters and the AC water pumps, bronze through-hull fittings, generator parts, a rebuilt AC compressor, the two massive house batteries she needed to wire in parallel as soon as she had time. The sheer bulk of all that familiar metal, safely lashed down in its proper place, comforted her.

In a moment she heard Smitty call, "Ready?"

"Do it!" she shouted back.

Fizz, pop. A blue arc sprang from the board. Chris recoiled and yelled, "Kill it!"

The arc winked out. Smitty's feet pounded the deck. "You okay?" He bent over the hatch again, Jacquie peering over his shoulder.

Chris blew out a breath. "Just scared me. It's a bad switch." She shrugged and gave him a rueful smile. "About the only replacement part I don't have."

"Murphy's Law."

"Murphy and I need to have a little chat," she grumbled.

"I can run into town and get one."

"To tell you the truth, I'd rather wait and rewire the whole damned thing up right," she said, wiping her sweaty hands on a cloth she tugged from her back pocket. "We can use the lamps instead. Better tape down that switch in the salon, though."

"Sounds like a plan. You care which flavor of tape I use?"

"Do we have anything that even vaguely matches the decor?" she asked, knowing they didn't.

"Not even, darlin'."

"What the hell. Use whatever you want."

"You gonna need me anymore after that? I got some panels yet to cut."

"Nah, go ahead." Chris wiped her forehead on her shirt sleeve again. No, she was better off with Smitty handling dangerous tools well away from her. Every time he hit a switch, she got zapped.

Chris started to stick her screwdriver in her back pocket and froze.

No, that didn't make sense, either. Why would Smitty try to kill her?

Suddenly she couldn't breathe. She tossed the screwdriver out of the hatch above her head, then grabbed the

hatch's sides and hustled out. The breeze struck her full
force, a wind smelling of rain again and the darkening sky
to the northwest showing the dissipated thunderheads had re-
grouped. Jacquie looked up from the book she appeared to
be reading, then glanced toward the pier. On the dock, Smitty,
now shirtless, hand sawed through a long panel of marine
ply, his muscles sliding easily beneath his golden skin.

Surely not. Smitty had struck her as a genuine guy from
the beginning. He had an ease about him that suggested he
wasn't nervous or hiding anything. Living in close quarters
with his partner for three weeks had given him ample opportunity to say or do something to incriminate himself, but
McLellan apparently hadn't picked up on anything.

No, it had to be someone else, maybe someone outside
the four agents she knew. She was just exhausted, and
nursing low-level terror was making her jumpy.

"I'm going below," Chris said to Jacquie. "I've got some
work in the engine room."

"All right."

Chris slipped down to the lower passageway, absently
noting the skeleton of the mahogany framework as she
passed. As was becoming her habit, she propped the engine
room door open with the crate of oil before she got to
work. She had only one thing to do: track down the damned
exhaust leak that had nearly killed her.

Obsession wasn't going anywhere until it was patched.
Chris had fought pinhole leaks before. Rust was just a fact
of life on a boat, and she'd come to have a healthy respect
for the way salt and water and metal combined into either
a battery or a mass of corrosion.

Chris stood back and evaluated the exhaust system as a
whole, an engineering strategy that had driven the roughnecks crazy—*just get on with it, sweetcheeks!*—but had

saved her a helluva lot of time and effort in the long run. In this case, it was simple: the exhaust blown from the engine ran through a wide metal pipe until the raw-water cooling system hooked in; then the steam exhaust mixed with the water, cooled down, passed into a standard marine water hose and exited the stern. The leak, Chris knew, must be upstream of the raw-water system, when the exhaust was still primarily smoke.

She first checked the bolts holding the metal exhaust pipe fitting to the manifold itself. No sign of the bolts having loosened, no crumbling mess of a melted gasket. The bolts were evenly rusted, too, suggesting they hadn't seen a wrench in some time. On to the exhaust pipe.

From the exhaust manifold to the raw-water system, the metal exhaust pipe was jacketed with several pieces of heavy-duty temperature-resistant material. The pipe could reach extreme temperatures and give you a third-degree burn in about two seconds flat if you brushed against it while Hortense was running. Chris would have to untie the tightly wired jacket holders—the ones that reminded her of office envelopes with their red strings—and check every inch of Hortense's considerably long pipe.

She decided to tackle the easiest-to-reach jacket first. It covered the two feet of pipe bolted directly to the manifold, with only a slender gap of about a quarter inch between it and the next jacket covering the ninety-degree bend where the pipe curved to run behind the engine. Chris had nearly unwound the first metal tie from its securing button when she saw the problem.

A perfectly round hole in the gap between the two jackets.

Chris stopped wrestling with the metal tie and pulled the jackets' edges back with her fingertips. Yes, it was a hole, not a shadow. Its edges were clean, not rusted at all, and as round as if it'd been drilled there. In fact, it looked exactly like a hole created by a five-sixteenths drill bit.

A pinhole leak she'd expected, someplace where the metal had been weak or had succumbed to fatigue in the harsh marine environment.

But not this. Not sabotage.

Can't you make this just a little worse? she prayed angrily. *Isn't there a hurricane out there you can throw at me? Or maybe you could sink my yacht, just for grins.*

She walked to the tool chest and opened the lid. The tools all sat strapped down against the yacht's movement. The drill lay mute and harmless in its bed. She lifted out a tray of wrenches to reveal the plastic case of drill bits. Hands shaking, she opened the set.

All bits present and accounted for.

She plucked the five-sixteenths bit from its holder and examined it. No tell-tale metal shards clinging to the blade, no nicks or scratches. It looked almost brand-new. And she couldn't remember the last time she'd used this particular bit.

She took it back to the engine. The bit slid neatly into the hole. She removed it again, went back to the tool chest. Compared to the other bits, it showed more wear, but nothing out of the ordinary. Nothing that might suggest it had been used to put the hole in the exhaust pipe.

What exactly did sabotage mean?

Heavy footsteps on the stairs. Chris froze for a split second, then quickly snapped the bit back in its holder. She closed the bit set, stowed the wrench tray, closed the tool chest. Another few seconds and she'd shoved the jacket edges back together on Hortense's exhaust pipe.

"Whatcha doin'?" Smitty said from the doorway.

Chris shoved her trembling hands in her shorts' back pockets and shrugged. "Thinking about going after that manifold leak. We can't leave New Orleans until that's taken care of, but I'll be damned if I want to go poking around a quarter mile of pipe."

"Oh." Smitty's bare chest glistened with perspiration and his jeans rode low on his hips. He ran his hand through his sweat-darkened hair. Under other circumstances, Chris would have thought he looked incredibly lean and sexy. "Let me grab some breakfast for dinner and I'll take care of it."

"That's okay," she said. "I can do it. It's probably a pinhole leak and just needs a welding job."

"Naaaah," Smitty admonished with a casual smile. "That's *nasty* work. There's some trim in the salon that needs a last coat of varnish. You do that and I'll do this. I'm guessing you've had enough engine work to last you a lifetime. You want some eggs?"

"I'm not hungry."

"Right-o, boss." He winked as he turned to go.

Ther be Dragynes here.

Chris stepped into the lower passageway and waited until she heard a frying pan hit the stove, then the coffee grinder growling its way through some beans. Smitty would be busy for a while, reading while he ate. He was a lot like her: he liked his schedule the way it was and no monkeying around with it.

Satisfied she knew where Smitty would be for twenty minutes or so, Chris collected fresh linens from the closet near Smitty's room, then walked to McLellan's cabin door and opened it.

His lingering cologne, all musk and leather, crashed over her. *Damn that man,* she thought as the scent insinuated itself in her senses. The same cologne he'd worn that night, that she'd carried on her skin after they'd taken each other. She closed her eyes against her body's thrumming.

She silently closed the cabin door behind her. The cabin had hardly seen any renovation—this side of the boat hadn't leaked much—and they hadn't had time to repanel and recarpet. The wide bed, roughly made in what Chris imagined was a man's way, looked abandoned. A towel hung crookedly on the rack visible through the open bathroom door.

Chris tossed the fresh sheets on the bed and looked around. The dingy curtains needed replacing. The cabinetry had been sanded down and simply needed a few coats of varnish to complete its restoration. She opened the clothes chest's bottom drawer. It held only a blanket and a stack of neatly folded golf shirts. On impulse, she removed the items, shook them out.

What are you expecting? she berated herself. *A clue? For the missing drill bit to fall out? If he'd sabotaged the engine, he would have destroyed the evidence, tossed the drill bit overboard or out with the trash.*

Nevertheless, she methodically opened every clothes drawer, then looked in the hanging locker, the nightstand, the bathroom cabinets, searching for something—anything—and finding nothing but expensive clothing.

She gave up and made short work of changing the sheets and towels, then hurriedly left the cabin. Once they were in the gulf again, when she knew Smitty would be on the flybridge for his watch, she'd search his cabin, too. She dumped the used linens on the washing machine in the little launderette, wondering if Jacquie could be prevailed upon to do the washing.

Inside her own cabin, Chris locked the door behind her. The wall-mounted lamp's light dispelled the growing gloom of evening, casting the room into the warm hues of red mahogany. The traditional blue comforter and blue-cushioned chair welcomed her.

This room, she thought as she surveyed it, had been her home for almost a year. There were the leaking portholes she'd reseated and sealed, there was the water-stained cabinetry she'd stripped and varnished. Chris sat on the bed, ran her hand over her quilt's compass rose pattern.

My home.

She pressed the hidden panel in the wall above the headboard. When it popped open, she could see the plastic strip tucked into the cubby hole. She needed to get it to Gus, preferably without anyone knowing, but hadn't figured out how to do that yet. A couple of hours of pondering and she'd have it. Time she didn't have, she thought as the hidden panel clicked shut.

In the nightstand drawer lay a handheld GPS. She fired it up. Even down in the bowels of the yacht, the little device was able to get a signal from the satellite. For the umpteenth time, she keyed in the lat-longs Natalie had given her. Same place, one of many private islands people had shelled out millions of dollars for. Yes, definitely U.S. waters there. The Coasties could ride in like the cavalry. Chris scanned the device's settings and waypoints—the little electronic beacons directing the way to the destination—to make sure she remembered exactly how to get there. Then she carefully erased Isladonata's lat-longs.

She switched off the GPS and placed it back in the nightstand drawer. Hiding. She was hiding and she knew it. She slid the drawer closed.

Face the facts.

Smitty had had plenty of opportunities to install the black box and run the wiring up to her office wall.

Smitty had started the engines when he knew she'd be in one of the engine rooms, and hadn't checked first to see where she was.

Smitty's broom had lodged against the engine room door.

Smitty had left her alone on the yacht once they had reached New Orleans, which had sent McLellan ballistic.

Smitty's page had pulled McLellan away from her last night and given Falks a chance to corner her.

Smitty hadn't been on the yacht last night when he should have been, and showed up just as she found Falks's corpse.

Could Smitty have been working with Falks to get the alleged thirty million dollars back—and prevent her from reaching Natalie? And prevent the DEA from getting its hands on Scintella?

Could he have killed Falks? And if they were working together, why would he have done it? Greed?

"Damn," Chris said, her voice loud in the silence.

Maybe Smitty was the mole and maybe he wasn't. She didn't trust Jacquie or Russ to be straight arrows, either, so going to them with her suspicions was out of the question. No, the way to handle this thing was to go forward as planned, to avoid tipping him off by acting as if everything was normal. But she'd watch Smitty the whole time, not be caught off guard again.

Chris leaned her head in her hands. Days like this, she just wanted to call it quits. Just give up the chase, give up the work. Go back to Galveston, forget everything, forget the fact her grandfather had given her only this yacht, forget this horrible mess Natalie had gotten herself into. All she wanted was to run her charter business and live a quiet life. Sometimes, like now, it seemed as though the only way Chris could ever do what she wanted was to leave her family behind.

Family. She hadn't had family since her mother succumbed to cancer and her father wrapped his car around a telephone pole. The only "family" she had was Natalie, who perhaps would learn from this experience and not leap into a bad relationship again.

Chris raised her head, clenched her hands into fists. If Natalie hadn't married Jerome Scintella after such a short engagement, they wouldn't be in this mess. Natalie might have seen past the dollar signs to the man and realized who he was.

Jerome Scintella.

The Ruger gleamed, lamplight caressing its lines like a lover's hand.

Chris hoped she'd never meet Scintella face-to-face. She wasn't sure what would happen if she did.

As she slid the nightstand drawer closed, she tried not to notice how the Ruger slumbered, so innocent, so peaceful, so beautiful.

So tempting.

Chapter 13

Sunset on the Gulf of Mexico, Chris thought as she stood at the flybridge helm, felt like the last stop before oblivion.

Ahead, miles of open water stretched all the way to night. A deep mauve and orange sky glowed in the west; low clouds streaked the horizon. A brown pelican arced, then tucked in its shoulder and dove. It bobbed up to sit quietly and held its chin close to its chest for a moment before lifting its beak to swallow. Then it lifted—heavy, improbable flyer—into the air again, as a pelican always had in these waters, and probably always would. The air smelled of nothing but mild salt and wild wind. *Obsession*'s hull neatly sliced the blue water, her bow wave splashing up, white and foaming, then falling back and disappearing as the yacht swept past.

Early that morning, *Obsession* had traveled through the main shipping lanes, passing hundreds of oil rigs that dotted the Louisiana coastal waters before breaking out into the wilderness of the gulf around noon. The run south at her cruising speed of seventeen knots had been a comfortable ride all through the afternoon. Now, two hundred nautical miles from the Keys and a hundred off Florida's west coast, it looked as if it'd be a fine night. They'd reach Key West by morning. Right on schedule.

Chris zipped up her light jacket a little in the crisp wind; her shorts-clad legs chilled pleasantly. The helm console gauges, gleaming green against the growing dark, showed *Obsession* in working order, shipshape in Bristol fashion. Hortense evidenced no sign of vibration. The new carbon monoxide idiot lights Chris had installed the last day in New Orleans were dull; thanks to Smitty's welding job, which Chris had double-checked, no more exhaust was being vented into the engine room.

And McLellan was still in Galveston, forced to stay there by Antonio Garza and Gus Perkins.

Her search of Smitty's cabin, in the middle of his first duty at the wheel, had turned up nothing. Much as her mental gymnastics had developed no theory, at least none that made any sense, about the exhaust pipe sabotage. It was as though the Sabotage Fairy had struck, then disappeared without a trace. Smitty's concerned report that night about the drilled hole had sounded genuine. If he had drilled it, wouldn't he have simply welded it over and said nothing?

Or was she just hopelessly naive?

Chris was getting used to the lump her Ruger made under her pillow. And waking instantly at the slightest creak of the passageway floor outside her cabin. Over the course of the day, she had already become as attuned to the movements of her passengers as she was to Claire's hiccup upon starting and the rhythms of bilge pump and air-conditioning.

And here was Russ, emerging from the pilothouse, right on time. "Good evening," she said.

He handed her a frosty bottled water. "Weather fax came in. It's clear sailing for the night."

"Good news."

"Heard anything from your sister?"

Chris shook her head. "Only a quick call in New Orleans to say she was okay. But I gave her the satellite phone number so she can reach us out here."

"Still on schedule?"

"She'll be on Isladonata in two days."

"I looked at one of your charts. It'd be hell trying to pick that island out of the five hundred sitting out there."

Chris nodded. "Thank God for lat-longs."

Russ lowered his stocky body onto the bench seat near the helm console and set his own coffee on the side table. "We probably all need to sit down and have a talk about strategy for getting in."

"Agreed," Chris said, wondering why when Russ suggested a war session it didn't feel as if he was trying to take over. Not like McLellan had. As the sun collapsed onto land, she wondered if she'd ever see McLellan again and felt again the hollowness. He would have loved this leg of the trip, all the fathomless water. Damn him.

"Your sister understands our situation, doesn't she?"

"She knows we're dead if she slips up," she said as she twisted the cap off her bottle.

"Good."

His stout nod and matter-of-fact manner reassured Chris almost against her will. He was all cop, carried himself with that confidence and bearing she associated with a state trooper's trustworthiness. But she hadn't decided yet whether she could trust him or Perfect Jacquie, no matter how friendly they appeared.

Hang on for the ride, she reminded herself. *When the plan breaks down, play it by ear.*

No matter how crazy that made her nerves. Chris glanced at the compass and nudged *Obsession* farther east. All the best intentions in the world to "play it by ear" couldn't easily override a lifetime of habit. She'd planned and executed plans since she was ten years old and watched her mother lose the cancer battle. Understanding things—that was the only way Chris knew how to deal with problems. If she could just get her brain around the facts, if she could mark out a plan for working through the problem, then she could manage—

"Jacquie said you and McLellan got into it over this whole protective custody thing," Russ said.

"You could say that."

"I know it's none of my business—"

"And it'll probably stay that way." Chris kept her voice even. Still being pissed about being held hostage wasn't really productive. Time to move on. "I'd prefer not to talk about it."

"I just wanted to say he's a good man. The best in his field, in my book. Knows what he's doing in a tight spot."

"Chalk it up to a little disagreement over what's best for whom."

The wind snatched Russ's laughter from his lips. "I got the impression the other night he had a decided interest in your personal welfare, Captain."

"Nice show," she agreed. "Backstage is a different story."

"I reckon it is."

Chris flushed with annoyance at his lightly sarcastic tone. "This started as my voyage, Mr. LeBlanc. My sister's life is at stake. I'm not interested in fighting Connor McLellan every damned step of the way because he's obsessed with whether I go to the store by myself or not. I can't waste time arguing over nonessentials."

"Nonessentials isn't what we're talking about." Russ stood up and leaned against the helm console, just where McLellan used to when he kept her company. "I think you've got some kind of idea about how this thing's gonna go and what everybody's gonna do and how it's all gonna turn out. It won't be anything like you expect. I promise you that. You're not bulletproof."

Chris tried to catch hold of the fear suddenly spiraling in her chest and missed. Was he threatening her? "What do you mean?"

"I mean you're not a cop and you're not a criminal. You don't know what these Isladonata guys might do. No amount of you walking around believing it'll be the way you want it to be is gonna change that."

"I've already had this conversation with Jacquie. I know I'm out of my league—"

"Connor McLellan is the guy who's going to even the score for you."

Chris ignored her trembling fingers as she said, "And Smitty."

Russ stared at her. "Yeah," he said slowly, "True. There's Smitty." He blew out a breath. The green instrument lighting cast his strong features as impervious as rock.

"I just want my sister safe and away from Jerome Scintella," Chris repeated. The words, echoing back at her from the limitless dark of dangerous engine rooms and handgun barrels, suddenly felt like a mantra that had lost its power. "Putting me under house arrest wasn't going to help that situation."

"You're wrong there. You're the one keeping your sister sane with your phone calls. You're the one keeping this tub afloat and running. You're the one who's going to make us look like we belong on Isladonata."

"Why don't you just take the lat-longs and call in the big guns?" Chris asked.

"Because your sister would be dead before the first chopper landed. McLellan insisted we do it this way, to give us a chance to get Natalie out before the shooting starts." Russ pushed off the console. "His heart's in the right place, whether you can see that or not. Your safety's part of the equation."

"I can take care of myself," she snapped. "I always have."

"Did you tell him that?"

"Not in so many words—"

"Because the last person who told him that was his brother. About four days before he died."

She caught her breath. "You knew his brother?"

"Jacquie and I were there when they pulled Sean out of the water."

"What happened to him?"

"He was a drug dealer, pretty high up in the organization," Russ said. "But Connor had convinced him to roll his boss. Sean died in a bad sting operation."

Chris clamped onto the wheel hard. "It wasn't an accident?"

"Three shots to the back of the head? No, it wasn't an accident."

She saw again McLellan's anguish, his dark anger over his brother's death, his clenched fist of rage.

Smitty had lied.

Before she could say anything to Russ, Smitty popped onto the flybridge, steaming coffee mug in hand.

"Are you harassing my girlfriend?" he asked Russ.

Chris felt the agent's scrutiny as he answered, "I don't think so."

Smitty bumped his shoulder companionably against Chris's, sending her nerves screaming. "First mate reporting for duty, darlin'. You ready to take a break?"

Chris managed a nod. She relinquished the wheel to Smitty, then automatically recorded the latest heading and position statements in the log book. Routine. Yes. That would calm her down until she could talk to Russ and Jacquie alone, when she was absolutely sure Smitty couldn't overhear them. Maybe Key West, when she could send him ashore for something.

"What's for dinner?" she asked as she stowed the book in the helm's cabinet.

Smitty rubbed his stomach. "Jambalaya and dirty rice, cooked up by our very own Miss Jacqueline Adair."

"I'm headed that way, too," Russ said.

When they reached the dinette, Russ slid his stocky frame onto the bench seat and grabbed his utensils with both hands, then looked expectantly at the galley like an anxious hound.

"What can I help you with?" Chris asked Jacquie, glad for the temporary relief of relative domesticity.

Jacquie's trademark scarf, a red one this time, wrapped tightly now around the neat bun she wore, bobbed as she opened the oven door to remove a deep pan. "Nothing right now." She parked the pan, overflowing with fluffy white bread, on a potholder. "All I ask is cooperation with the dishwashing later."

"Smells great," Chris remarked. "Beats the TV dinner Smitty microwaved for me last night."

Jacquie's brows quirked as she ladled steaming jambalaya from a metal pot into bowls. "I'm not even going to tell you what I think about Smitty's food of choice, even though he seems to like the good stuff."

"As long as somebody else cooks it," Russ volunteered, accepting a bowl from Chris.

"I heard that!" Smitty yelled from the pilothouse. He stuck his head through the galley door. "I'm moving to the lower helm. It's gettin' kinda windy up top."

"You just want to eavesdrop on us," Jacquie accused. "What are you afraid you're going to miss?"

Smitty winked at Chris. "The good stuff."

"How windy is it?" Chris asked him, ignoring the fear threading her spine.

"Very. Damn near blew my do off." He passed his hand over his barely thinning hair. He disappeared from the galley, presumably gone forward to the pilothouse helm.

Not far enough away to have a private conversation. Yet.

"Why are you getting up?" Jacquie asked her as Chris scooted out of the dinette.

"I need to check the sailing tender. I didn't lash her back down after we took her out in New Orleans."

"I got it." Jacquie waved her hand at Chris to sit back down, then swept off her apron. "You've been working. Eat."

"Nice little sailboat," Russ said conversationally as Jacquie slipped out the sliding salon door and up the rear flybridge steps. "She speedy?"

"Flies when she's got her shoulder in, yeah. A little tricky when the wind pipes up."

"The best kind of sailin'."

A sudden snap, like a breaking board, sounded directly overhead.

"What the hell?" Russ said, sliding from the dinette seat.

Sudden movement—the briefest glimpse of falling, a woman's body—outside the galley windows caught Chris's attention.

"Jacquie!" Chris shot out of the dinette and ran into the

pilothouse. "Circle slow to starboard!" she ordered Smitty as she punched the Man Overboard button on the GPS mounted over his head. "Jacquie's gone in." Chris slapped the searchlight on and aimed it down into the water. "Russ, see if you can spot her." As Russ grabbed the searchlight lever, she darted out the pilothouse's door onto the starboard deck.

Outside, she scanned the surface for a flailing hand, a flash of scarf. Nothing. *Obsession*'s engines growled steadily as Smitty backed them down to a low RPM. Jacquie didn't call out or scream. The searchlight's broad beam illuminated only the long, rolling waves. The moon lingered overhead, casting feeble diamonds on the water. Chris suddenly couldn't remember what color Jacquie had been wearing. *Obsession* circled. The searchlight's beam traveled slowly over the waves, penetrating the water at the crests to reveal small fish swirling.

Then she saw it: a red shirt wafting just beneath the surface.

"Kill the engines!" she shouted. "Russ! Can you see her?"

"Got her!"

Chris ran to the bow and jerked open the emergency gear cabinet. She cinched the rescue harness on and hauled out the two hundred foot coil of high-strength lifeline. The life ring went over her shoulder and another coil of lifeline snap-shackled onto it.

Back at the open deck door, she dropped the life ring on the deck and knelt to tie the two lifelines onto a mooring cleat.

"Russ!" she said. When he came out on deck, she said, "Show Smitty where to keep the light. I may need you to throw this to me when I get there."

"Let me go in—"

"Have you rescued anyone before?"

"No, but—"

"Smitty!"

Just inside the open door, Smitty's face shone pale beneath his tan. "Ma'am."

"You were search and rescue. You gonna go in after Jacquie?"

The fear—no, the terror—she saw in his frozen expression, the redness around his eyes, told her everything she needed to know about his Coast Guard days. Post-traumatic stress.

"Forget it," she snapped. "And kill those engines like I told you."

"Ma'am," he said in almost a whisper.

She handed Russ the life ring and its coil of line. "If I yell at you, throw it high and past us. Got it?"

He nodded.

She turned and dove.

The water iced her veins the moment she hit it. She swam toward the halo of light where Jacquie's shirt billowed, like a falling skydiver's, beneath the waves just out of reach. Tugging a little more lifeline out, she dove under.

The light disappeared. Her eyes stung in the salt water. If this was just the shirt and Jacquie had gone down... The shirt fabric brushed her hand. She grabbed and pulled. It was heavy, thank God.

Chris drew Jacquie to the surface and turned the woman's face up, into air. Unconscious. *Have to do this the hard way.*

She caught Jacquie around the chest and swam toward *Obsession.* The water wavered beneath the searchlight. *This woman weighs more than she looks,* Chris thought abstractedly. *Have I swum that far? Where's the damned boat?* She turned her head. Another fifty feet. *Easy enough.* She snuffled water, coughed.

Her arms were burning by the time she reached the yacht.

"The life ring won't work!" Chris shouted up. "She's out cold. Grab a harness from the kit up front."

"I'm on it." Russ's authoritative voice reassured her.

Chris held hard to the end of the lifeline tied to the mooring cleat while the waves lifted and dropped them. She tipped Jacquie's head back against her own shoulder, trying to keep the woman's face out of the water. *Obsession's* house lights illuminated a slight halo around her hull, easing the dark. Behind her, the lifeline floated like a streamer, carried away by the current. Jacquie bled from a nasty cut behind her ear, probably from hitting the deck rail on the way down when she fell. Chris tried to remember whether sharks cruised this far north.

A rescue harness splatted the water next to her, lifeline attached. Chris wrestled the harness around Jacquie's inert form, fighting not to lose her. Once Jacquie was secured, Chris cinched the harness snugly and fastened the buckle. "Okay! Pull her up!"

Chris held Jacquie's head out of the water as the harness, its lifeline attached at the waist, began to draw her out of the water. She looked up. Russ hauled Jacquie out hand over hand. She'd forgotten to tell him to use the crane on the coach house roof. Still, he was a strong man. He could handle the weight. He grabbed Jacquie's harness and pulled her into the pilothouse.

Chris waited to be hauled out next, bobbing and resting, letting the adrenaline drain away. Clouds streamed away from the moon. Behind them, stars dimpled the sky. What could Jacquie have done to make her fall? she wondered. In a moment, she heard Russ and Smitty talking.

Then Smitty's words chilled her to the bone. "I'll start the engines."

"No!" she screamed as one engine fired up, "the lifeline could get caught in the props!" The deep, explosive rumble drowned out her voice.

In an instant, the harness yanked the breath from her. The lifeline razed her fingers as she lost her grip. Black water covered her head.

She dragged, scraping against the hull. She caught hold of a through-hull fitting, but her fingers couldn't grip, couldn't hold. The roar of the whirring blades filled her skull. Dive. Dive. Swim deep, swim behind the props, foul their blades with the line and stop them spinning.

She swam what seemed like *down*, trying to keep distance between her limbs and the rushing water. How much line had wrapped around the propeller? The harness caught her. She tried to unfasten the snap shackle but the line was too tight. She'd have to get close to the blades to get loose.

Was she getting pulled backward? Forward? Up? Without the boat close by, she couldn't tell. How much line did she have left? Ten feet? Less? The mental image of her foot getting chopped—slice and dice—by the bronze blades made her draw them in close to her body. She opened her eyes. Blackness everywhere. Her lungs burned. She stroked forward.

Her head hit the hull. Pain scorched her skull. She felt the tug. The props would eat her alive. She struck out with her arms, trying to keep her legs tucked in. Her head ached. She concentrated on the props' roar. Try again. Swim around it, put it behind you, then go up.

Suddenly the tugging stopped. She put one hand on the hull. *Obsession* still vibrated strongly. The engines ran but the boat didn't move. The lifeline had fouled the props. The boat wouldn't chop her to bits.

It'd hold her under until she drowned.

She started to see red. The lifeline.

She grabbed the line and pulled herself toward the now-still props, relieving the tension, hoping the line wouldn't suddenly break and drag her face-first into suddenly freed and spinning blades. The snap shackle on her harness caught on the harness ring. She tried not to panic. Sort it out. Her fingers studied the harness fitting, the shackle. Twisted.

She yanked the shackle around and unhooked it. Free.

One hand on the hull, she swam out from beneath the yacht and surfaced, coughing. *Obsession,* turned slightly by the wave action, presented her backside, giving Chris the full benefit of her exhaust.

"Chris!" Russ's voice echoed weirdly from the yacht's stern and heaving water. "Chris!"

Still heaving for breath, she floated, vaguely aware of Russ scrambling down the ladder to the swim platform. She heard his voice—he kept talking—but wanted only the cool night wind blowing the fumes away from her face, to feel the last of the salt water trickling from her sinuses down her throat, to lie here with the air scraping in and out of her burning lungs.

She wanted Connor.

"Chris!" Russ shouted again, sounding desperate.

Chris roused herself, treaded water. "I'm not coming close until Smitty kills the engines!" she shouted, trying to pitch her voice over the noisy exhaust. "You shut down those goddamned engines and bring Smitty's ass back with you!"

If Russ hesitated, Chris didn't see it. She'd tread water all night if she had to, but she wasn't going near the swim platform as long as Hortense and Claire were capable of spinning propellers. As long as Smitty was out of sight. She sniffed hard, ignoring the salt burn in her nostrils. If she could just breathe. Her lungs felt so tight.

The exhaust pipes' deep spluttering died, leaving only the flat clap of wave on fiberglass. Dark movement on the aft deck, then the deck lights popped on, revealing the two men standing together until Russ dropped onto the swim platform again. Chris dipped her head back to let the water sweep her hair from her face. She watched the men for a long moment, made sure Smitty wasn't going to move from the deck rail, then breaststroked to the teak platform. Russ grasped her arm and hauled her from the water as if she weighed nothing. Her breath hitched a little, but she got control.

"How's Jacquie?" She started stripping the rescue harness off, angry that her voice sounded so raspy, so weak.

"Hurt pretty bad, but alive."

Chris swung up the steps to face Smitty, who squared off against her in a defensive posture. Fighting to have her voice here, on the deck, she tightened her abs for support as she said, "Did you hail the Coast Guard?"

"I haven't had time—"

"Bullshit!" Chris clenched her hands into fists and willed herself not to strike him. "Do you even know how to use the VHF radio? How about a freakin' phone?"

"Wait a minute—"

"Jacquie's barely alive and you don't have time to hail the *Coast Guard?* What the hell were you doing that you didn't have time to call for help?"

She brushed past him and strode down the side deck to the pilothouse, aware that both men were following. Jacquie lay on her back on the pilothouse's bench near the helm console, the ugly cut behind her ear bleeding through the T-shirt bandage someone had made. "Hang on," Chris told her. "I'm gonna get help."

Glancing at the GPS for their current position, she

grabbed the satellite phone from its holder. "This is motor vessel *Obsession* with a Coast Guard emergency. Requesting Coast Guard assistance, over."

"This is Captain Anderson of the U.S. Coast Guard," blared the phone's speakers. "What's the nature of your emergency? Over."

"We've recovered a man overboard who requires medical assistance." Chris gave as much of Jacquie's information as Russ knew, then relayed *Obsession*'s position.

"Bring your vessel east on heading one two five. Our chopper should meet you in twenty minutes."

"No can do. We're dead in the water with lifeline fouling both props. It'll take twenty minutes just to cut it all out."

"Roger that. Make that ETA thirty minutes."

"Thirty minutes," Chris repeated.

She slotted the phone handset back into place, then glared at Smitty. "*Now* would have been the time to start the engines."

"Hey, I didn't know—"

"You don't know a helluva lot for someone who was Coast Guard." Chris automatically checked her watch to note the time, then pivoted to face Smitty. "Does 'kill the engines' mean anything to you, *Coastie?*"

"Come on, Chris—"

"This is the second time you've nearly killed me because you couldn't follow a simple order. Give me one good reason why I should keep your ass aboard instead of tossing it straight into the fucking gulf."

"Look, Chris, I know you're upset," Smitty said, his hands raised as if to fend her off.

"I'm not upset, you moron, I'm furious." She jabbed a finger at his chest but stayed out of his reach. "Confined to quarters until we reach land. Then you're *off* my vessel."

"No way." Smitty shook his head. He glanced at Russ, looking for support. "I'm going to do my job."

"And what's your job, buddy?" Russ asked softly from where he sat at Jacquie's side.

"What do you mean?" Smitty asked, eyes wide.

"You lied," Russ said. "You told her you served. I know from your records you couldn't even finish training."

Relief swept through Chris's body in a great rush. Russ understood. He knew. Or at least he was beginning to see.

"Why'd you do that?" Russ continued, his gray-green gaze spearing Smitty. "What did you hope to gain by lying?"

"Look," Smitty said with a feeble shrug, "Connor wouldn't have taken me if he'd thought I couldn't handle crewing. I did fine with that at Cape May—it was just the rescue operations...." His hands clenched and unclenched several times. "You just don't know what it's like to go out there and throw yourself into all that water and—"

"She did." Russ nodded at Chris.

"That's not the problem," Chris said, starting to shiver in the pilot house air-conditioning. "The problem is you've told me a helluva lot that's not true."

"Like what?" Smitty challenged, his expression very much like that of a disgruntled teenager testing parental boundaries.

"You told me McLellan's brother shot himself."

Russ pulled his Glock from its holster, held it steady. "You were on that sting, just like us. You know what happened to Sean."

"Yeah, exactly what he deserved. You play with guys like that, you take your chances. Just because it was pretty boy's brother, everybody's a bleedin' heart."

Chris froze. "Falks called McLellan 'pretty boy' the other night."

"Aw, shit." Smitty's disgust showed in his snarl. "You're kiddin' me, Nancy Drew."

"Where's the best place to put this asshole?" Russ asked without taking his eyes off Smitty.

"Bunk cabin upstairs," she said quietly, her throat aching. "There's not a hatch big enough to climb out."

"This is crazy! Damn, Russ—"

"Let's go." Russ motioned Smitty to precede him out of the pilothouse.

"Wait a minute," Chris said on a hunch. "We need to make sure it's clean."

On the way down to the bunk cabin, Chris ducked into the office to grab the yacht's key ring. Inside the small room, she quickly upended the cushions, dug around in the little hanging locker. Then her hands brushed something hard near the clothes rod.

"Gotcha!" she said in triumph.

"What is it?" Russ called from outside.

She peeled away the tape that held the weapon to the locker's ceiling. "Ditty revolver." It tucked neatly into her waistband. Super lightweight.

"Hey!" Smitty protested. "You think that's mine? That isn't mine!"

Chris finished her search and emerged, gave Smitty plenty of room to pass, stayed out of his reach. Russ shoved Smitty, hard, into the cabin.

"You come outta here, I shoot you on sight. Got that?"

"When do I get my piss breaks?" Smitty asked.

Chris ignored his sarcastic tone. "You don't. Piss out the window."

Smitty dropped onto the bunk, stared at the windowless wall in front of him. As she closed the door, she saw his eyes shift, meet hers, filled with anger. And something more: resentment. Loathing. The same look she'd seen from Natalie on the rare occasions Chris hadn't given her younger sister what she wanted. But he was much more dangerous than a spoiled child. The door clicked closed.

She turned the key. The lock shot home and suddenly Chris could breathe again.

Chapter 14

"How's she doing?" Chris asked the nurse as the woman thunked a big plastic Super Big Gulp cup, emblazoned with the Tampa Bay Hospital logo and filled with crushed ice and water, onto the wheeled adjustable tray next to Jacquie's bed.

The nurse slapped a blood pressure cuff around Jacquie's arm. "Let's just see." She hit the switch on the measurement machine and watched its lights until it beeped. The Velcro scritched as she removed the cuff. "Good as gold." The nurse scribbled on a chart.

Chris sat back in the uncomfortable guest chair at the bed's foot and eyed the pink-and-purple flowery scrubs the nurse wore. She was half-glad Jacquie wasn't awake to see them. *Not your style at all,* Chris thought to Jacquie.

She studied the bandage on Jacquie's head, which had turned out not to have as disastrous a wound as had first appeared. By the time *Obsession* had reached Tampa Bay at dawn, Jacquie's injuries had already been examined and treated. Jacquie had even managed a wave with her good hand when they came into her room. A broken forearm and wrenched shoulder were the worst of it. Jacquie's arm would be in a sling for a few weeks, then she'd be in physical therapy after that.

"If she wants more pain medication when she wakes up, buzz me," the nurse said.

"Thanks."

Russ caught the door on his way in as the nurse sped away. He closed it quietly. "She doin' all right?" he asked in a low voice as he walked to the bed.

"The nurse keeps telling me that. Pain killers are still on offer."

"Good." Russ leaned over Jacquie, studying the bandages and stiff sling. "At least it's not her shooting arm."

"What'd you find?" Chris asked.

Russ finally looked her way for the first time since entering the room. "Not much. It looked like the sailing tender's boom might have been rigged up under pressure so if somebody moved it, it'd hit whoever happened to be on the wrong side. But I couldn't find the trip wire."

"It might have snapped off into the water when the boom swung," Chris suggested.

His expression hardened as he shoved his fists into his pants pockets. "Swung like a damned catapult. The impact's what knocked her off the flybridge. If she'd been about your height…" He glanced at Jacquie, still sleeping peacefully. "Probably would have taken her head off."

Chris swallowed. "Sounds like Smitty's work to me."

"Well, we can't say that yet." Before Chris could protest, he continued, "Local office is sending out internal investigations to take a look around."

"What about Smitty?"

"I gave him to our guys here. It's out of our hands now."

Chris sat forward in her chair and scrubbed her face with her hands. "So they'll decide whether to keep him in custody based on the circumstantial evidence your investigators might not find? Hell, Russ, the 'accidents' are just guessing on my part."

Russ shook his head. "You got more on him than you think. We're checking on a few things. The investigators are gonna wanna talk to you."

"When?"

"In a couple of hours. What's it been since you slept? Thirty-six hours by now?"

Chris leaned back in the guest chair and tried to calculate mornings and nights and hours, then realized it didn't matter. "I can sleep on this lovely sofa bed here if I start losing it." She nodded at the vinyl-covered sofa, thought about closing her eyes, about drifting off, then caught herself before she did. "How long do you think the investigators will take? Our window's closing. We've got to get to Isladonata in two days, three at the absolute latest. They know this is a priority for us."

He pursed his lips as if he was about to give her bad news. "They will now."

"What do you mean?"

"It's…complicated. McLellan can explain it."

"No," Chris said, standing up. She didn't want to meet this new challenge sitting down, no how, no way. "Smitty apparently told me the truth when he said this mission was under the radar. So I want *you* to explain it."

Russ spread his hands. "Hey, this is not my deal—"

"But you're *here*. You're in it, just like me. Is it true

McLellan set this up outside the DEA because he was afraid of the mole scuttling it?"

His solemn, square-jawed face confirmed it even though he said nothing.

"Okay, let me speculate," she went on. "McLellan's keeping this mission a secret for the reasons you're not discussing. Fair enough. So the cash Antonio Garza handed me for the yacht restoration didn't come from the DEA, but from McLellan himself. And chances are," she pursued, "the DEA would never allow a civilian like me to get involved. A snitch, sure. Someone on the inside, fine. But all I can give you is regular contact with Natalie—"

"And sometimes that's enough. A regular source of good information is an expensive asset on the street," Russ explained. "Hell, if I were Connor, I'd be willing to pay."

"And Falks showing up in the first place was another good clue, huh?" she asked, letting the sarcasm creep into her voice.

"It meant the connection between you and your sister was good, yeah. Falks would never have bothered you if your sister wasn't serious about leaving Scintella."

Chris fought the tears stinging the backs of her eyes. Which felt worse, believing McLellan had used her to get his hands on the missing thirty million or knowing he'd used her for the information she *could* give him?

And when you were weighing that kind of betrayal, what difference did it make whether the betrayer was a good guy or a bad guy?

"But you're overlooking one thing," Russ said. When she didn't invite him to enlighten her, he added, "Had Connor not taken this on, you'd be dead already."

And out of my misery. "Why didn't he just tell me?" she

demanded. "What's so difficult about being up-front with this kind of information?"

Russ's lips thinned and she knew he was through with this conversation. But she knew, too, could see in his eyes, that there was more he was unwilling to tell her. A lot more.

"Come on back to the marina with me," he said. "Sleep in your own bed tonight. I'll stay the night here with Jacquie."

"You don't have to do that," Jacquie murmured.

Her faint voice might have been a shout given the way Russ's head snapped around. "*Chère*," he said, smiling as he went to her. "You're back with us again."

"I hadn't gone *that* far."

"Far enough to scare me to death."

"Your nose is growing, Pinocchio," she muttered. "You probably had dibs on my Glock."

"And your ergonomic desk chair," he said. "Want some water?"

"Love some."

He adjusted the wheeled tray's height, then drove it around the bed where she could reach it with her good arm. She picked up the Super Big Gulp and sipped delicately at its fat blue straw. "Very nice," she said. "Now catch me up on all the news."

As Russ described his morning studying the sailing tender and gave his theory on the rigged boom, Jacquie nodded, her dark eyes thoughtful.

"Yes, there was definitely a twang, like a high-tension wire giving," she said. "I didn't see anything. Smitty had already gone below so even the instrument lights were out." She paused, then her lips drew into a chagrined line. "If I'd had Chris's eye for the mechanical, I might have recognized what would happen."

"That's why she's an engineer and you're not," Russ said.

"And we didn't anticipate Smitty's attack on Chris," Jacquie admonished. "Which means you and I aren't very good at what we do."

"He's a good salesman," Chris said quietly. "I bought his story about the Coast Guard even though I should have known before we ever reached New Orleans."

"Why?" Russ asked.

"There's a dead spot on the ICW where GPS occasionally doesn't work. All the cruisers know about it and we figure it's the Navy or the Coasties testing GPS-jamming devices. Smitty didn't know anything about it. I should have realized it then."

"You had a lot going on at the time from everything I heard," Jacquie said. "That was the night of the accident at sea, wasn't it? When Smith tried to kill you?"

"Did McLellan tell you that?" Chris asked, startled.

Russ nodded. "Smith's good at seizing opportunities. McLellan's theory is that he spotted a chance to do what Falks hadn't succeeded in doing while keeping his own position intact. Connor swears there was time for Smitty to have blocked the engine room door."

"All speculation, of course," Jacquie added. "Connor figured Smith might overplay his hand while he was gone and asked us to keep an eye on you. We just didn't count on Smith to play it the way he did."

McLellan had been watching out for her. Chris ignored the train of thought pulling out of that particular station and got back on the right track. "What about my sister? Are we still going forward if the DEA doesn't haul you all in under arrest?"

Jacquie and Russ exchanged a solemn look. Then Russ snorted. "Of course."

"I'm still in, as well," Jacquie said, raising her good

hand—her gun hand—to forestall Russ's protests. "You'll need glamour to get into Isladonata, and I can play debutante like nobody's business."

Russ frowned, looking as if he was building up a good head of steam. "You're not in any shape."

"It's my arm in a sling, not my face."

"Need a designer sling," Russ muttered.

"Better to hide my Glock," she shot back.

"McLellan can't ask you to do that, can he?" Chris asked.

Jacquie raised a brow at Chris. "It's his call, but I'm ready to go." Even under the bandage, the agent's demeanor reflected a steel will. "Provided we're not all thrown in the brig before then."

"We'll nail Scintella's ass to the wall," Russ said. "We've come too far not to."

"And get your sister out," Jacquie said in a firmer voice.

Chris nodded. Jerome Scintella was a terribly dangerous man, she'd learned from personal experience over the past three weeks. A plant in the DEA, a hired gun to terrorize her. Probably more guns on the way to kill her in retribution for Falks's death.

Scintella was dangerous enough that three career DEA agents were willing to risk life, limb and their jobs for a mission outside DEA provenance. She didn't know anything about how the agency worked, but it sounded as if they might end up subject to disciplinary action. Maybe fired or jailed.

Tears stung her eyes as she said, "Thank you."

"Thank you for answering my questions, Ms. Hampton." The DEA internal investigation officer clicked his pen closed and stuck it into his breast pocket. He smiled reassuringly at her before glancing out *Obsession*'s salon window at the late afternoon sunshine.

"So what does all this mean?" Chris asked. "What'll happen to Smitty?"

"I'll have to review all the information you've given me before making that call," he said as he rose.

Chris nodded. She wanted to ask about McLellan, what would happen to Russ and Jacquie, but she didn't dare stir trouble. The agents might still get out of this with their jobs intact, and she didn't intend to jeopardize that possibility.

"And we have to look into this." He brandished a baggie containing the rectangle of black plastic Chris had given him, the one with the fingerprint. "I'll let Mr. LeBlanc know if it turns up anything significant."

Chris knew it would. The print on it would tell her who had planted the transponder. All her money was on Smitty.

The officer's boots clomped across the salon floor, clattered as he stepped on the fiberglass deck, then punctuated his stride in gunshots down the wooden pier. Chris relaxed back into the plush sofa. On the mahogany table, the brass compass, showing no hint of tarnish after she'd scrubbed Falks's blood from it, winked at her as the light streamed in from the west-facing side of the yacht. A huge weight of dread had lifted from her shoulders, and now she was free.

Smitty was gone.

Chris tried to be angry with McLellan for hiding so much of the truth from her—the mole, the mission's being outside the DEA, his brother's having died in a DEA sting operation gone bad. For keeping her hostage for a full day. She couldn't. She was just too damned tired to be pissed.

Russ had been right. She was an engineer, not a cop. Why people did what they did was a mystery to her. Their actions she could understand: the sheer mechanics of behavior, do this, say that. But the motivation? She wasn't made like these people. Everyone around her—Russ,

Jacquie, McLellan—knew the games and unspoken rules. They easily navigated the ambiguities, the hazy morality. They spoke a language she didn't understand. She was in a place and among people where she didn't belong.

Ther be Dragynes here.

Dragynes, dragynes everywhere, and not a one to trust.

She sighed. How was she supposed to navigate waters like these, with charts that made no sense, with unmarked hazards and threats? All she knew was that somewhere out there in the confusing morass of secrets and lies and monsters, her little sister waited for her.

Chris couldn't let her down.

She was coming to realize that trust wasn't part of the equation. She had only to get to the next stage of the journey, and if a DEA agent who liked to keep secrets could help her do that, she'd take it. If a pair of his DEA buddies, who let him call all the shots, could make it possible for her to get onto the island, she'd accept their help.

But that didn't mean she'd be stupid.

She rose to close the salon curtains. Outside, red and orange streaked the pristine blue of a sky darkening to purple. She paused. Yes, a perfect sunset, like a gift. Like so many gifts she was beginning to see she'd been given.

This yacht. Its restoration. The hard work left to do that sat so well on her soul, so satisfying. The promise of Nat's homecoming. The end of one horrific journey and the start of another. It'd be either wonderful or deadly, and she didn't much care which, as long as it'd all be over.

She flicked the curtain closed, then turned toward the dockside windows and forgot about how tired she was.

Connor McLellan stood outside on the pier, hands in his slacks pockets, looking doubtful about being there.

Heart pounding, Chris slid the salon's side door open.

His head turned slightly, as though he'd been looking elsewhere and she'd startled him. He didn't smile. She stepped out to the deck, then raised the hinged deck rail gate to let herself onto the pier.

As her shoes touched the dock, he said, "You're okay."

She nodded. After a moment, she replied, "You know about Smitty?"

"Yes."

For a long minute they simply faced each other. Chris didn't know what to say. She knew what she wanted to say, but none of it seemed appropriate. McLellan's lips thinned as he raised his head to gaze west, toward the fading sun.

"Come inside," she interrupted. "The no-see-ums get bad."

He studied her, his handsome face registering indecision between his brows. "For a few minutes. I need to talk to you."

They stepped inside the salon, McLellan closing the sliding door behind them.

"You want a drink?" Chris asked.

"No, thanks."

"Have a seat." Chris gestured to the salon's chair. It seemed silly now; he lived aboard, in her home, and would until Natalie was rescued. Treating him like a visitor seemed strange.

He waited until she sat to speak. "I need to be straight with you."

"About more than one thing, from what I hear."

He nodded, accepted her accusation. "I had to be careful. I had to make sure you were safe."

"Right. I figured that out when you lost me that morning in New Orleans."

"I didn't lose you." He studied his clasped fingers. "I was at the yacht when Eugene Falks went inside."

Everything inside her faltered: air, blood, muscle, sinew,

bone. With startling clarity, she saw herself, a small, pale figure behind gray walls, electric fences and razor wire, facing endless days. Her mouth went dry. "You think I killed him."

He said nothing.

Hot tears spilled from her eyes. "I had no reason to."

"You had plenty of reason," he replied quietly. "He threatened your sister. He threatened you. He threatened your boat. He demanded something you claimed you didn't have—"

"I *didn't* have his money." Chris shot out of her chair, not caring about tears and pain and fear anymore, and paced to the aft deck door before turning. "I *don't* have his money. What does it take to convince you people of that?"

"Christina—"

"I didn't kill him! You believed me before. Why don't you believe me now?" Then at his stony face, "What did you find out in Galveston?"

"That you have a lot of influence with Gus Perkins." His eyebrows quirked, as though with chagrin. "That you've worked hard all your life. That you were just starting to get what you really wanted when all this went down."

"And you think I'd risk my sister's life for *money?*"

"Maybe you thought you could get away with both. Maybe you needed the money to finance your dream."

Chris squared her shoulders, straightened her spine. This was no different than dealing with Falks. With her grandfather. Here was yet another man with all the supposed answers telling her what she was doing and who she was. As if he knew her at all.

She leveled her gaze on him. "If you honestly believe that's who I am, there's nothing I can do or say to change it."

McLellan grimaced, as if in pain. "You thought *I* was the mole."

"Smitty led me to believe you were."

"He fooled a lot of us."

"And you think I'm trying to fool you now."

Neither spoke for a long time. McLellan's expression, his posture, everything about him said he hated suspecting her. Even though she knew he wasn't the bad guy, even though he knew the one who'd betrayed him was someone else, the distrust gaped like a chasm between them. This was a *job* to him, she reminded herself.

"I want to believe you, Christina."

At her name, she paused, hating the way he kept making this situation personal, afraid he wouldn't. "You're still not telling me the truth now. You think I can't see that?" she whispered, digging the chasm deeper.

"I didn't want to scare you worse than you already were. After that night— I couldn't tell you the truth after Falks was killed. Everything changed. I had to look seriously at the idea you and Natalie were scamming Scintella like Falks claimed."

Chris's short laugh sounded like death. "Well, I can't prove a negative, can I? No matter what I say, I'm guilty."

"I'm willing to take the chance you're not."

"I'm honored. And you're still hiding something."

McLellan scrubbed his cheek with his hand. "Scintella was the money man for a guy called Linus von Brutten. Von Brutten had a lot of irons in the fire, but the worst was a biological weapon."

"Good God."

McLellan nodded. "Untraceable poison. Scintella's smuggling helped fund von Brutten until he was killed last year. Now Scintella's working for someone else, but we don't know who."

"So the money that disappeared belongs to this someone."

He stood, shoved his hands in his pockets. "We're playing in a whole different ballpark now. When it was just Scintella, that was one thing. But when we're talking about men like von Brutten…" he trailed off, head shaking. "My point is, the money Jerome thinks your sister stole was payment for a cocaine shipment. The courier never showed up."

"Falks said it was intercepted by Natalie's accomplice."

"It doesn't matter who Scintella thinks intercepted it. He's got hell to pay on his end, so as long as he thinks *you* have it, your life is in danger."

"Par for the course." Chris wiped the residual tears from her face. "What made you suspect Smitty was the mole?"

"When he showed up at *Obsession* the night Falks was murdered and asked what you'd done. That question didn't sound right. Like he'd said it for my benefit. It got me thinking about other things that seemed wrong. Like the broom in the passageway. There's no way it would have lodged itself there." He reached as if to stroke her hair, but didn't. "He had time. I was wrestling the gas can out of that damned lazarette on the aft deck."

"Between us hitting the oil rig debris and his coming up to the flybridge, he could have drilled the hole in the pipe."

Connor frowned. "But wouldn't you have noticed the exhaust when you went below?"

She shook her head. "I'd killed the engines. No real fumes until he started them again."

"You found the hole?"

"I pretended I hadn't, so he could patch it himself without realizing I knew."

His gray eyes warmed with admiration. "Good girl." Then his pride faded into something else, an intensity she sometimes glimpsed. "God, I didn't want to leave you with him. But Garza threatened to shut us down after you called

Gus. I convinced him to wait until Smith made a mistake. I thought Smitty wouldn't try to kill you until we'd reached the island. He hasn't admitted to killing Falks yet. I didn't see him go aboard, but he had the opportunity."

Chris drew in a sharp breath. "I hate to dig my grave any deeper, but they both worked for the same man. What would be Smitty's motive?"

"Same as yours. Thirty million dollars is a lot of money."

"Would Scintella let him get away with that?"

"Not for long." McLellan turned his head to stare out the sliding door to the aft deck. Outside, boats nodded with the waves. "Smitty's capable of killing a man." He abruptly met her gaze. "I don't think you are."

"Nice vote of confidence in my innocence."

Her sarcasm fell unnoticed between them as he said, "That's the other reason I'm here. You're not going to Isladonata."

"Yes, I am."

He abruptly stood. "No." His hard jaw meant it. "Now that we've caught the inside man, there's no reason for you to put yourself in danger."

"How are you going to get there?" she challenged, rising to meet him. "You'll blow the surprise if you use anything but a luxury yacht."

"That's a chance I'll take."

"You'll put my sister's life at risk!"

"We'll handle it."

"Absolutely not." Chris shook her head. "I told Natalie I'd be there and I'm going to be there."

"You're acting like you have a choice."

When the winds blew against her, she knew how to take another tack. "You'll at least have the DEA there to back you up, right? Now that they know?"

He frowned, studied the faint brown stains left on the beige carpet where Eugene Falks had bled and where no amount of cleaning would scrub away the death. The DEA didn't know.

"Why are you going in alone?" Chris demanded. "Don't you want to arrest Jerome Scintella?"

"Christina." Suddenly he strode to her and his strong hands grasped her arms, making her look him in the eye. His face, subtly lined with strain, seemed haunted. His fingers tightened painfully but she didn't move, didn't make a sound. He abruptly released her. "Sean was executed by Eugene Falks," he said flatly. "On the orders of your brother-in-law."

Chris stepped back, felt the sliding glass door at her shoulder blades. She reached a hand to steady herself. No, McLellan didn't want to arrest Scintella. He wanted to kill the man. It was written in the fine lines around his mouth, in the darkness she'd so often glimpsed in his eyes. It was what he'd come so close to telling her once.

It was why he'd run this mission outside the DEA in the first place. Why he hadn't told her everything. Why he'd hidden Scintella's part in Sean McLellan's death.

This wasn't a setup to arrest a drug lord. It was a vigilante mission.

And there was no way Natalie would survive, not when McLellan was on the blood trail.

"I want to get Natalie away from him," she said evenly.

"The man's a drug lord, Christina!" Fury bristled in his every move as he paced. "He doesn't care who lives and who dies as long as he gets what he wants. Natalie means nothing to him. *You* mean nothing to him. He doesn't care."

"What difference does it make?" Chris shouted back. "You're just going to kill Jerome, anyway! You're no different than Falks. Natalie doesn't mean anything to you and I sure as hell don't."

Connor stopped his pacing, spun on his heel to face her. "Is that what you think? You believe I want to kill my brother's murderer?"

"I don't know what I believe anymore. Who can I trust? *You?*"

Now, all the fury, all the frustration, seemed to drain out of him, leaving him weak. He dropped onto the sofa, leaned his head in his hands.

"You didn't tell me the truth about why you were on my boat. In my *home.*"

"I wanted to keep you safe," he said quietly. "I didn't do a very good job of it, but I didn't expect my own partner to be the guy I should have been watching."

As he bowed his head in what might have been shame or resignation or defeat, Chris felt her own anger fade. Betrayal she understood. Putting your trust into someone close to you, then having that person undermine your every move. *Oh yeah, Granddad, you taught me that a long, long time ago.* It wasn't a lesson quickly forgotten.

"I'm sorry," he said. "That's part of what I came here to say. I'm sorry. For all of it."

She stood, looking down at the *dragyne* that had frightened and confused her, that she couldn't stop thinking about and wanting. Everything she feared in those dark waters, she realized, didn't have to be evil. Not when the *dragyne* had held her so close, desperation in every rough caress, or when he'd whispered her name over and over until he could no longer speak.

There were times when you had to give up wanting the maps and charts, when you had to go with what you knew to be true: landmarks, the signs you could recognize, your own gut instinct. Didn't every navigational chart she'd ever used have the warning in the small print? *Open your eyes.*

She knelt in front of him where he sat with his elbows propped on his knees, his hands hanging useless in front of him. "I trust you." And she knew when she said it that it was true.

As if of their own accord, his fingers reached out. She raised her hands to meet his, tentative, wishful, fearful. His touch strengthened, exploring. *Yes,* she thought. *It's okay.* Still, he didn't raise his head to look at her. She disentangled her fingers to stroke his jaw. Suddenly he hauled her to him, his strong arms wrapped tightly around her, crushing her against him.

Here, she felt safe. *Here,* she knew she was all right while everything she feared raged around them.

He held her while she wept out the pain and confusion of the past weeks, the terror she had faced and the terror still in front of her. His broad hands stroked her back, his soothing murmurs washed over her ears. She heard her name and felt his own trembling. She felt his pulse beating in his neck against her cheek, his chest rising and falling like the inexorable tide.

He held her when her tears dried and she pulled far enough away to find his lips, he held her when her hands raked through his hair, when her breath let go. He held her when his mouth strayed to the tender skin of her throat and her head tipped back. He held her when he laid her down on the long sofa's lush seat. Outside the still-open curtains, she could see how the faraway stars gleamed and glittered; *this way,* they called, beacons of light in the great unknown darkness. *This way.* Then he held her when he showed her a heaven far more exquisite.

Chapter 15

Chris braced herself on her elbow and trailed her fingers down Connor's chest. "I lied," she said softly.

"About what?" He reached up and pivoted the air-conditioning vent so it blew somewhere other than directly onto her bed, onto them.

"About the first time not meaning anything."

"That's not what you said. You said not to pretend it meant more than it did." His arm, wrapped around her shoulders, pressed her closer. "What did it mean?"

Chris felt the tears coming, and let them. Words caught in the back of her throat. With Natalie, yes, she could say something of what she felt. But with a man? This man? "A lot," she finally managed.

He stroked her face. "So you almost trust me."

"Why do you say that?"

"You're still not talking about how you feel." He drew her down and kissed her lightly. "It's not easy, is it?"

She shook her head, laid her cheek on his chest.

He tightened his hold. "It just takes time."

"We don't have much of that," she reminded him.

"We will if I come to Galveston."

"You still want to do that?" Hope flared, fearful and painful, in her chest.

"Might as well. I'll get fired for going off on this little jaunt, so I won't have a job." He shrugged, his shoulder flexing under her temple.

"Would they do that?"

"Probably. A career change wouldn't hurt."

"So you want to leave the DEA."

She heard the weariness in his voice as he replied, "Imagine playing Whack-a-Mole with drug dealers. For every lowlife drug runner you take down, another pops up to take his place. The problem's not the supply. It's the demand." He paused for a long moment. "Sean understood that before I did. The problem was *he* was the supply I was trying to shut down. We have to start choking off the demand at the source, with the kids."

"Your Spanish is good."

"Yes. Why?"

"I bet Garza or Gus could set you up with a youth outreach agency down in Galveston."

His short chuckle was skeptical. "Like I'm good with kids."

"Hey!" She lifted up and glared at him. "You were damned good with that kid in the boatyard. Don't under-rate yourself. I'm serious," she said firmly, suppressing a laugh at his look of incredulity. "You got him doing something different. And your experience with your brother counts for something, doesn't it?"

"Sean wasn't a teenager." But the hesitant speculation in his voice told her she'd gotten *him* thinking.

"There's just the matter of where you're going to live," she said.

"Yeah, there is. I sold my house."

"*Sold* your house?"

"I had to pay for all this somehow." He waved his hand at *Obsession*. "I got lucky. I had an old house on a double lot in the Houston Heights. The people who bought the property are tearing down the house and putting up a huge Victorian."

Chris stared at him, trying to get her brain around his admission. "So you don't have a place to live?"

"Don't look so shocked," he said gently. "It's just a house."

"Did you grow up there?"

"There and other places. My folks moved back east after we graduated college, so Sean and I shared it until he took off."

"And it's been your home since then."

"As much home as any place has been."

Chris lowered her head back to his chest, hearing deep inside his breath moving like the sea in a conch shell. The conversation moved her, frightened her, but she didn't know why. Why should she care whether or not Connor had felt at home in his city house? He was obviously okay with it.

"Natalie won't want to live here with you," he said abruptly.

"How do you know?" she asked, a little annoyed that he'd guessed what she'd secretly been thinking. "She's always liked living with me."

"She won't be the same woman you knew six months ago," he went on. "Sean wasn't the same man."

"It sounds like your brother was gone a lot longer than Nat," she pointed out, letting her fingertips play across his collarbone.

He sighed. "Sean started leaving long before he stepped out the front door for the last time. It took me a while—years—to understand that he got to make his own choices, and it wasn't my job to judge them." When Chris raised her head to protest, he added, "The only thing I get to do is figure out what I want for myself. Everyone else gets to go their own way. Even if the path looks to me like it's leading straight to hell."

Chris leaned away, propped herself on her elbow again. "But you tried to talk him out of his drug involvement, didn't you?"

His gorgeous eyes darkened with what looked like defeat or wisdom or acceptance. "It didn't help. He needed to do what he did, just like Natalie needed to go marry someone she didn't know. Just like she needs you now to come rescue her and you need to go do that." His voice dropped, as if afraid to say the words. "Like you always have."

"What are you saying?"

"That you have a choice."

Chris irritably rolled onto her back, then pulled the sheet over her breasts. "But you've taken that choice away, haven't you?"

"Christina, it's so damned dangerous."

"She's in over her head," Chris said stubbornly.

"So are you," he whispered. "Aren't you where you want to be? Trying to help her again?"

"That's different."

Connor pivoted to his side and draped his heavy arm over her waist. "All I'm asking you to do is keep an open mind about your sister when she comes home. In my experience, they keep making the same decision over and over."

"I'd be naive to expect anything different," Chris said, ignoring how naive she feared she could sometimes be.

"Naive is okay," he said, leaning down to kiss her shoulder. "Willfully blind is something else."

"Willfully blind is something I can't afford right now."

Connor slowly peeled the sheet down. "No, we can't. That's why I want to come to Galveston with you. So you and I can see how things might turn out." He paused his visual exploration. "You'll have to help me find a place to stay. You know the area and I don't."

She shrugged, liking how his mouth felt on her skin, especially when it traveled southwest a few inches and lingered. When he raised his head and she remembered they were having a conversation, she said, "I know of a place offhand. Cheap. Kind of small. Landlady can be a pain."

His lips tickled her breastbone. "As long as it's near you, I can handle it."

"How about your old cabin?" she asked. He stopped what he was doing to meet her gaze. "Until we decide you should move into mine."

"Are you sure you want me?"

"Are you sure you want *me?*"

Her uncertainty must have shown in her face because he caught hold of her wrists and rolled on top of her. "What do you think?" he whispered, pressing in until she gasped. "Because I think I'm already home."

Chris woke by degrees. Cool air blew over her bare shoulder where the sheet didn't reach. She opened one eye. Light filled the porthole windows, at the wrong angle for morning. All was quiet but for the steady hum of the air-conditioning unit.

Alone. She knew without looking that Connor wasn't in bed anymore. Her head felt stuffed with cotton. She'd slept hard and awakened feeling five miles into a ten-mile hangover. The bedside clock read three in the afternoon. Connor was probably at the hospital to see Jacquie. She rolled onto his side of the bed, wrapped her arms around his pillow, buried her face in it. His scent belonged here, she thought, breathing it in.

She smiled against the fabric, thinking about his promise to come to Galveston after the trip, see how things went. If last night was any indication, she thought as she rolled onto her back and stretched, things would go just *fine*.

God, that man was good with his mouth.

She shivered, then dragged herself out of bed. In half an hour, she was showered, clothed, and ready to head to the hospital, where she planned to argue heatedly for them to keep to the current plan and take *Obsession* down to Isla-donata. She intended to be there when Natalie was rescued.

But she'd have to plot the course first. Always be prepared. She pulled the nightstand drawer open to get the handheld GPS.

It was gone.

Connor.

Maybe he'd simply taken the GPS to the hospital with him, she told herself. Maybe he'd just carried it upstairs, played around with it a while to get acquainted with it. Maybe—

Maybe you're just fooling yourself and he's gone to kill Scintella now.

"Don't jump to conclusions," she said aloud. "It takes time to set up a raid." Right. What she needed was a plan. "Call a cab, get to the hospital, see if he's there."

While she waited for the cab to arrive, she quickly searched the salon, galley and pilothouse. There were signs he'd eaten (clean dishes in the drainer) and signs he'd made some calls (the fruit bowl shoved aside and the ball-point pen uncapped next to the notepad, the pad indented with his handwriting). No GPS.

She grabbed a No.2 pencil from the pencil cup and used the old sketch trick to see the numbers he'd written on the pad. With trembling hands she dialed the number on her cell.

"Tampa Bay," a harried-sounding male tenor said.

"Tampa Bay what?" Chris asked. "What do you guys do?"

"Impound yard, lady. You gotta claim?"

"No, wrong number. Thanks."

On the shore, a car horn honked. Her cab was waiting. She stuck the paper into her purse with her cell phone. Stepping outside, into sunshine, her now-dry Keds soaked up the dock's heat. It felt good—hot and familiar. What wasn't familiar was the woman walking slowly toward her, dressed in yesterday's red shirt and white shorts, her wrinkled red scarf wrapped elegantly around her head, hiding the bandage, and her arm in a sling.

"What are you doing?" Chris shouted as she jogged toward Jacquie.

"Russ took off after leaving me some not-so-subtle hints he and Connor are going to the island alone," she said when Chris reached her.

"You shouldn't be here."

"The hell I shouldn't."

Chris measured the hard glint in Jacquie's tired eyes and pulled the note paper from her purse. "Connor called an impound yard."

"What's the number?"

Chris hit redial on her cell and handed it Jacquie. While

Jacquie talked to the yard, Chris settled up with the cabbie in the parking lot. As he drove off, she hoped they wouldn't end up needing him.

"Thank you for your help," Jacquie was saying as Chris returned. She savagely punched End and handed the phone back. "They've commandeered a seized drug running boat, the bastards."

Chris chucked the phone into her purse and they turned back toward *Obsession*. "Is that legal?"

"Connor pulled some strings to do it."

"When?"

"Four hours ago. They showed up at the impound yard and took possession of something called a Baja Outlaw."

"That's a Cigarette boat." Big boat, powerful engines, no mufflers.

"Fast?"

"About as fast as you can get." Chris worriedly slipped her hair from its ponytail, then wound it back up again. "Connor's still hiding this from the DEA."

"The boy's stubbornness is going to get him killed."

"Not if I can help it."

Inside *Obsession*, Jacquie settled on the salon sofa. "How far out are we from Isladonata?"

Chris stepped into the pilothouse to retrieve the chart from the chart table's under-desk storage area and paused. Something was missing. She scanned the helm. It took several moments, but her brain finally ticked over and realized what was wrong.

The engine keys were gone.

"Shit." She raced upstairs to the flybridge helm. Nothing there, either.

"He's taken the engine keys," she called to Jacquie as she reentered the coach house.

"He really doesn't want us tagging along."

"Well, he'll have to try harder than that," Chris snapped, trying not to be furious.

"Why?"

"You can jump-start a diesel engine with a freakin' screwdriver."

Jacquie's brows shot up. "He's underestimated you, girlfriend."

"He wouldn't be the first. I'm going to get my sister, dammit."

"You and me faking our way onto the island? Damn right we'll get her."

Chris quelled the hope that flared in her at Jacquie's decisiveness. Girl Power. Girls and Glocks and Rugers, she corrected herself.

She set the antique compass to one side and spread the chart over the coffee table. "Will the Coasties work with Connor if he's not on an official raid?" She tried to keep her voice calm, ignored the deep ache she felt from yet another of his betrayals, no matter how well-intentioned.

"Doubtful. He might call them in after the bust."

"If he shows up without me and without someone in uniform, Natalie won't know to trust him."

"They're planning on arresting Jerome Scintella and his gang," Jacquie pointed out as she leaned forward to look at the map. "Natalie won't have to trust them."

"And if things go wrong?"

"My bet's on Connor and Russ. Connor's probably going to have backup we don't know about."

"His backup before was Smitty and you know where that got him." *Correction. Where it got me.*

Then she heard herself say, "He's not going to arrest Scintella. He's going to kill him." And the logical conclusion of that path was that their talk of living in Galveston had been nothing more than his attempt to persuade her he wasn't going to murder Jerome Scintella. So she wouldn't try to stop him.

Jacquie looked up from her perusal of the chart, eyes narrowed. "Why do you say that?"

"Why else wouldn't he make this official?"

"That's not Connor," Jacquie said flatly. "He'd never do that."

"Have you talked with him about his brother?"

"I was there. I worked that sting operation." Her level gaze, just this side of hostile, met Chris's. "Yes, I've talked to him about his brother."

"No. I mean *talked* to him. Has he told you how he feels about what happened? What he wants to do?" *Has he looked at you with that terrible inevitability, as if he had no other choice than to spill a man's blood?*

Jacquie's face went still, as if Chris had said more than either of them had intended. "He's a good agent. He wants justice."

"I don't care what he wants," Chris lied, "as long as Natalie comes out alive."

"He'll get your sister out all right. His conscience won't let him do anything else."

Sudden tears stung Chris's eyes. How much she wanted to believe that. How afraid she was to take that chance.

"You have him wrong, Chris," Jacquie said, chin lifted. "He won't feel worthy of his badge—or you—if he doesn't save her. It'll be his brother all over again, except worse."

"How could it possibly be worse?" Chris asked, feeling a fierce tug at the idea of Natalie's being hurt or killed.

"Sean had gone down a long road without Connor. Family can be like that. After a few years of absence and silence, you start wondering not just what they're doing but who they are. You wake up one day and they're strangers. Then you wonder if you ever knew them at all." She was silent for a long moment, and Chris didn't know if Jacquie was talking about how she saw her own family, or maybe how her family saw her.

"But Connor knows you," Jacquie continued, the faintest tremor in her voice. "And he knows if he loses Natalie in this raid, he stands a very good chance of losing you. It's one thing to lose your past and someone you don't know anymore. But losing your future?"

"You love him," Chris said suddenly, her heart clogging her throat.

"And it has never done me any good whatsoever." Jacquie absently tapped the chart with her fingertips. "He's never looked at me twice." She raised a brow at Chris. "You have nothing to worry about where I'm concerned."

"But I've got a lot to worry about with him," Chris said. "Not the least of which is that he stole my GPS."

"So that and a fast boat gives him what? A hell of a good head start?"

Chris shook her head. "The GPS he stole has decoy lat-longs programmed in it. They're going to the wrong island."

Isladonata rested, an emerald on a topaz bed. In the dawn, mist blanketed the coastal forest that abruptly ended at sheer cliffs on three of the island's faces. As Chris guided *Obsession* southwest to the island's southern face, she raised the binoculars. The treetops sloped down, toward what looked like might be a lagoon. Two buoys, green on the left, red on the right. Bingo.

Of course, if she could see the buoys, someone on the island could see her.

Obsession might have been spotted by security, but no one was saying. Chris flipped from VHF channel 16 to channel 13, just in case the island used a different frequency, but both were silent except for the occasional crackle of static. She backed off, kept the yacht in position a mile away from the red and green channel markers. The swells here were long and broad; *Obsession* serenely rode the waves.

Jacquie joined her on the flybridge. Her arm sling was wrapped with a decorative black, white and red scarf that appeared to be part of her sundress. The dress, deep-necked, fitted snugly around her trim waist and flared at the hip, looking sexy and simple enough to have cost a small fortune.

"Ralph Lauren?" Chris guessed.

"Donna Karan. Wait till you see the hat." Jacquie gave her the once-over. "You look pretty sharp yourself."

"Monkey suit," Chris remarked, resisting the urge to straighten her lightweight royal blue blazer over her crisply pressed white slacks. "Are you going to this party as a model?"

"Maybe a prostitute. We'll see how it goes. I'm versatile."

Chris gave the dress a critical eye. "You don't look like a high-dollar whore."

"I hope not. But you look like a captain who knows what she's doing."

"Wait till you see the hat," Chris replied. "They'll have binoculars on us," she reminded her. "Here goes nothing."

Chris levered the throttles forward. Hortense and Claire rumbled reassuringly and in moments *Obsession*'s bow sliced the pristine water, nose pointed directly between the distant buoys. Chris smoothed her ponytail, then flipped the captain's cap onto her head.

Jacquie turned her back to the bow, then pulled her

Glock from her sling. Keeping the firearm low behind the helm console, Jacquie pivoted to face front and laid it in one of the cubbyholes, out of sight but close at hand.

"This is nuts, you know," Jacquie remarked conversationally.

"You were the one preaching Girl Power when we talked about it," Chris said, wishing her nerves weren't jumping under every patch of skin.

"Yes, well, at the time I expected a little Boy Power right behind us. Too bad my boss didn't agree with me." Jacquie smiled and lifted her face toward the sea, pushing out her gifted chest in a nice show for any vigilant island security forces. "I'm going to end up fired if not worse when we get back."

"Your boss'll be pissed?"

"Thoroughly. One rogue agent is enough. An injured rogue agent getting herself killed in action because she disobeyed a direct order to stay put will get *his* ass in hot water." She sighed. "With any luck, we'll find Natalie and get out before anyone notices she's gone. Or that we're gone."

"My luck hasn't been that good on this trip." Chris slipped on her sunglasses as the growing light sparkled hard on the water. "Let's work off your luck for a change."

Jacquie tapped her forearm cast.

"That was meant for me, remember."

"Meaning my luck's just as bad."

"How are you doing on pain?"

Jacquie shrugged her good right shoulder, winced. "Still flying on the last pill, thanks."

Obsession swayed slightly as she passed over the waves sliding across her path. About half a mile out now, Chris judged. She checked her speed and backed off to a stately ten knots. No need to look like they were in a hurry.

"Anything yet?" Chris asked.

Jacquie took a long look through the binoculars. "There's a lagoon beyond the breakwater. I'm seeing some big boats moored in there."

"Any sailboats?"

"Two really tall masts."

"Deepwater lagoon, maybe," Chris said. "In general, the taller the mast, the deeper the keel."

"Good Lord." Jacquie panned the binoculars. "You weren't kidding about it being a resort. It's built up a series of terraces—"

Chris jumped when the VHF blared with a man's booming voice. "Approaching vessel, please identify yourself." She turned down the volume.

"Show time," Chris muttered. She put Hortense and Claire in Neutral, then picked up the VHF mic. "Motor vessel *Obsession* requesting permission to approach and dock."

Silence for several long minutes. "*Obsession,* there must be a mistake. We don't have you down for an arrival today."

Jacquie put both hands on her hips. Chris held the mic open while Jacquie screeched, "What does he mean we're not on the schedule? Maurice told me specifically today and if he…"

"Isladonata," Chris said over Jacquie's continuing outburst, "would you mind rechecking your paperwork? Over."

"*Obsession,* we've checked."

"I'll *wait,* if you'll just check it again," Chris said, putting a pleading note in her voice as Jacquie kicked her tirade into high gear. Chris let her finger hang on the mic for a couple of seconds before she released it, giving the security office plenty of time to share her pain.

"Who's Maurice?" Chris asked with her best ventriloquist lips.

"A boy I dated in high school!" Jacquie said, waving her good arm, outraged, in the air.

"I'm sorry, *Obsession,*" the male voice said, and seemed to mean it, "but I don't have you on the list."

Jacquie grabbed the VHF from Chris's hand. "Jacqueline Cummins!" she shrieked into the mic. "Maurice said he'd put my name on the list for Jerome Scintella's party. Cummins! Go check your records again, moron."

Chris tried not to roll her eyes. Jacquie's choice of pseudonym wasn't just funny from a porn point of view; Cummins was also the brand name of a popular diesel engine.

"Ma'am, we don't have your vessel's name."

Chris grabbed the mic from Jacquie's hand and suffered a mock slap for her trouble before Jacquie stamped toward the flybridge's aft section.

"You see what I'm working with here," Chris said to her sympathetic listener. "Do you have the girls' names on your list?"

"Uh, no." The voice sounded doubtful.

"I guess they've all arrived already."

"Uh, no, they haven't. They're not due until the big party tomorrow."

"Okay, so Miss Cummins's agent told her to come early. It's a simple mixup and you'd be doing me a huge favor if you just let me drop Miss Cummins off now."

"Ma'am, if you're not on the schedule, there's nothing I can do."

"I don't think you understand. Mr. Scintella specifically requested Miss Cummins's…ah…services. Letting us through may be a breach of protocol but I don't imagine Mr. Scintella would be glad to hear you've turned her away." She paused. "It's up to you."

"*Obsession,* please stand by."

Chris remained at attention while Jacquie started on another one-sided screaming match. If lungs and foul language were the keys to getting your way, Chris reflected, the door was opening even as Jacquie spoke. Jacquie charged the helm and grabbed the throttles, throwing *Obsession*'s nose to port.

"Don't make them think twice about letting you in," Chris said as she wrestled Jacquie's hand off the controls. She gave Jacquie a shove onto the bench seat near the helm and pointed at her sternly. Jacquie crossed her legs and turned away, for all the world like a spoiled brat. She reminded Chris, surprisingly, of Natalie in a postadolescent huff.

Chris straightened *Obsession* back out to face the breakwater's opening squarely. It'd been nearly five minutes. They waited another five before the VHF cracked and spat.

"*Obsession,* you may approach and dock at the pier, slip four on the starboard side. Welcome to Isladonata, Captain."

Chris didn't bother to suppress a grin. The security officer would know her relief intimately. "Slip four on the pier," she repeated. "Thank you, sir. *Obsession* out."

Jacquie stood and came to lean on the helm console. "So we're in." Her lovely dark skin had a grayish cast and a light sweat sheen.

"Do you need to lie down for a while?" Chris asked.

"I'm all right. I should be able to keep them busy while you look for your sister. If I can get them to tell me where Scintella's rooms are, I'll meet you there." Jacquie's smile looked wan. "I promise to stay conscious and able to get back to the yacht."

"Good, because I'm not leaving without you. Now sit down."

Chris scanned the island's layout. The sheer cliffs and coastal forests gave way to a natural break, where a lagoon stretched, cool and blue, into the island's interior to wash up at pristine white sands. On the starboard side of the break, a security building had been set into the rock. As *Obsession* motored past the buoys, Chris raised a hand. A man behind the window waved back.

Inside, sleek luxury motor yachts, much larger than *Obsession,* lay at their moorings. The pier, Chris noted wryly, was for the small fry. A pair of dockhands emerged from a boathouse, coming to catch the yacht.

The satellite phone buzzed. Natalie? Chris grabbed the handset. "Hampton," she said.

"I need Adair," the voice said. "She aboard?"

Chris handed the handset to Jacquie, then dropped the wheel to pivot *Obsession* on the engines, turn her toward the assigned slip. Just another day in paradise, she thought as she took in the blue sky and clear water. Then Jacquie said, "Shit! Are you sure?" and paradise faded into a hot and muggy hideout for thugs and murderers.

"God bless," Jacquie said. She dropped the handset back in its cradle.

"What's wrong?"

Jacquie's already paling face had gone almost gray. "We may have got it wrong about Smitty."

Chris's stomach clenched hard. "What do you mean? He tried to kill me!"

"Yeah, but he didn't plant the transponder."

"They matched the fingerprint?"

Jacquie nodded. "It's Connor's."

Chapter 16

"That doesn't make any sense," Chris said.

"It does if he's covering his bases. He's a sharp guy. Maybe he anticipated you taking off without him."

"You think he's following our signal here?"

Jacquie shielded her eyes with her good hand and scanned the resort marching elegantly up the little hillside. "It's a good guess."

"He's on his own, then. I just want Natalie."

"I bet that's what he's counting on."

As *Obsession* motored to the pier, Chris glanced over the massive vessels moored in the lagoon, trying to gauge the island's party mood. Helluva lot of fiberglass. One hundred feet, Italian design. One hundred and ten feet, design unknown though reminiscent of a French yacht she'd seen once. A ninety-footer, an ocean-capable Cape Horn with its distinctive blue hull. And a gargantuan one hundred-fifty foot yacht with three decks, Italian design, flying a Venezuelan flag. Jerome's South American contact, maybe.

Armed men stalked the various yachts' decks. "Expecting trouble," Chris observed. She scanned the shoreline, noting all cover ended at the wide, bare expanse of beach. "Where's the safest place to be when the shooting starts?"

Jacquie smiled. "Idaho. The second best place is here, on the getaway vessel."

The two dockhands, wearing walkie-talkies on their belts, hustled out to meet *Obsession*. Chris maneuvered the yacht into the tight slip and held her in position. One young man made hand motions for Chris to bring the nose further to starboard so his buddy could grab the line she'd laid out. Following the signals, she jockeyed *Obsession* around in the slip until all four lines were secured.

The signaling dockhand cupped his hands around his mouth. "Nice landing, Captain!"

Chris touched her brim. She shut down the engines and took her first good look at Isladonata's resort.

The resort's main building climbed, as Jacquie had said, up several terraces. Each terrace had its own rooms with windows facing the lagoon. Man-made waterfalls cascaded down the stepped landscape at irregular intervals, sending a fine mist into the air. A beautifully carved stone stairway wound up the terraces, past the individual rooms, to a large archway supported by pillars on either side. A short man dressed in a white suit trotted from the archway down the long stairway toward the pier.

"Welcome to Fantasy Island," Jacquie said as she followed Chris down to the deck. "Here comes Tattoo now."

Chris shot her a nervous glance. "You get your Glock?"

"Too bulky. I'm armed."

Jacquie raised her skirt enough to flash Chris a glimpse of a pearl-handled revolver strapped to her lower thigh before gracefully stepping onto the heavy-duty portable stairs the dockhands had secured in place on the floating pier. One of them took Jacquie's hand to steady her on the way down; she flirted with the young man, making him blush.

"My apologies, Miss Cummins," the white-suited man said when he reached her. He raised her proffered hand to his fleshy lips. "We had no idea Mr. Scintella had made special arrangements for anyone's arrival. I'm surprised he didn't mention someone of your extraordinary beauty."

Jacquie smiled warmly, preening a little at his attention. "I understand these things can happen."

"Captain, you won't mind…" He gestured to the dock-hands who stood poised and ready to board. "Security precaution."

"Of course," Chris replied, and stepped aside to allow the dockhands to board.

"Shall we?" Tattoo offered his arm to Jacquie.

"I'll wait. I may need the captain to fetch something for me."

"We have servants—"

"I prefer my own servants." Jacquie flashed a smile. "I'm sure you understand. May we wait here until your little search is done?"

Tattoo inclined his head.

When the two young men climbed up to the deck, Chris saw the firearms strapped behind the radios. She followed them inside the pilothouse, then back into the salon area as they performed a random search of cabinets and hatches. One disappeared downstairs while the other stood in the salon's center.

"Expecting trouble?" Chris asked conversationally.

"Routine," the fresh-faced young man replied. "You wouldn't believe the lowlifes who try to sneak into this place."

"Did you have to search the big yachts, too?" she asked, as if seventy feet were rubber ducky size.

He shook his head. "They have gentleman's agreements. It's just the drop-ins we search."

"Get many of those?"

"Not usually."

They filed outside and disembarked. Chris walked down the stair unassisted and earned only a haughty smile from Tattoo, who still waited with the chattering Jacquie on the dock. Chris fell into step behind them as they turned toward the hotel, glad she wasn't the center of attention. Jacquie might be cool as a cucumber but Chris had to clench a fist against her trembling. *I do much better,* she suddenly realized, *when someone's trying to kill me.*

On the long walk up the winding stone stairs, Tattoo inquired politely after Jacquie's health, how she injured her arm, was she in any pain. Jacquie tucked her good hand into his crooked elbow and beamed at him, the slightest hint of smokiness in her voice. "No pain whatsoever," she crooned.

The archway Chris had seen earlier led to a wide, breezy veranda where empty deck chairs faced paradise. Tattoo explained the resort had been designed and built by an architect who was particularly attuned to weather, hence the way the stone walls captured and funneled wind through the rooms. Freshwater springs fed the cisterns.

"Sweetest water in the world," he boasted.

He led them around the foyer's ménage à trois fountain, then into a luxurious living space decorated with fine, old furniture. While he shuffled papers on a Louis XVI desk for a few minutes, Chris had plenty of time to lean in the doorway, studying the foyer's layout and the two stairways she could see from her vantage point.

Jerome Scintella would have the best rooms in the place, Chris guessed, probably as high as possible. Which meant Natalie would be the princess in the freakin' tower.

"Not many people around," Chris remarked, and earned Jacquie's glare. Right. *Servants* should be seen and not heard.

Tattoo ignored their exchange to respond politely. "Most of our guests are on diving expeditions today. We offer a full range of activities and entertainment." He smiled warmly at Jacquie. "And are quite happy to accommodate any entertainment our guests see fit to bring with them."

"Mr. Scintella has arrived by now, of course," Jacquie said. At Tattoo's nod, she added, "I would like to see him after I've been shown my room. Does it face the lagoon?"

"Yes, ma'am. You're in the east wing."

"And Mr. Scintella?"

"In the main building, in the uppermost suite."

Jacquie glanced in Chris's direction. "Bring my bag," she ordered. "I have a gift for Mr. Scintella."

Chris touched her cap's brim and strode out. She made short work of getting to *Obsession* and retrieving the carry bag she and Jacquie had prepped earlier. Heavy damned thing, but then it would be. They'd wrapped up the brass compass as Jerome's "gift." That weight, plus the carry bag's stout canvas straps, ensured Jerome would go down easily with a well-aimed swing. Chris took the time to go to her cabin, remove the canvas bag from its cubbyhole. It fit neatly in its holster under her arm, hidden by her blazer.

Was Connor on his way?

No time, Chris reminded herself as she stepped off *Obsession.* She didn't have time to think about how Connor had lied to her again. Put him away, out of her mind. Where he belonged.

Her sister needed her. That's all that counted.

Back up at the foyer, she paused in Tattoo's office doorway. He and Jacquie were gone, presumably viewing Jacquie's room. Chris skirted the fountain and headed directly up the first staircase, the one she hoped led all the way to the highest terrace. The spiral stone steps led up to the next level and presented her with two breezeways, one extending far along the front of the resort and the other, much shorter, angling back along the side with slightly less impressive views.

She eased down the short passageway, paused at the single arched doorway. The door was half-open. *Calm,* her mind ordered, growing cool as steel. Focus on Natalie. Go through every room until you find her, get her ass onto *Obsession,* then have the lines untied and the engines running by the time Jacquie gets back to the yacht.

Tears squeezed from her eyes and she irritably brushed them away. No time to be weak. *And screw you, Granddad,* she cursed before his voice could inhabit her mind, tell her she lacked nerve.

That's right, old man. I'm a mechanic and a captain and whether I get through this alive or not, I'm going to at least try. Chris adjusted her blazer and dropped the canvas bag from her shoulder, holding it by the straps, ready to swing. She could do this. If anyone asked, she was trying to find Miss Jacqueline Cummins.

She nudged the door fully open. *Opulent* was the wrong word for what she found inside, but it was the right idea. Opulent in an island kind of way. Fresh and clean, lots of light pastels and dusky highlights, white floors and walls with a Mediterranean feel. Empty. She searched quickly

but found no other exits or stairs to the upper terrace. She
slipped out, drawing the door back to half-open.

A guttural roar exploded in the lagoon as a Cigarette
boat broke past the buoys. The fast boat threw a high wake
as it slithered sideways in a quick turn and powered toward
the pier. The motors screamed when the pilot threw them
into reverse to stop the boat at the dock's end. Six men
dressed in black leaped from the cockpit onto the pier,
drew their guns as they ran toward the resort.

One of the men was tall, black-haired, with strong arms
she knew very, very well.

Chris shrank back against the stone wall. So McLellan
had arrived with reinforcements. Did this mean he'd con-
tacted his superiors at the DEA after all?

Pistols cracked above her head, backing her up to the
relative cover of the stone staircase. Shooters on the upper
terrace. Shooters where she'd hoped to find Natalie. A man
on the dock stumbled—not Connor—and went down,
stayed there. Her hands trembled even though she held
tightly to the canvas bag with both. *Deep breath.*

None of the men on the various moored yachts had
moved. Not their battle.

Shouts and shots echoed through the breezeways. The
rhythmic clatter of a submachine gun, stone chipping and
falling. Running feet. Chris leaned her cheek against the
cool stone.

Oh God, I can't do this.

Then the high-pitched scream of a terrified young
woman, directly overhead.

Natalie.

Chris ran down the steps to the foyer, then back up the
second stairwell she'd noticed earlier. Those stairs led to
an interior garden filled with lush vegetation, a marble

fountain, and decorative bench seats. Chris quickly scanned the area and found what she was looking for: steps to the highest terrace. The stairs, cut into the stone, ran along the cliff wall that backed the resort.

She sprinted up the first few steps, then got hold of herself. Brains, not brawn. She stopped. Deep breaths. She unbuttoned her tunic, drew the Ruger. It felt heavy, solid, in her grip. A gun in one hand, a helluva a swinging weapon in the other. Steady, no rushing. Her pounding heart had her breathing hard. *I can do this.* She flicked off the Ruger's safety. *For Natalie, I can do this.* Three steps from the top. The underside of a wrought iron table emerged. Two steps. Dense foliage blocked everything to the right, but to the left, the table was joined by a handful of chairs. A doorway began to take shape directly ahead.

Should she call out? Would Natalie hear her? Or would Chris just be giving herself away?

Last step. She was on the upper terrace. Beyond the table and chairs, a hot tub squatted in the midst of a teak deck. Half-full drinks still waited; wet footprints led into a distant doorway. The door ahead of her was open, revealing a short hall and blue sky. A walk-through to the balcony.

Below, footsteps pounded stone, then dirt, as men scrambled. She had to find Natalie, fast.

"Chris!" a voice hissed.

Chris's head snapped around. Natalie, her dark hair falling in lush waves over her shoulders, pelted toward her from a doorway hidden by the bushes at the stairway's head.

"Oh, God, Chris, I'm so glad you came!" Natalie cried softly, throwing her arms around her sister. "I've been so scared."

"I know. We have to get out," Chris said, backing away so Natalie would let her go. "There's a bunch of men here—"

"They killed one of Jerome's guards!" Natalie said, tears streaming down her lovely face. "The guard on the roof fell all the way to the—" She stared at the gun Chris held. "God, Chris, you have a gun!"

"It's okay. I'm going to get you out." Chris glanced over her sister—light cotton dress, flat sandals—and holstered the Ruger, tugged the blazer over it. "We'll have to run for it."

"I'm not sure I—"

"Natalie!" Chris snapped, trying to keep her voice low. "Don't get difficult on me now. I need you to cooperate."

"I'm not trying to be difficult, I just—"

"She's not going anywhere."

Chris turned and faced the man who, from Natalie's descriptions, could only be Jerome Scintella. Handsome in a fleshy way, broad-shouldered, with sensual lips that curved into a smile that was borderline cruel. His Polo shirt was stretched taut over a bulky chest; his slacks suggested powerful thighs.

He was unarmed.

That huge, that mean-looking, he didn't have to be.

"Mr. Scintella, it's nice to finally meet you," Chris said. Play for time, wait for Jacquie. Use the Ruger as a last resort.

"I wish I shared your sentiment," he replied.

His voice sounded like gravel. Too much shouting, she thought. Too many late nights partying hard and ordering executions.

"Natalie's coming with me," Chris said.

"If you can afford her."

"Natalie, move back."

Chris felt her sister step away as the familiar preternatural calm descended. She knew suddenly what a mother felt protecting her child, knew she'd allow and submit to horrific things if only her loved one stayed safe, unharmed. But horrific things hadn't happened yet. Not yet.

"I still want my thirty million dollars," Scintella went on. "And since Falks told me you have it, I have to assume it's somewhere on that pretty boat you've been working so diligently to repair."

"That's what Falks was looking for the night he broke in, wasn't it?" Chris said.

Scintella shrugged his massive shoulders and took a step toward the stairway. "I hear he plays a little rough with his targets. Other than that, I don't really know what Falks gets up to in his spare time."

Chris tucked her left hand into her blazer. "Nothing now. He's dead. Step away from there."

Scintella smiled, toothy and grim. "Natalie's told me about you. Tough nut to crack." He didn't move, widened his stance slightly, like a gunslinger. "You bitches stick together like glue."

"Sisters do that." *Stall,* she thought. *Give Jacquie a chance to work her way here.* "You don't seem upset about ole Eugene."

"Replaceable." The casual twitch of his lips sent a shudder down Chris's spine. "Not like that nice yacht of yours. It'd be a shame to see it torn all to bits, wouldn't it?" He took another step, close to cutting off the stairway.

Chris pulled the Ruger from her blazer and held it steady. "I said back off."

"You didn't tell me she carried a gun, sweet cheeks," he called to Natalie. "I shouldn't have listened to you. This island's been a fucking disaster since you talked me into coming here."

"It's not my fault things went bad!" Natalie's hand touched Chris's back. Making contact. Staying grounded.

"It doesn't matter," Chris retorted. "The DEA's here to arrest you."

"My men will take care of that. The agents will be dead soon."

Connor.

Chris gritted her teeth. First things first. Chris felt her arm tiring, knew Scintella could see her hand starting to tremble with the weight. The Ruger was a damned heavy firearm. It was only a matter of time.

Then he reached behind his back.

"Chris!"

Scintella spun toward Jacquie's voice. His hand, Chris saw, had been reaching for a gun tucked in his waistband. Jacquie's diversion was enough.

In a single smooth motion Chris slipped the canvas bag from her shoulder, felt the compass straining the bag's straps as it dropped. Then it caught at the bottom of her swing, arcing forward in what felt like slow motion but must have taken only a second as she hoisted the bag up, levered it directly between the man's legs. The heavy bronze compass caught him square. He grunted, then went down gasping, clutching himself.

Jacquie bent and liberated his gun. "Remind me to stay on your good side," she told Chris without humor. "It'd have been easier just to shoot him."

"What the hell's going on downstairs?" Chris asked, trying to still her trembling hands against the adrenaline rush.

"McLellan's boys crashed the party. They're looking for Jerome."

"Are they okay?"

Jacquie shot her a worried look. "I saw Russ, but not Connor."

Natalie clutched Chris's arm. "What's going on? Who are these people?"

"The DEA," Chris said absently. Her mind was on Jacquie, how pale she'd become. "You're not looking good. Can we get out now without getting shot at?"

Jacquie nodded, sweat starting to shine on her face. "I'm okay. I say we wait a little while to see if they eliminate enough of the bad guys to walk out later. Scintella's men might start shooting at anyone they don't recognize." Jacquie frowned at the man still writhing on the deck.

"Where can we wait that's safe?" Chris asked Natalie.

Nat pointed at the walk-through. "There's an alcove out front. We can see the lagoon from there but it's inset far enough into the cliff we can't be seen from below."

"I don't like the dead end, but I'll take what I can get for now," Jacquie said. "I'll handle Scintella. You go on out. I'm right behind you."

"What's she going to do?" Natalie stage-whispered as Chris drew her into the cool hallway.

"I don't know, but it'll be the right thing. She's one of the good guys. Here, carry this." She handed the canvas bag to Natalie, whose arms jerked when the full weight hit. "I could use a break."

Chris motioned Natalie to stay put while she ducked out to check the balcony. A bench, some potted plants. No people. They could put their backs to the wall and have a clear view of anyone coming out of the hallway after them. But Jacquie was right. It was definitely a dead end. "Come on," she said.

She settled Natalie on the bench, then sat next to her, gun in hand. "How are you feeling?" she asked.

"So much better now you're here," Natalie said. Her face glistened with fresh tears. "I was so worried about you."

"Me?" Chris leaned forward enough to see down to the

pier, where a small group of armed men congregated. Scintella's thugs? "Why would you worry about me?"

"I-It's a long way to come by boat." Her wide eyes shone. "Anything could have happened."

"Anything just about did happen," Chris remarked dryly. "More than once. But the important part is that I'm here now, and I'll get you home safe and sound." She stroked her sister's cheek as she always had.

"Home." Natalie's brows drew together, what their grandfather had called her Hampton pride-line prominent between them.

Chris leaned forward to survey the lagoon once more. The men had scattered, leaving only one on the dock. From here, she could see the lower terraces and how the waterfalls spilled down in cooling arcs. Banana tree leaves rasped when the wind kicked up, and the pungent spice of jelly palm fruit wafted in her direction. Tattoo was right. The resort was designed perfectly for catching the breeze.

Which was why she heard McLellan say in a low voice, "Are you sure you want to do this?"

Chris instinctively dropped to a kneeling position behind the rail and put her forefinger to her lips, hushing Natalie. Connor's calm, deep voice had come from the doorway to her left, this terrace level. Glad of her soft-soled boating shoes, she padded toward the walk-through. On the passageway's other side, two long strides would bring her to the doorway facing the lagoon.

"Yes, I'm sure," Smitty replied softly. "It's the only way to get what we want."

Her blood ran cold in her veins. McLellan had brought Smitty to Isladonata? Because he needed Smitty as a ticket in, or because they were working together? She fought back a sudden burn of tears. Had McLellan bugged her boat because he and Smitty were working together?

She heard Smitty's soft laugh, then the distinctive clicks of a revolver being cocked. "Say goodbye, pretty boy."

"No!" she shouted and spun into the doorway, gun drawn, willing herself to see everything at once.

Smitty, standing. McLellan, sitting on the edge of a chair, hands in the air, feet under him. Smitty's arm swung toward her, then back before McLellan could launch himself at his ex-partner. Everything settled again into stillness: Smitty aiming at McLellan; Chris aiming at Smitty; McLellan wound like a spring, every muscle tensed and ready.

"Drop the gun, Smitty."

"Christina, just walk away."

"Shut up."

"Take Natalie and leave!" McLellan shot her a desperate glance full of everything Chris was secretly afraid wouldn't be there: fear, longing. Love.

"I don't think you're in any position to be givin' orders to the lady anymore, *pardner*," Smitty said.

"I won't let you kill him," Chris said evenly, "so put the gun away."

"Isn't Scintella looking for you?"

"Not anymore."

"I'm so scared!" Smitty mocked. "Did you shoot him with your big nasty gun?"

Chris spared a small smile. "Not quite." She held the Ruger steady with both hands, exactly as she'd been taught. *Breathe.*

Smitty inclined his head to her. "Move along now. I got business to finish."

"Put down your gun," Chris insisted.

"I can't just let him walk."

"Why do you want Connor to die?" she stalled. *Come on, Jacquie, quit fiddling with Scintella and figure out what's going on here. I need you.*

Smitty shook his head. "To tell you the truth, I don't care whether he lives or dies."

"Then why are you doing this?" McLellan asked softly.

"It's just business, man. You know that."

"Yeah, business. How long have you been working for Scintella?"

"Long before your brother went down. That was a sad piece of work. I'm sorry I had to do it. He was a good kid."

McLellan inhaled sharply. "You pulled the trigger? I thought Falks did it."

"Falks missed the first time. I had to clean up after him. So much I had to clean up, time after time after time. Gets tiring, man."

"So tiring you got rid of him?" McLellan asked softly.

Smitty burst out laughing. "Hell, yeah! You didn't think *she* did it, did ya?" He shook his head. "No nerve. She's stubborn, but that ain't the same." Smitty cast a dismissive glance in Chris's direction. "You just go on now. This isn't about you."

Chris took a step forward into the room, keeping the gun steady. "You tried to kill me."

"You don't have the balls to pull that trigger, darlin'," he said. "I watched you. I know you. You're an upright woman, know the difference between right and wrong. You ain't gonna shoot me. You think you will, but you won't." His smile was almost pitying. "You don't have the nerve."

"Then you've got me wrong."

"Nah, I don't think so."

"Why the hell did you try to kill me?"

Exasperated, he said impatiently, "Because you kept gettin' in the way, sweetheart. You just didn't have what it takes, just like I told—"

A deafening report echoed around the room. Chris flinched. Smitty stared at her, red spouting from his neck, spraying over the light pastels and white tiles. He clasped his free hand against his throat. His mouth opened, but nothing came out except dark, dark blood, then his gaze slid past Chris and registered surprise. His arm came up, his gun aimed at McLellan.

Chris squeezed the trigger.

Smitty's revolver tipped forward, slipped from his fingers as he grabbed at his own chest, twisted a handful of reddening shirt in his fist. He fell to his knees, cartilage cracking on the tiles. He went down, face-first, into a pool of blood.

Stunned, ears ringing, Chris slowly turned her head, almost afraid of what she'd find. Natalie, shaking, held Jacquie's pearl-handled revolver in her fingertips as though it were poison. *Please,* Chris prayed, *not this. Not this. She can't take it.*

McLellan put his arm around Chris, pulled her close and pressed his lips to her hair. She merely nodded. She was okay. It was Natalie she worried about. He let her go to gently tug the revolver from Natalie's hand. Natalie turned into Chris's embrace, weeping.

"It's okay, baby," Chris murmured, holding Natalie close with one hand, her gun in the other. "It'll be just fine."

Chapter 17

Chris stood alone on *Obsession's* bow, looking at the mess of the resort. A contingent of black-suited Coasties swarmed over the pier and hotel, prodding handcuffed men in black to the Coast Guard ship waiting at the dock's end. Tattoo was being questioned by a stocky man with a crew cut Chris mistook for Russ until she saw Russ sitting on a bench next to Jacquie. Both agents were listening to the interrogation, apparently adding their questions to the list Crew Cut was asking. Stretchers bearing the injured were being carried to the upper terrace roof, where a Coast Guard helicopter waited, its blades limp.

Behind her, the lagoon was virtually empty. The huge yachts had apparently picked up their owners and left at the first sign of orange and white. Mooring buoys floated forlornly in the blue water. Even the tall sailboats had gone.

Finally, McLellan walked down the pier beside a cuffed

and slightly limping Jerome Scintella. Scintella spared Chris only the smallest glance, then stared straight ahead. At the dock's end, McLellan formally handed him over to a group of men dressed in black with DEA emblazoned in white on their caps and wearing badges on their belts.

So he'd chosen to let Scintella live, to give him justice rather than death.

McLellan strode back toward the resort, tall and handsome and looking exactly like the officer he was, but halted at the bowsprit and looked up at her.

She called down to him, "Who said, 'Fear makes demons out of angels'?"

He frowned. "Sounds like Shakespeare."

"I'm just trying to figure out which you are."

"Safest bet's neither." He watched the armed DEA agents escort Scintella inside the cutter, then said, "Got a minute?"

"Come on up."

As he climbed aboard, she thought, *Screw the plan.* None of her plans had made any difference to what had gone down. What mattered was that Natalie was safe. The things she and Connor had said to each other… well, there wasn't much point in getting into it right now.

When he joined her on the bow, his gaze swept over her. She'd shed the stuffy captain's blazer and wore her normal tank top and shorts.

"You're not hurt." He sounded like he wanted to reassure himself.

"Scintella's in custody."

He turned to lean, like her, on the steel railing, watching armed men in black escort unarmed men in black onto the Coast Guard cutter. "Yeah." He tipped his hands up, studied his fingers. "You were right."

"About what?"

He was quiet for a long time, then said, "I wanted to kill him. I didn't plan it. Not consciously. But when you'd brought Natalie and Jacquie down and I was cuffing him, looking at him, I—" he broke off. "I thought how easy it'd be to just put one bullet in him, call it self-defense." He turned to look at her. The breeze lifted his hair across his forehead, blew his shirt collar against the strong column of his neck. "I killed the old dream instead."

Chris, trembling, stroked his arm and in an instant, she was in his embrace, burying her cheek against his chest, smelling his scent. How tightly his hands gripped her, like a drowning man, she thought. But neither of them would drown. Not today.

And now, after seeing Smitty again, after trying to protect Natalie, after the gunfire and the running and facing down Jerome, she understood why he'd stolen her GPS and her engine keys, tried to keep her away. Hell, yeah, she was angry about it, would be for a while. But she felt his fear for her in his kiss, in his rough hands moving over her back.

"It'll be okay," she said when he finally released her lips. "We'll be okay."

He nodded, pulled her tight against him. "We'd better."

"Tricky with the transponder," she grumbled.

"Tricky with the GPS. Damn near put us fifty miles off."

"No less than you deserved."

"Spare set of keys?"

She held out her hand as she glared up at him. "Trade secret." When he dropped her engine keys into her palm, she said, "Still coming to Galveston?"

"Damn right I am. By way of Key West. I've got the debriefing from hell so I'll be a few days behind you."

"Is your career over?"

A hint of shadow crossed his eyes. "We can talk about it in Key West."

"I'll see you there."

"Don't be late," he murmured, still not letting her go. "I stuck my neck out—again—to convince my superiors to let you bring *Obsession* back yourself. We both have a lot of explaining to do." Then he kissed her hard, quickly. "Be careful getting there."

"I promise," she said in a low voice, liking how his eyes warmed when she said it.

"Chris!" Natalie called from the dock, a big, muscular man by her side. "Are we going yet?"

"Soon!" She reluctantly pulled from McLellan's arms. "Who's that?" she wondered aloud.

"The Hulk is some guy called Gabriel."

"The guardian angel. He was noticeably absent when I found Nat."

"We found him in the communications room, on the horn with the Coast Guard to let us know Scintella was on the island."

"A bona fide good guy."

"Appears to be."

Crew Cut, the man Chris had earlier mistaken for Russ, cleared his throat behind Natalie, who spun on her heel. While he spoke to her, her body relaxed slightly and she became more animated, more like the Natalie Chris knew. *She's enjoying the attention,* Chris thought. Is that what had drawn her to this dangerous life? The thought she'd be important?

"And who's that?" Chris asked, studying Crew Cut. Close up, she saw the man had about fifteen years on Russ.

"Homeland Security." At Chris's wide eyes, he added, "Smuggling and border control was rolled into Homeland Security. His name's Shoemaker. He worked the von

Brutten case. He's taking over." He toyed with her fingers. "I'm going to miss you on the trip to Key West. Even with one of our agents aboard."

"It's a short run," she replied. "Just a few hours. It looks like we'll have Gabriel, too."

"Are you going to take Russ and Jacquie with you?"

"Russ needs to fly Jacquie straight back. Her head injury's giving her some stick." She squeezed his fingers. "Thanks for making it okay for me to bring *Obsession* home."

He nodded. "I know how important she is to you." He opened his mouth as if to say something, but changed his mind. Then he said, "Do what you need to."

Chris smiled and squeezed his fingers back. "I always do."

Hortense and Claire started easily, still warm from their journey south early that morning. In the pilothouse, Chris automatically checked engine hours in the log, then switched on the VHF radio and radar. She'd pilot from inside for a change, get out of the sun. Her sunscreen had worn off long ago and her natural light golden color was darkening more than she liked. The black-uniformed DEA agent stood on the bow, apparently assigned to keep her from sneaking off somewhere, from skipping her appointment with the powers that be.

Natalie slipped her arm around Chris's waist and leaned her head on her shoulder. "Thanks for coming to get me," she said. "I don't know what I would have done without you."

Chris held Natalie for a long moment while they both cried. The lingering scent of Nat's perfume—peaches, like their mother's—cocooned Chris in painful memories that Natalie would never have: making caramel apples, folding laundry together, being held tight after a fall. Chris had at least had a mother for a few years. Natalie had only had Granddad.

"You did fine," Chris said softly. "Just fine."

Natalie pulled away. "I'm okay. Just kind of shocked, I guess." Her pretty brown eyes filled with fresh tears and her chin trembled. "But I killed Smitty."

Therapy, Chris thought. Something to help her deal with the guilt. "You knew him?" she asked gently.

When Natalie nodded, her brown curls bounced. "He was around a lot, did a lot with Jerome. I can't believe I shot him."

"I was going to have to," Chris murmured. She took a deep breath, letting the memory play like another dream. "I did."

"You're a better shot than me." Natalie sniffed.

Chris glanced quickly at her. Was she in some kind of low-level shock? "I have some prep work left to do before we go. Where's Gabriel?"

"Checking the boat out. He always scopes out the place I am, no matter where it is."

"That's a guy who takes his job seriously."

"That's what I pay him for. Can I get a drink?"

"Fridge for soft drinks. The wet bar's got the hard stuff."

"I need the hard stuff. You want anything?"

"I'm driving, remember? I'll be right back."

Chris slipped down to her cabin. Just a minute to regroup, to be quiet. Gather her thoughts. The image of Smitty turning, blood pouring from his neck, filled her mind and chilled her soul. She could use her own therapy session or two, she was sure. Unbidden, the image continued, playing without her permission. That look of surprise on his face, as if he hadn't expected little Natalie, the quintessential girlie-girl, to pull the trigger. The Ruger's kick as she squeezed the trigger at point-blank range. The widening red splotch on his white T-shirt.

Chris clasped her hands together to still their shaking. *Get a grip,* she thought wearily. Four or five hours at sea, then she could fall apart. Preferably in Connor's arms.

If Natalie was okay. If she could leave her alone.

First she needed to get away from this damned island.

When she went back through the salon to go into the pilothouse, Natalie waved to her from the aft deck where she sat back in a deck chair, a tumbler in her hand. Gabriel towered over her chair. He was too tall for the aft deck, Chris noted. He had to keep his head cocked slightly to one side so he wouldn't scrape the ceiling.

"Did you know there are two bullet holes in the stern?" Natalie asked Chris when she joined them.

"Show me."

"Just look over. You'll see them."

Chris leaned far over the railing. Two bullet holes. Unbelievable. She studied the splayed edges of cracked fiberglass around the holes that rode high on the stern. The bullets were probably buried somewhere in the lazarette. In fact, she'd bet on it because she smelled gas, where one must have punctured the gas can. At least there was enough metal down there to have stopped the bullets passing through the lazarette and into the cabins.

She could stop to clean it up, but she wanted to get away from Isladonata. Now. She wanted to erase every trace of the island's existence—hell, of the trip, except for the hard work they'd done on *Obsession,* and Connor— from the yacht and her heart and her soul.

"The holes are fine," she said. "Let's get out of here. Will you help cast off?" she asked Gabriel.

The bodyguard waited for Natalie's nod to say, "Yes, ma'am," but didn't move.

"Chris," Natalie said, "let's talk about where we're going."

Chris walked into the salon as she said, "Key West. Then Galveston."

"I don't think we should," Natalie said, following her inside, the massive Gabriel in tow. "I think we should go to Jamaica."

"That's not the plan."

"I know it's not *your* plan," Natalie said, "but I'm counting on it."

"We can't just go to Jamaica. We have to go to Key West. Fill out forms, give more statements, whatever the DEA wants us to do. The agent they've assigned to us will make sure of that. They're going to want to interview you about Jerome's friends."

"I don't know anything about his friends. Look, the emergency's over." Natalie smiled, tossing her lush curls over her shoulder. "Now we can do what we want."

"You think this is some kind of vacation?" Chris asked, angry. "I nearly got myself killed coming after you. You have no idea what I've had to do to get here!"

Natalie nodded her head sympathetically, her expression that of a much older, wiser woman. "Yes, Chris, I do know."

And suddenly Chris saw in her mind's eye the charts and maps fading, all the trusted navigational aids losing their magnetic north, the stars fleeing, and knew she looked into the eyes of a *dragyne*. "Tell me," she said softly. "Tell me what you've done."

"I told you she was sharp." Natalie smiled up at Gabriel. The man folded his heavy arms over his chest and said nothing.

"Is he really your bodyguard?" Chris asked. *And where's the DEA agent?*

Natalie tucked her leg under her as she sat on the sofa. "He's my business partner after Smitty didn't work out."

Her eyes filled with tears, but didn't spill. "I'm sorry he tried to hurt you. That wasn't part of the plan."

Chris gritted her teeth, clenched her fists. Calm. She had to stay calm. "So Smitty worked for Jerome or for you?"

"Jerome first, then me." Natalie leaned forward. "Jerome's an idiot. His brother said so to his face. I was there. But Jerome wouldn't listen to me. He said…terrible things to me, called me names, told me I was stupid. You know what that's like."

With a slowly dawning dread, Chris nodded. "Just like a man to think he's right all the time." She glanced around the salon. No agent. No good guy in black anywhere.

"Jerome couldn't handle the pressure. His family was trying to get him to hand part of his territory over to his younger brother but he wouldn't do it." Natalie sipped her drink. "*You* wouldn't have been so selfish. You'd have given me a chance."

"Like the one you hope I'll give you now."

"Exactly."

Chris was silent for a long moment, trying to quell her rising anger. "So you did steal Jerome's money." *And cause Falks to come after me. And scare me to death. And cause Smitty to want to kill me.*

"I needed seed money for my venture. The inheritance just wasn't enough."

"Smitty was *your* business partner."

Natalie's eyes shone with excitement. "He intercepted the courier and I sent the money to you. Great plan. It worked beautifully."

"It worked?" The fury welling in Chris exploded. "Eugene Falks attacked me as a warning to you not to get involved! He threatened me and you over this money! Was that part of your plan?"

"Oh, God, no! Chris, I would never have done anything to get you hurt." Natalie leaped from the sofa and threw her arms around Chris. "I just wanted you to come and get me, take me away from Jerome! That's all."

Natalie's arms felt suddenly like a vise. Chris pried herself from her sister's grip. "Then why was Smitty trying to kill me?" she demanded.

"He told me he didn't think you'd go along with my business venture." Tears trickled down Nat's face, dragging her mascara in dark runnels over her cheeks. "He thought you'd turn us in. I kept telling him you wouldn't do that, but he wouldn't listen."

"Then why get me involved at all? Why didn't you and Smitty just leave Jerome and go off on your own?"

Natalie's tears waned and she sniffed. "Because we had to do something about Jerome. I couldn't just leave him. He'd never let me go. And even if I got away, he would have ordered me killed. I had to get someone else to take him out."

Chris thought about McLellan escorting Jerome Scintella down the pier toward the waiting Coast Guard cutter. How easy it would have been for Natalie and Smitty to connect the dots between Chris and the DEA, knowing Chris would turn first to Gus Perkins, her sailing instructor, then to his old HPD partner. The same partner who'd tried to help McLellan dig his brother out of Scintella's drug cartel.

"That's a helluva chance you took," Chris said. "What made you so sure Jerome would end up arrested?"

"Smitty would have found a way of handling that." Natalie's confidence struck Chris as awful. Frightening. "He was DEA from way back, of course. The right word in the right ear would have done it. The fact you ended up with him aboard was perfect. Better than we could have dreamed."

"Until Smitty decided I wouldn't play the game."

Natalie's normally open and happy face darkened. Their grandfather suddenly stared out from her visage, chilling Chris's blood in her veins. "That's why I had to kill him," Natalie said, her voice sharp, unforgiving. "How *dare* he try to hurt my sister."

"He didn't expect you to shoot him," Chris said, taking an involuntary step back.

"He should have," Natalie asserted. "He knew how I felt about having you with me." Her frown deepened. "But he was wrong about you, wasn't he? You'll help me now."

Chris looked at her sister, this woman Connor had warned might be different. But Connor was wrong. Nat hadn't really changed. Natalie was her grandfather's granddaughter, through and through.

They'd played this game more than once, Chris suddenly realized. Over the shoplifting, over cars and clothes and a condo, Natalie reaching for all she could get, Chris coming along behind to clean things up, make things right. Natalie had seen what Jerome's power and wealth could do, and coveted them for herself.

There was no way in the world Chris could fix this.

Oh, Natalie, Chris despaired. Then, *Damn you to hell, Grandfather.*

"No," Chris said quietly. "Smitty was right about me. I won't do illegal and immoral things to help you make a lot of money."

Natalie smiled. "You and I make a great team." She held her hand out to Chris. "Come on. We can have anything we want if we work together."

Anything we want.

No more watching Natalie get the terrific toys and vacations and attention while Chris got nothing. No more waiting to be noticed by the people who accepted Natalie so much more easily because she was the *real* Hampton. No more fighting with men to get ahead, to get what she wanted, for their respect.

She could have anything she wanted.

Except a life she could live with. Except Connor.

Chris slowly shook her head. "I'm sorry, Natalie. I can't do that. I *won't* do that."

"Chris, please," Natalie said. "It'll be so much easier if you just go along. I want you with me on this. We have the money already—"

"The thirty million dollars?"

"I sent it to you ages ago."

Natalie turned the antique brass compass upside down. The dial thunked into the lid, making Chris wince. Chris forgot it was an eighteenth century artifact when Natalie took a tiny key from a chain around her neck and fit it into an almost invisible pinhole slot. She turned gently and the compass housing's false bottom flipped open. Inside lay a black velvet bag.

Natalie untied the bag's string top. The bag's contents clicked, like a child's stash of pebbles or a serial killer's collection of human teeth. Then she upended the bag and the mahogany table was suddenly strewn with dozens of gorgeous, glittering, cut diamonds.

"I had to send them to you," Natalie explained matter-of-factly, as if it were a given. "Jerome was looking for them. He would have found them if I'd kept them." She closed her eyes and smiled, almost beatific-looking in her contentment. "The irony of you hitting him with them was splendid. Such poetry." She opened her eyes and her gorgeous eyes and brows looked more to Chris like those of a predator than the sweet girl she remembered—or thought she remembered. "Go to your cabin, Chris. We're taking the yacht to Jamaica."

"Where's the DEA agent?" Chris asked.

"We've taken care of him."

The bodyguard unfolded his massive arms. Chris lifted her chin. Natalie wouldn't kill her or allow her to be killed, she knew that. Chris angled her back to the salon wall.

"Lock her in one of the cabins," Natalie ordered Gabriel. "We'll go to Jamaica ourselves. She'll come around."

"If you do that, Connor will come after me," Chris said.

"That hunk you were with?" Natalie shrugged. "You'll find someone else. I mean, look at you. A little makeup and the guys will be falling over themselves. Don't worry about your hunk. We'll take care of him, too."

No, Chris thought. She wouldn't allow Natalie to do this, to hijack her vessel, kidnap her, kill the man she wanted. If she went along with this…dream…Natalie would never let her leave. She looked at the sister she no longer knew—perhaps never had. Beautiful Natalie. Chris turned slightly, found the light switch Smitty had taped down.

In her mind's eye, Chris saw electricity racing from the switch along the wiring to the lazarette, saw the gas fumes hanging like a cloud in the small storage space, saw the bright blue arc of the bad relay.

The bodyguard moved deliberately toward her. Behind him, the new curtains moved slightly in the island's breeze. There was the gleaming mahogany trim, so painstakingly stripped and varnished and remounted. The galley whose coordinating colors she'd chosen herself. Below, her cabin, throw pillows and her mother's quilt laid over the bed exactly as she liked, the first real place she'd ever had of her own, inviolate, untouched by her grandfather's iron will.

And here the map truly ended. All known paths, all known routes, every plan she'd ever had disappeared from the endless blue and undocumented waters. *Ther be*

Dragynes here. Because sometimes facing a *dragyne* meant giving up everything you wanted, everything you feared, to do the one right thing you had to do.

"I'm sorry, Natalie," Chris whispered, tears rolling down her face, blurring the vision of the huge man reaching for her. "I'm so sorry."

She flicked the switch.

She heard first her name, *Christina,* then familiar arms picked her up. He smelled right, too, Connor, and then sunshine fell on her face. She heard a woman crying, then men shouting, their shoes scraping. She lay still for a long time, listening.

"Get him out of here," she heard Connor growl, then more footsteps on the wooden dock.

The arms lifted her again, carried her a little farther away. The right side of her face hurt, but something cold was being pressed to it. Moving wasn't an option. The woman was still weeping—Natalie?—but the weeping was going away, as if the woman was being taken off somewhere.

Chris forced her eyes open. Connor's body blocked the sun, shaded her. His hand held a compress against her cheek. She tentatively touched the back of his hand.

Connor's head turned. "Hello, love."

"I'm okay," Chris said, not moving. If she moved, she'd throw up. She wouldn't do that, not on Connor's nice shoes.

"What happened to me? Was it the explosion?"

He shook his head. "That ape hit you. When the explosion happened, he took off, but we caught him."

"How long's it been?" she asked.

"Since the explosion? Just a few minutes. You haven't been out long."

"Where's Natalie?"

"With Russ and Jacquie."

Chris swallowed, then steadied her voice. "You have to arrest her. She was working with Smitty. The whole thing was her idea. Get Jerome in trouble, get him arrested or killed so she could…" She tried to say more, but her throat closed.

"Hold still, love."

She closed her eyes, felt him move slightly and then speak. Russ's voice in counterpoint. Footsteps heading off. Chris lay quietly, for how long she didn't know. She heard the Coast Guard cutter's engines fire, heard the water churn as it pulled from the pier and headed out of the lagoon. Still Connor waited, occasionally wetting the cloth he held.

"You're going to have a helluva black eye," he murmured once.

"In the grand scheme of things, that's not bad."

She opened her eyes. All she wanted was an icy bottle of Coke and to lie on her quilt in the air-conditioning that always blew on her.

Her quilt. She struggled to sit up, pushing away Connor's hands. "Stop," she told him. "Let me see my boat."

With a sigh, he gave up and helped her sit, braced her against his chest. From where they were, she could see all of *Obsession*'s starboard side.

Her bow tipped high in the air, levered there by the water flowing unimpeded into her exploded stern. The ragged remnant of an attempt to keep her afloat—yellow float gear strapped to her hull—made ghostly shapes beneath the clear blue water. Her decks lay nearly underwater. The bit of aft deck that wasn't already submerged had been blackened by fire and smoke. When the breeze picked up, the eye-stinging smell of burnt fiberglass carried to Chris.

Connor wrapped his arms around her. "We tried." He

pointed to the rigid inflatable and the sailing tender lying on their keels on the dock. "Your office equipment is in that big box there."

"What about my quilt?" Chris asked numbly.

"The lower passageway went under almost immediately."

She nodded. So Claire and Hortense had drowned first. Her mother's quilt lost. Everything she'd worked for, gone.

She watched *Obsession*'s beautifully polished coach house ease deeper. The yacht's windows gleamed as brightly beneath the crystal clear water as above it. Another few minutes, her bow tipped level—the water inside had evened out—and she sank, leaving only bubbles and the flybridge helm for Chris to see.

Six months later

Chris sat on the Galveston Marina's only bench, watching the seagulls lift from the breakwater and arc easily toward home, wings barely moving. She wrapped her jacket around her chest against the cool winter breeze. The boats in this marina were mainly sail, and their halyards clinked companionably against their masts. It was a comforting sound, she thought. Like children's chatter. When halyards clinked, all was right with the world.

"You beat me here," Connor said as he dropped onto the bench beside her and leaned in for a quick kiss. "Have you been waiting long?"

She shook her head. "Just wondering why you wanted to meet here after work."

He draped his arm across the bench behind her. "Makes a nice change from just going straight home, doesn't it?"

She thought about their tiny apartment, not much bigger than *Obsession*'s salon, galley, and dinette put together.

Neither had had the heart to really work at furnishing it, making it a home. It was merely a space in which they lived. Even making love there felt temporary, as if they were on vacation and biding their time, enjoying each other but waiting for a better place. Not to mention it sported a view of the refineries steadily pluming white smoke into the clear Texas sky. Here, a tern cried and streaked past with a wriggling fish in its beak while a pristine cloud loomed in the distance.

"Very nice change," she admitted and leaned into him. "How was work?"

"Emilio's making some progress."

"In his English or otherwise?"

"He's not wearing gang colors yet."

Chris tipped her head back to look at him. The tension that she'd learned to read around his eyes was gone, leaving only the character lines she thought were so sexy. "You're doing a good job."

"It's up to him, like it always is." He caressed her shoulder.

They still didn't talk about Natalie. She did that once a week in Houston, when she told a different facet of her story of betrayal and fear and guilt. It'd been a long time since she'd woken herself or Connor with her nightmares. In a few weeks, the counselor had said today, the story might change to one of acceptance and letting go.

And who knew? When Natalie was eligible for parole in a few years, she might have become someone different. Someone who didn't refuse visits from the sister who'd turned her in, betrayed her.

"It's a nice evening," Chris said now.

"Do you want to have more evenings like this one?"

"You mean come here every day?"

He smiled and nodded. "Something like that."

She thought about her long work days at the office, analyzing plans and calculating precisions, the chopper rides out to the rigs where old enemies took one look at her and chose not to argue. Coming out here for a few minutes' rest felt like just something else to do. She wanted to put Nothing at the top of her to-do list for a few more months.

"Not after a hard day at work," she admitted.

"I'm not talking about that. I'm talking about you quitting."

She turned and stared at him. "I thought we're saving the last of your house money for emergencies. We can't afford for me not to work."

"We could if we lived aboard again. Cheaper living on a boat."

Chris's chest tightened. How great, how comforting, it would be. On the water again. She shook her head. "We can't afford to buy a boat."

He leaned close, kissed her ear before he whispered, "True. But I had something else in mind."

"Like what?"

"A fixer-upper." He lifted his head and pointed toward the breakwater where a yellow Sea Tow center cockpit tow boat was angling a much larger vessel down the channel. "You know, one that's just floating and we'll have to do all the work ourselves."

"That's a full-time job," Chris protested, one eye on the tow boat.

"And why you should resign your job. It's going to take a lot of work to bring her back. Like that one." He pointed at the towed vessel as she rounded the breakwater and eased down the channel past the dock where they sat.

She was an elegant little motor yacht, forty-five feet,

classic aft cabin design. Old, Chris judged, *Obsession*'s age, still a fiberglass hull. Streaked and dirty, rusty. No doubt water-damaged.

Beneath the grime, Chris knew she was gorgeous.

"She's not *Obsession*," Connor began but Chris interrupted.

"She's *ours?*"

"If you want her."

Chris stood, shaded her eyes with her hand to take in the boat's lines. How pretty her bow was, how gracefully the deck line swept back to the stern. Sweet thing.

It took Chris a moment to realize she was smiling. Then she turned to Connor. "Where did you find her?"

He shrugged, glanced away like someone who didn't want to tell. "Somebody owed me."

"Ah, jeez, this is a seized yacht, isn't it?"

"The government thought it was okay for you to sink yours in service of justice, so I thought they could at least do you the favor of replacing her."

Which was a fine gesture because they both knew U.S. law demanded that boats seized, damaged or destroyed during the execution of a drug-related operation were forfeit. Chris had filed the necessary paperwork for recompense because she, as *Obsession*'s owner, had been only peripherally involved. But given her relationship with Natalie, she doubted she'd ever see any of the tens of thousands of dollars she and Connor had put into the yacht.

But if she did, here was a brand-new project. Hell, even if she didn't, here was a brand-new project.

She waved to Gus, who was standing on the yacht's flybridge making hand motions to Chris about the motor yacht. Yes, she agreed, the yacht was a junker, but a junker with a lot of class underneath.

Connor led her down the pier to the slip where the Sea Tow captain, using his own boat, started to pivot the yacht into the slip. Gus climbed down to the deck to throw bow lines to Chris and Connor where they waited to tie her off.

"Engines?" Chris asked.

"Not Detroits," Connor warned, "but I got a good deal on some rebuilt six-vee-seventy-ones. You probably need to check them out before I write the check."

"It'll cost a fortune to haul the existing engines and bed new ones," Chris protested.

"Taken care of," Connor said. "Your buddy Dave is going to let us use the boatyard and his equipment for nothing. We'll just have to work at night and on Sundays when his guys aren't there."

They caught the lines Gus tossed, then cleated off the vessel. Chris caught the distinctive whiff of *old boat,* a combination of mustiness and damp wood and cracked hoses. She ran her hands over the yacht's railing, the first spark of real excitement flaring in her chest. *Yes,* she thought. *We can do this.*

"She's a mess," Gus said, removing his baseball cap to scratch his bald head, "but I guess you've seen worse. Should clean up pretty, though." He jumped from the deck to the pier and nodded approvingly. "Smooth as silk cutting the water. Wave chop on the way here didn't seem to bother her much, either."

"Thanks for helping bring her down," Connor said, shaking hands with the old man.

"My pleasure, son." He hauled Chris into a bear hug, patted her hair. "Helluva present and what my girl deserves after all she's been through. Y'all be good." Then he climbed nimbly into the Sea Tow boat for his ride home.

Connor stepped aboard their new boat and turned to

Chris. "She'll be a lot of work, but I thought we could work on her together. Make her ours."

Ours.

Their home. Their choices, their colors and textures. Their work and priorities. Doing it for no other reason than because they wanted it, without deadlines and fear and hidden agendas.

"Starting from scratch," she said, almost in wonder.

"From the water up," he affirmed.

She took the hand he offered and stepped aboard. He opened the sliding salon door. The musty smell was strong, but the boat would air out in a few days.

"I don't mind camping out on the floor if you want to move in right away," Connor said. "We can start with all the main systems. Hell, we could tear out any of these non-load-bearing walls and reconfigure the entire interior if you want. Redesign her the way that makes sense for us. And our charter business."

"Would you still work at the center?"

He nodded. "Good for my soul. Just like this work would be good for yours."

Chris looked around at the battered wall panels. The electrical control panel would be a mess, she knew. A serious rewiring job. All the plumbing would have to be rerun, the framework examined for rot, the cracked windows repaired or replaced. The carpet was a mildewed disaster; the sofa and chair were fashion horrors from the Sixties. Water and holding tanks would have to be replaced. If any of the piloting instruments worked, it'd be a minor miracle.

Not *Obsession,* but then, Chris thought, maybe she'd moved past that, moved on to some new part of her life where she didn't have to worry and plan and make sure everything was just so. Her maps were gone, her compasses gone, and she had only her own experience and skills and the landmarks she knew to be true to guide her. Like the solid, trustworthy man who stood in front of her, waiting to see what she was going to say.

She studied him, standing next to her in the spacious and decrepit salon. Yes, she thought, tears creeping into her eyes, he did know her. Smitty had known what she wasn't, but Connor knew what she was.

"Let's do it," she said.

"I'm glad you like her," he said, pulling her into his arms. "Welcome home."

* * * * *

Excitement, chills, thrills and hot romance—
that's Silhouette Bombshell,
and there's more coming your way!
Turn the page for an exclusive look
at one of next month's titles,
DETOUR
by Sylvie Kurtz.
Available August 2006
wherever Silhouette Books are sold.

Chapter 1

Thirteen had always been a lucky number for me. And today it didn't let me down. I spotted my elusive target the second I walked into the old warehouse housing the Black Bridge Gym in Nashua's downtown hospital district. There, Finnegan Murdock, aka the Hammer, taught a Wrestling Federation-style class at night.

Finn stood in the middle of the ring, grunting as he pounded his opponent's face to a simulated bloody pulp. The slap of his foot against the mat made a wet thwack mimicking the sound of fist-on-flesh that echoed in the cavernous room. I aimed the hidden camera in my parka lapel square at him.

"Push off," Finn instructed the apprentice wrestler at his side, then hefted the man's body over his head. He spun the apprentice around and launched into a series of instruction on the art of mock anger and crowd rousing at the eleven brawny male wrestler-wannabes peering up at him from the ring's edge.

Finn, all two-hundred and eighty-five pounds of him, stood as erect as a Colossus in his skimpy black spandex leggings and silver tear-away wife-beater shirt, sweat gleaming off his bulging pecs and delts under the stark fluorescent lights. The sharp angles of his bald head, beady steel-gray eyes and hook nose probably accounted for his stage name. So did the hammerhead shark tattoo on his steroid-enhanced chest.

As he twirled his student over his head, he caught sight of me in the shadows of the ring. Uh-oh. Not good.

"Who the hell are you?" His gravelly voice rocked through the air.

Tapping my chest innocently with a hand, I stood up. "Me? I'm Jennifer Jones."

"Who let you in here? How'd you get past the guard?" He glowered as he dropped the man he was holding to the mat and stepped to the ropes. He shook a finger at me. "Wait a minute, I know you. You're the broad who wanted help changing a flat tire yesterday afternoon."

I gulped, then pasted on my best bubblehead smile and batted my eyelashes at him. "What can I say? I'm a fan. Can I have your autograph?"

Suspicion dawned in his beady eyes. "Someone, get her!"

I didn't hang around to argue. I booked out of the joint, knowing he'd come after me and, this time, the bloody pulp face wouldn't be faked. He couldn't afford to let me show the images I'd caught on tape to his insurance company.

Sierra Martindale, private investigator, was once again on the run and loving it.

Finnegan Murdock was a part-time wrestling instructor and a full-time mechanic for an oil-change company in Hudson on the other side of the Merrimack River. Nothing wrong with multi-tasking. I was rather good at it myself. The problem was that Finn was supposed to be in so much pain from his on-the-job shoulder injury that he couldn't possibly heft the poundage required by his work.

My job was to get him on tape to prove insurance fraud. A bone my brother Van, a lawyer, had thrown my way, knowing things were a little tight for me at the moment what with my boyfriend Leonardo's betrayal last Thanksgiving.

So here I was, hauling ass through the back black door of the corrugated metal building into the frigid January night air, where my breath steamed like exhaust. The offices of Martindale & Martindale were about six blocks away on Pearl Street and, on these cold days, I couldn't trust my van, Betsy, to start, so I'd walked. With the spur of adrenaline giving me wings, I was getting a lead on the muscle-bound thugs pounding the pavement after me.

Unfortunately, they shot out the front door, forcing me away from my family's law office. I ran down Harbor Avenue, hoping to get back on course on East Hollis Street. I hadn't counted on my pursuers splitting into two packs and cutting me off. I ended up racing down Hudson Street, boots slipping on snow, down the ramp near the train tracks and onto Temple Street where I had two choices: take the bridge across the Nashua River to Canal Street—which would put me way off course—or take the walking path, with the river on one side and a steep embankment on the other, that would get me to the library and Pearson Avenue and back to Main Street, almost home.

I chose the path, tripping over discarded beer bottles and nearly colliding with a bum on the narrow snowbound path. The cold air burned my lungs and I tasted blood in my throat. Sweat drenched my shirt and I unzipped my parka. But I kept running.

Then I just couldn't.

And that wasn't normal because I was in top shape. I mean, way better than average. I'd done every sport I could from the minute I could. My mother had called me Fidget from Day One. My brother accused me of living life with pedal jammed to the metal and not paying attention to any of the roadside signs. A gross over-exaggeration, by the way. On top of that, I also ran to get rid of the toxic build-up of frustrations.

I know. Hard to believe that someone like me would need that coping mechanism. After all, I came from a reasonably well-to-do family. I got a top-notch education at local private schools. And when I turned twenty-five next year, I would come into a sizeable inheritance.

But trust me, I was a snarl of frustrations. Guy troubles. Job troubles. Family troubles. They all wove together like a tightly-knit scarf. So I ran. And running had never failed me.

Until now.

Like cement that had suddenly turned to concrete, my legs refused to move, my lungs refused to fill and my heart refused to settle. It pounded like a mad drummer out of step with the rest of the band. I'd probably pushed myself too far too fast after the bug that had flattened me for most of last week. All I needed was to catch my breath and I'd be okay.

Using the last of my strength, I hiked down an alley thick with shadows and scrambled over a wooden privacy fence. Then gravity took over, pulling me down on the other side, just as the posse of wrestlers tromped by with all the finesse of stampeding cattle. Lucky for me a pile of garbage bags cushioned my fall.

With thick fingers, I managed to extract my cell phone from my parka pocket and press Speed Dial 1.

"This better be important, Sierra," my brother barked at me.

"I'm in trouble," I managed to puff out, hand splayed over my hammering heart to keep it from flying out of my chest.

Immediately, Van's voice deepened with concern. "Where are you?"

"I, uh, I'm not sure." I forced myself to look around. Like teeth on an old skeleton, the fence seemed to fall away, spinning and blackening the world around me. My heart beat all out of synch. And my breath was as thin as smoke. "Near the library. Office building. Parking lot."

"Sierra?"

"Van. I don't. Feel so good."

He swore, and Van rarely swore. "Hang on, Sierra. I'm coming."

I tried to answer, but my suddenly thick mouth wouldn't cooperate.

They told me I died that night. But I don't remember any bright light calling me home or my life flashing in front of me. Just everything kind of fading away and the scary out-of-whack rhythm of my fibrillating heart pulsing in my head.

I didn't know it then, but I'd just hit the mother of all speed bumps.

BRINGS YOU THE LATEST IN
Vicki Hinze's
WAR GAMES
MINISERIES

Double Dare

December 2005

A plot to release the deadly DR-27
supervirus at a crowded mall? Not U.S.
Air Force captain Maggie Holt's idea of
Christmas cheer. Forget the mistletoe—
Maggie, with the help of scientist
Justin Crowe, has to stop a psycho
terrorist before she can even think of
enjoying Christmas kisses.

Available at your favorite retail outlet.

Stability is highly overrated….

Dana Logan's world had always revolved around her children. Now they're all grown up and don't seem to need anything she's able to give them. Struggling to find her new identity, Dana realizes that it's about time for her to get "off her rocker" and begin a new life!

Off Her Rocker

by Jennifer Archer

HARLEQUIN® *Romance*

A family saga begins to unravel
when the doors to the Bella Lucia
Restaurant Empire are opened...

The Brides of Bella Lucia

*A family torn apart by secrets,
reunited by marriage*

AUGUST 2006

Meet Rachel Valentine, in
HAVING THE FRENCHMAN'S BABY
by Rebecca Winters

Find out what happens when a night of passion is followed
by a shocking revelation and an unexpected pregnancy!

SEPTEMBER 2006

The Valentine family saga continues with
THE REBEL PRINCE by Raye Morgan

www.eHarlequin.com   HRBB0706BW